SPECIAL MESSAGE TO READERS

THE ULVERSCROFT FOUNDATION
(registered UK charity number 264873)

was established in 1972 to provide funds for research, diagnosis and treatment of eye diseases.
Examples of major projects funded by the Ulverscroft Foundation are:-

- The Children's Eye Unit at Moorfields Eye Hospital, London
- The Ulverscroft Children's Eye Unit at Great Ormond Street Hospital for Sick Children
- Funding research into eye diseases and treatment at the Department of Ophthalmology, University of Leicester
- The Ulverscroft Vision Research Group, Institute of Child Health
- Twin operating theatres at the Western Ophthalmic Hospital, London
- The Chair of Ophthalmology at the Royal Australian College of Ophthalmologists

You can help further the work of the Foundation by making a donation or leaving a legacy.
Every contribution is gratefully received. If you would like to help support the Foundation or require further information, please contact:

THE ULVERSCROFT FOUNDATION
The Green, Bradgate Road, Anstey
Leicester LE7 7FU, England
Tel: (0116) 236 4325
website: www.foundation.ulverscroft.com

THE FOOTBALL POOL MURDERS

Most people would regard winning a fortune on the football pools as a stroke of very good luck — but for three particular people, their big win is anything but lucky. For after receiving their presentation cheques from the pools company, each of them disappears mysteriously, their cheques uncashed. Some time later they are all found dead — victims of strangulation. Are these murders the work of a religious maniac who violently disapproves of gambling? Superintendent Budd has good cause to wonder, as he tackles one of his most baffling cases.

GERALD VERNER

THE FOOTBALL POOL MURDERS

Complete and Unabridged

LINFORD
Leicester

First published in Great Britain

First Linford Edition
published 2015

*A catalogue record for this book is available
from the British Library.*

ISBN 978–1–4448–2268–7

Published by
F. A. Thorpe (Publishing)
Anstey, Leicestershire

Set by Words & Graphics Ltd.
Anstey, Leicestershire
Printed and bound in Great Britain by
T. J. International Ltd., Padstow, Cornwall

This book is printed on acid-free paper

To

W. W. SAYER

Author and innkeeper whose beer
and books are both excellent

CONTENTS

1

Out of the Blue

Mr. Alfred Gummidge opened the door of his small, drab, and dismal house, and stepped quickly out into the narrow, drab, and even more dismal street.

It was raining heavily, but Mr. Gummidge, although he had neither overcoat nor umbrella, was blissfully unaware of this. He would have been equally unaware if it had been snowing, sleeting, hailing, or performing any other kind of climatic acrobatics. His mind was in such a state of exaltation that he was completely oblivious to externals, and if the muddy, dirty street up which he hurried had suddenly and miraculously changed into an enchanted garden, it is doubtful if he would have noticed the difference.

At that moment the whole world was an enchanted garden in the view of Mr. Gummidge. His eyes gleamed behind his steel-rimmed spectacles, and his breath came unevenly, as he strove to suppress the excitement that seethed within his narrow breast. Never before, not even under the influence of the beer at the Red Lion, had he experienced such a wonderful feeling of elation. An hour ago he had been a very ordinary, middle-aged plumber, who, by dint of hard work and rigid economy, had succeeded for twenty-four years in scraping together sufficient money each week to keep himself, his wife, and three children more or less adequately housed, clothed, and fed. Now —

The thought of the miracle which had happened that evening increased his pace to a jerky trot. He turned the corner, crossed the glistening road, and shuffled along towards the lights of a public-house that shone, blearily, through the wet murk. Outside the entrance to the four-ale bar he paused, drawing in his breath with the quick, sharp intake of a man who has just plunged into icy water, and then, pushing open the swing door, he entered.

It was only a quarter to seven and the bar was, in consequence, nearly empty.

2

But among the four men who stood by the stained counter was a friend of Mr. Gummidge's, a man who lived a few doors away in the same street.

''Allo, Alf!' he greeted, in surprise, as he caught sight of the newcomer. 'You're early ter-night, ain't yer? What's up? 'Ad a row with the missus?'

Mr. Gummidge shook his head.

'The missus ain't in,' he replied, in a voice that shook a little. 'Gorn ter the pitchers. Listen, Joe — I've done it! I've got an awl c'rect in the penny points pool!'

The look that swept across the other's face was one of mingled disbelief and almost stupefied amazement.

'You've — what?' he got out.

'Got an awl c'rect!' shouted Mr. Gummidge, plunging his hand in his breast pocket and producing a folded and familiar-looking paper. 'Look at it, Joe! Take a look at this 'ere!'

He spread the coupon out on the bar and pointed triumphantly with a stubby finger in verification of his statement.

'Gor luv us!' ejaculated Joe, in awe,

3

staring down at the paper. 'You — you sure yer ain't made no mistake?'

'Course I'm sure!' said Mr. Gummidge. 'Didn't I get the results on the wireless 'alf an hour ago? An' didn't I check up me coupon ter make cert'n? Course I did! There ain't no mistake, Joe. That there seventh line's an awl c'rect.'

'Well, I'll be — ' Joe prophesied a future event that was extremely unlikely. 'What a bit o' luck! — 'ere, let's 'ave some beer!'

'You'll 'ave it with me, Joe,' said Mr. Gummidge firmly, as his friend called to the potman. 'Two pints o' bitter, Tom, an' 'ave one yourself.'

'Well, 'ere's all the best, mate,' said Joe, raising his glass. 'Blimey, you'll be rollin' in it! Smallwood's pays thousands on the penny points pool.'

'It'll come in 'andy fer me old age, Joe,' remarked Mr. Gummidge, trying to keep his voice normal. 'It's bin a bit of a struggle now an' agin ter make ends meet, as you know. An' the missus 'ull be able ter 'ave all the things she's wanted — an' young

4

Elsie an' Jack an' Ted. 'Ave another?'

Joe 'had another,' and by the time it was consumed several more friends of Mr. Gummidge's had come in. They were told of his good fortune, and more beer was ordered. Mr. Gummidge became the centre of a congratulatory group that steadily increased in size as the evening wore on. The news of his luck spread to the saloon bar, and the landlord came to insist on Alf's having a drink at the expense of the house. At nine o'clock Mr. Gummidge remembered that he had a wife and family who were as yet unacquainted with his unexpected windfall. Rather thickly, for by this time he had consumed many pints in celebration, he explained this to his friends.

'Mus' go along 'ome an' tell the missus,' he said, surveying the assembled company with slightly glassy eyes. 'She don' know yet.'

'Don't be in a 'urry, Alf!' protested his friend Joe. 'It's early yet, an', blimey, you don't go pullin' off the penny points ev'ry day o' yer life! 'Ave one more — '

'Don' want no more!' said Mr.

Gummidge obstinately. 'I'm going now. Mus' go an' tell the missus. Goo'-night. Shee you all ter-morrer.'

He pushed his way through the throng towards the door, turned to call a final 'goo'-night,' and passed out into the rain.

Sarah would wonder what had become of him, he thought, as he hurried homewards. But wait till he walked in and told her the news! Course, she wouldn't believe him at first; but when she did — He chuckled in anticipation of her delight and forced his rather unsteady legs into a stumbling trot . . .

★ ★ ★

Miss Mote sat in the small sitting-room of her tiny cottage, staring into the fire and listening to the first news on the wireless. Beside her chair, on a little table, lay in readiness a pencil and a copy of that week's football pool coupon which she had sent on the previous Thursday. At the end of the news the results would come through, and she would be able to check her attempt.

Miss Mote was a regular follower of the pools. Every week she invested the sum of two shillings, and at the end of every week she listened hopefully in the anticipation that fortune would smile on her. On two occasions that season she had won small sums, once for the 'three draws,' and once for the 'four aways.' The larger dividends had never come her way, but there was always the chance, and the interest of making her selections passed many a lonely hour, for she had little other amusement now.

The cultured voice from the loudspeaker began to read the Stock Exchange prices, and Miss Mote twisted round in her chair, picked up her pencil, and drew the copy of her coupon towards her. There were, she reflected as she waited, millions of people all over the country doing exactly the same as she, at that moment. And to thousands of those millions the next half-hour would bring a small fortune, for to the majority even a few pounds could be classed in that category.

A few pounds would mean a lot to her. Just the difference between the bare

7

necessities of life and those little luxuries that make existence so much pleasanter. To some, of course, would come a huge sum — an unbelievable sum — a fortune that they could never hope to acquire in any other way. She passed a thin hand over her sparse grey hair, and settled herself more comfortably in her chair, her pencil poised over the paper in front of her, as the loudspeaker became momentarily silent. Perhaps the wheel of fortune would turn her way.

The loudspeaker suddenly broke into speech again:

'Sport. Association Football results. The League, Division One . . . '

Miss Mote, her faded eyes screwed up in an effort of concentration, her lips moving gently as she silently repeated the words of the announcer, rapidly noted down the results. 1 1 2 × 1 1 2 2 . . .

She gave a little sigh of relief as she came to the end of the long list. Why did they always read the results so quickly? It was very difficult to follow. She rose, switched off the wireless, came back to her chair, and began to sort out from the full list those results which interested her directly. The three draws — how had she fared with those this week? One right; two right — oh dear, what a nuisance — one wrong! They might as well *all* have been wrong. The four aways *were* all wrong! Well, that was that! It was hardly likely she would be lucky with the points pool. The first line was definitely wrong. Only six right out of the fourteen. The second was a little better — eight. Miss Mote caught her breath suddenly, and for a moment the printed form swam before her eyes. The third — the third line was *right*!

She blinked down at the coupon, her frail little body trembling with excitement. There must be a mistake! She couldn't have got a winning line in the points pool!

She checked the results again. There wasn't a mistake! Her forecast *was* correct.

She leaned back, suddenly breathless and a little sick. It was incredible, but it was true! She had won the first dividend. There would be a telegram on the Monday to tell her so, and on the following Thursday the cheque would be presented to her . . .

How many times had she seen the photographs of the fortunate people who had previously won large amounts, taken grouped together with the celebrity who had presented the cheques and envied them. And now she would be one of them.

Who would hand her *her* cheque, and how much would it be for? The first dividend was always for a large amount — sometimes it ran into many thousands. Many thousands! Just to imagine having all that money, *real* money! There were so many things she wanted to do and had not been able to . . .

She got up feeling that the world had suddenly become unreal, stirred the tiny fire until it flamed cheerfully, and went out into the small kitchen to make herself a cup of tea. She felt in need of a stimulant.

Outside, the wind sighed mournfully round the little cottage, and the rain beat heavily on the window-panes, but Miss Mote heard neither. Cosily ensconced in

10

her chair before the fire, she sipped her tea and dreamed — pleasantly . . .

★ ★ ★

'Wake up, darling!'

At the sound of his wife's voice, Harold Walbrook stirred uneasily in the big chair, grunted unintelligibly, snuggled his head deeper into the cushion, and continued to sleep.

'Wake up, dear!' repeated Molly Walbrook severely. 'It's nearly six, and you've been sleeping since three. You can't want to sleep any more.'

'Um-m-m-m-m!' remarked her husband, partially opening one eye and immediately closing it again. Deciding that drastic action was the only way of coping with the situation, his wife calmly removed the cushion from beneath his head. He snorted, opened his eyes, and blinked up at her.

'Have I been asleep?' he said, with a prodigious yawn.

'Well — ' began Molly sarcastically, but he interrupted her, hoisting himself out of the chair and peering at the clock.

'Good lord! It's nearly six!' he exclaimed. 'The football results'll be through in a few minutes.'

'That's why I woke you,' she said, as he bent over to the wireless in the corner and switched it on. 'I wonder if we'll have any luck this week?'

'You never know,' he replied, stretching himself. He came back to the fireplace, and looked about on the mantelpiece. 'What happened to the copy of my coupon? I put it behind this photograph — '

'It's in the drawer of the sideboard, dear,' said his wife. 'I put it there when I tidied up. Wouldn't it be marvellous if we got one of the really big dividends?' Her eyes sparkled at the thought.

'It'ud be a miracle!' he answered, slipping an arm round her waist and lightly kissing the top of her shining fair head.

'But' — she twisted round to face him, her hands gripping the lapels of his coat — 'somebody's got to win it, darling. It might just as well be us. Oh, it would be wonderful! We could move into a larger flat, and I could have a maid and lots of new clothes and that mink coat we saw in Regent Street, and we could buy a car, and — '

'And in the meantime I can hear the kettle boiling its head off!' broke in her husband practically.

'Oh!' She suddenly came back to earth, and disengaging herself from his embrace, ran into the kitchen to attend to the urgent demands of the noisy kettle.

When she came back with the laden tray of tea-things he was listening to the first news.

'While you check the results,' she said, as she poured out the tea, 'I'll change my frock. If we're going to the pictures we want to get there early or we won't get a seat.'

He nodded, and took the cup she handed to him.

'We can leave soon after half-past six,' he said. 'That ought to be time enough.'

The news and the tea came to an end together. As she washed up in the little kitchen, she could hear the monotonous voice from the loudspeaker droning out the results.

'Arsenal 1, Chelsea 1; Birmingham 2, Everton 1; Derby County 3, Charlton Athletic 0 . . . '

She was putting on her hat before the mirror in the bedroom when her husband's excited shout reached her.

'Molly!'

He came rushing in before she could answer, caught her round the waist, and whirled her round and round the room in a mad waltz.

'What on earth — ' she began breathlessly.

'You can have your new flat and your maid and everything you ever wanted!' he cried. 'The miracle's happened, darling! I've got an all right forecast in the penny points pool!'

'Oh, Harry!' she stumbled and sank down on the side of the bed, staring up at his flushed face, her hat perched drunkenly over one eye. 'You — you haven't — '

'I have!' Her expression and the ludicrous angle of her hat made him suddenly burst out laughing. 'You ought to see yourself,' he gasped. They began to laugh together . . .

* ★ ★

Sir Hector Blatherwaite, M.P., cleared his throat and surveyed his small audience, grouped before him in the big room at the Astoria Hotel, London, for a moment in silence. There was nothing formal about this gathering. It held a spirit of good comradeship, and was more like a family party than anything else, although most of the people present had never met before and had been unaware of each other's existence.

Mr. Alfred Gummidge, unusually tidy in his Sunday-best, his white hair close-cropped to his bullet head, a cigarette glowing under the canopy of his shaggy moustache, sat a little awkwardly at a small table, and waited without any expression at all for what was to happen next. Miss Mote, very neat in her threadbare black, her hands folded in her lap, still looked a little dazed and bewildered, much as Alice must have done on her first introduction to Wonderland. Harold Walbrook and his wife were smiling, a happy and excited couple with flushed faces and shining

15

eyes. The executives and officials of Messrs. Smallwood's Pools, Ltd., genial and self-possessed, since this function was no novelty to them, presided over the whole with an air that was almost paternal.

Sir Hector cleared his throat again and began to speak.

'I'm very pleased,' he said, 'to be present on this occasion, which will probably be a unique one in your lives. Not only does it give me the opportunity of adding my congratulations to those of Messrs. Smallwood's on your winning such a large dividend in their pool, but it enables me to become the concrete vehicle of placing these big sums of money in your possession.

'Before I present you with the cheques for your winnings, however, I should like to impress upon you that money is less easily acquired than spent. Fortune has favoured you with an opportunity that is very unlikely to occur again in your life-times. Let me urge on you all, therefore, to treat this good fortune wisely. By all means spend some of your money — there are, no doubt, many things you have always wished for which you are now in a position to have — but put the greater part of it safely away. Invest it so that it will bring you in a permanent income.

'To help you, Messrs. Smallwood's have prepared a little booklet containing sound advice. Let me beg of you not only to read it carefully, but to follow the advice it gives. There are plenty of unscrupulous people in this world lying in wait for those who have, like yourselves, unexpectedly come into money, and who are unversed in the ways of finance. Avoid them. Or if you cannot avoid them, do nothing without consulting someone who knows and whose advice you can trust.

'This money is, of course, your own, and you are entitled to do as you please with it, but I do earnestly hope that you will bear in mind what I have said. It gives me great pleasure to present these cheques on behalf of Messrs. Smallwood's Ltd., and I wish you good luck and long lives to enjoy the fruits of your success.'

Sir Hector Blatherwaite completed the presentation, the winners, holding their cheques, were grouped around him, and a photographer, who had been in readiness, took several flashlight photographs.

Mr. Alfred Gummidge stowed his cheque carefully away in an inside pocket and returned to his table, where a waiter was hovering to find out what he would like in the way of refreshment.

Miss Mote, still clutching her cheque, as though by the very physical contact of it she would assure herself that it was real, went nervously back to her seat and sat down, to gaze surreptitiously at the slip of paper which represented the enormous sum of ten thousand four hundred pounds.

Harold Walbrook rejoined his wife with a smile, showed her the cheque, and then put it away in his wallet.

The little books, which Sir Hector had mentioned in his short speech, were distributed, and the serious business of the afternoon was ended.

At five o'clock Sir Hector Blatherwaite, refreshed with two large whiskies-and-sodas, shook hands all round and took his departure, and half an hour later the little gathering broke up. The three special investigators — ex-C.I.D. men — who had brought the prizewinners from their various homes and whose duty it was to see them safely back again, escorted their charges to their different railway stations, and prepared to remain with them until they reached their own front doors.

That they had carried out their instructions to the letter, in each case, was proved later. But their responsibility ended when the people in their care had crossed their own threshold, and what subsequently happened, happened after that.

2

Into the Dark

Mr. Budd laid down his pen, gave a prodigious yawn, and stretched himself.

'That finishes the Clauton business,' he grunted, with a sigh of satisfaction, throwing the report he had just signed into a wire letter-basket.

'An' a good thing, too,' remarked Sergeant Leek feelingly. 'P'r'aps we'll get a bit o' rest now.'

'P'r'aps *I'll* get a bit o' rest, you mean!' growled his superior, producing one of his thin black cigars and searching for his matches. 'You never get anythin' else but rest, because you never do anythin' . What's the matter with you? Night starvation?'

'I only get tired when I've bin workin' hard — ' began the lean sergeant, in protest.

'Then how can you ever be tired?'

broke in Mr. Budd. 'Workin' hard! You've heard people talk about it!' He found his matches, lighted his cigar, and blew out a cloud of acrid smoke. 'Look at this job I've just cleared up. What did you do? Nothin'! An' even that you did wrong!'

The melancholy Leek had no answer for this paradoxical statement, so he contented himself with a resigned sigh and hitched himself farther on to the hard chair on which he was perched. Mr. Budd, having no other scathing remarks to make for the moment, leaned back, hoisted his feet on to the desk, and closing his eyes, smoked in somnolent comfort.

The soft 'buzz' of the house telephone disturbed his peace, and with an unintelligible grunt of annoyance, he sat up and reached for the instrument.

'Hallo!' he growled. 'Oh, yes, sir! Yes, sir, I'll come right along now.'

He hung up the receiver, and looked regretfully at his partly smoked cigar.

'I've got ter go along to the Assistant Commissioner,' he announced. 'Which I s'pose means more work. You wait 'ere,

21

an' don't go over-exertin' yerself while I'm gone.'

'I wonder what 'e wants ter see you about?' said Leek curiously.

'Wants to arrange about gettin' you inter a nursin'-home for sleepin' sickness, I expect!' said Mr. Budd, laying down his cigar in the ashtray, and moving ponderously to the door. 'Or maybe he's arranged with the Office o' Works to 'ave you put in Trafalgar Square as a statue symbolical of peace! How the devil do I know what he wants until I've seen 'im?'

He left his bare little office and made his way to the Assistant Commissioner's room. In answer to his knock, Colonel Blair's voice bade him come in. The stout superintendent entered, and as he closed the door behind him, the Assistant Commissioner's neat, grey head was raised from the littered desk at which he sat.

'Sit down, Budd!' He waved an immaculate hand towards a chair facing him. 'You're not on anything at the moment, are you?'

'No, sir.' Mr. Budd shook his head.

'I thought not.' Colonel Blair helped himself to a cigarette from a box in front of him and lit it. 'Well, I've got a job for you. Do you know anything about football pools?'

Mr. Budd, in the act of compressing his huge bulk into the inadequate chair in which he had been told to sit, paused, half-in and half-out.

'Football pools, sir?' he repeated. 'You mean the coupon things?'

The Assistant Commissioner allowed a thin stream of smoke to escape from his lips, and nodded.

'Well, I can't say as I know much about 'em first hand,' replied Mr. Budd, lowering himself the rest of the way into the chair. 'I know of 'em, of course, sir.'

'You know the principle on which they're run?' said Colonel Blair, and the stout superintendent admitted that he did. 'Well, then, I needn't explain,' continued the Assistant Commissioner. 'There are several concerns running them, and the biggest of these is Smallwood's. Last week the first dividend in their penny points pool was divided amongst three people' — he paused, and consulted a slip of paper on his blotting-pad — 'a man named Alfred Gummidge, a plumber, living at No. 9, Reed Street, Darlington; a middle-aged spinster, Miss Louisa Mote, of Hawthorne Cottage, Meopham, a village near Gravesend, in Kent, and a clerk called Harold Walbrook, in the employ of the Magnum Insurance Company, of High Holborn, who lives at No. 7, Brockvale Mansions, a block of flats in Balham.

'These three people on Thursday last, were each presented with a cheque for ten thousand four hundred pounds, the amount of their winnings. The presentation was made at the Astoria Hotel by Sir Hector Blatherwaite, M.P., who had been invited by Messrs. Smallwood's for this purpose — they usually endeavour, I understand, to get a celebrity to perform this ceremony — and afterwards the three winners were conducted to their respective homes by the special investigators in the employ of Messrs. Smallwood's. These men are all ex-detective officers, and their job is to inquire into the bona fides of winners, bring them to London to have the cheques presented to them, and take them back again afterwards. They are instructed not to leave them until they have seen them to their own front doors.'

The Assistant Commissioner stopped to inhale a lungful of smoke, and Mr. Budd waited without comment for him to go on.

'In these three cases, the men carried out their instructions as usual,' continued Colonel Blair, 'but on the following day — the Friday — all three of these people disappeared!'

If he had intended to startle Mr. Budd, he failed. The heavy-lidded eyes opened a trifle wider, but the big face remained expressionless.

'Interestin' an' peculiar,' murmured the stout man. 'And queer.'

'It is — very queer,' agreed the Assistant Commissioner, leaning forward and turning over the papers in a folder in front of him. 'Alfred Gummidge left his house at a quarter to eleven on the Friday morning to go to a plumbing job. He never arrived there, and he hasn't been seen since. Harold Walbrook left his flat on the same morning at ten minutes to nine to go to his office as usual. *He* never got there, either, and has vanished completely. Louisa Mote's disappearance took longer to discover, because she lives alone, and apparently has few friends. When, however, the local milkman found the milk had not been taken in for two days, he thought she might have been taken ill and informed the police. Her cottage was entered, but there was no sign of her, neither has anything been seen or heard of her. The local police in each instance have made extensive inquiries, but without results. These people have vanished into thin air without leaving a trace. Messrs. Smallwood's are, naturally, very concerned, although no responsibility rests with them, and it is due to their pressure that the local police have called in the aid of the Yard. I want you to take charge of the inquiry.'

Mr. Budd gently massaged his cascade of chins, and frowned. He foresaw a difficult task before him.

'I'll do me best, sir,' he said. 'I s'pose

there's no likelihood that these three people 'ave just gone off on their own somewhere?'

'I shouldn't think so.' The Assistant Commissioner shook his head. 'In the case of one, that might be a plausible explanation, but it's too much of a coincidence to suggest that three distinct and separate people, each a stranger to the other, should suddenly decide to break their domestic ties. No, I don't think there's anything in that idea. Besides, they would have left some trace.'

'I agree that it don't seem reasonable,' said Mr. Budd. 'But we've got to consider everythin', an' people do queer things when they suddenly get hold of large sums of money an' ain't used to it. What 'appened to the cheques, sir?'

'They were in the possession of the people who vanished,' answered Colonel Blair. 'But they are quite useless to anyone at the moment. Messrs. Smallwood's have stopped payment on them until such time as these people shall reappear, or give a satisfactory explanation for their absence.'

'So they'd be useless to anybody who thought they might get hold of this money by kidnappin' these people an' pinchin' the cheques,' murmured the stout super-intendent.

'Quite!' declared the Assistant Com-missioner. 'And so far as my information goes, there has been no attempt made to cash them.'

'Which seems to wash out robbery as a motive,' remarked Mr. Budd. 'That's what we've got to find, sir — the motive. If we can get hold o' that, we'll be half-way towards clearin' the thing up.'

'That's what makes the whole thing so extraordinary,' said his superior. 'There doesn't appear to be any motive.'

'Well, sir,' replied Mr. Budd, stroking his broad nose, 'there must be a reason. Unless, of course, we're dealin' with a lunatic, an' that don't seem possible, because we'd 'ave to s'pose there was three of 'em! One person couldn't be in three places at once.'

'There's one thing that might be worth noting,' said Colonel Blair, crushing the stub of his cigarette out in the ash-tray at

28

his elbow. 'How did the person or persons responsible for the disappearance of these three people know that they had won a large dividend? The names are not publicly announced until some time after, and then only in a sort of weekly magazine which Smallwood's send out with their coupons.'

'Yes, that's somethin' worth thinkin' about, sir,' said Mr. Budd thoughtfully. 'Always supposin' that it *was* because these people 'ad won dividends that they disappeared.'

'The coincidence seems too great to suppose anything else,' answered the Assistant Commissioner. 'Well, you've got all the information I can give you. The local police in each district may be able to augment it a little, but not very much, I'm afraid.'

'There's just one thing, sir,' murmured Mr. Budd, gathering from the other's tone that the interview was at an end, and beginning to hoist himself out of the tight clutches of the chair. 'How is it there's bin nothin' about this in the papers?'

'Because the police consider it better to

keep the whole thing as quiet as possible,' replied Colonel Blair. 'In which I think they showed very good judgment. Nobody, with the exception of the relatives of these people, and Messrs. Smallwood's, are aware of what happened. How long it can be kept quiet is another matter. The newspapers are bound to get hold of it before long, but before they do, the less publicity the better. There's either nothing very much in the disappearance of these people, or there's something very big. I'm inclined to think there's something very big, myself.'

'Well, sir,' said Mr. Budd, softly scratching one fat cheek, 'it looks like a tough proposition.'

'I think it is,' said the Assistant Commissioner gravely. 'A very tough proposition.'

It was not long before they both realised how true this prediction had been.

3

Miss Mote Returns

Brockvale Mansions was a large block of flats situated in a quiet road off Balham High Street, and held one thing in common with many another large block of flats, in that it had apparently been designed with the express purpose of looking as ugly as possible. Built of a particularly unpleasant shade of red brick, broken at regular intervals by reinforced concrete balconies, it was roughly square in shape, and reared its unprepossessing bulk from a narrow strip of garden, barely three feet wide, that was separated from the pavement by very green and very forbidding iron railings. Behind these was a very yellow gravel path and a number of dusty and wilting shrubs that looked as though they were thoroughly ashamed of being there at all.

Mr. Budd brought his dingy little car to a gentle stop outside the entrance to this uninspiring building at four o'clock that afternoon, and squeezed himself with difficulty from behind the wheel.

'Why do people live in these sort o' places?' he grunted disparagingly. 'The thing looks like a soap factory.'

'I s'pose they've got to live somewhere,' said Leek, as he joined his superior on the pavement.

'What's the matter with a nice little house an' a bit o' garden?' said the big man, mentally comparing this barracks of a place with his own neat villa at Streatham, with its trim little garden full of the roses which he loved and tended with such care. 'I can't understand why people want to live like bees, all boxed up together.'

With the melancholy sergeant at his heels, he moved ponderously over to the gloomy entrance. The vestibule was bare and cold. There was no lift, but a flight of stone stairs, protected by an iron rail, led upwards. Mr. Budd sleepily surveyed an indicator screwed against the wall, and discovered that No. 7 was on the second floor.

'Come on,' he muttered, and began slowly to mount the stairs.

After his interview with the Assistant Commissioner, he had gone back to his office, acquainted the interested Leek with the reason for his summons, and, thinking the matter over, had decided to start his inquiries at the Walbrooks'. The first essential in a case of this kind was to acquire as much information as possible. It was no good trying to evolve theories on nothing, and nothing was, at present, just about all he had to work on.

These three people had each received a cheque for ten thousand four hundred pounds from Smallwood's Pools, they had been taken back to their homes, and they had vanished into thin air. And that was all that was known. Until some further facts came to light, or could be patiently discovered, there was no indication of the how, why, or wherefore.

Was there something that connected these people other than their mutual good fortune? The police had already gone into that and discovered nothing, but was there something that perhaps the people themselves didn't know about? The organisation necessary to spirit these people away must have been considerable, and the practical carrying out of the scheme must have involved the use of several persons.

Unless, therefore, there was some large material gain accruing, surely no sane person would have gone to all the trouble which this wholesale kidnapping must have necessitated? But what material gain could anyone hope for? The three victims had all been in poor circumstances, and it must have been evident to the meanest intelligence that the cheques they had won would be stopped immediately their disappearance was known. It was the motive that had to be looked for, and it was the hope that he would be able to pick up something that might suggest a motive that had brought Mr. Budd to Balham.

A little breathless from his climb, he presently found himself standing outside a neat, green-painted door with a highly polished brass '7' screwed a foot from the top. Two similar doors on the broad stone landing were numbered '5' and '6'. There was no knocker, but, set in the wall to one side of the door, was a bell-push.

Mr. Budd pressed it, and waited. He waited for nearly a minute, but nothing happened.

'P'r'aps there ain't no one at 'ome,' said Leek pessimistically.

The stout superintendent made no reply, but pressed the bell-push again and kept his finger on it. There was another interval of complete silence, and then a quick footstep sounded within, and the door was opened. A slim girl, who would have been pretty but for the whiteness of her face and the redness of her eyes, looked at them inquiringly.

'Mrs. Walbrook?' asked Mr. Budd, and when she nodded: 'I'm Superintendent Budd, of the Criminal Investigation Department, New Scotland Yard — '

'Oh,' she interrupted him quickly, 'you have news of Harold — my husband?'

She broke off, and Mr. Budd shook his head.

'No, I'm afraid not, ma'am,' he said sympathetically. 'But I'm in charge of the case, an' I'd like to ask you one or two questions.'

The animation that had momentarily lighted up her face died.

'Come in,' she invited listlessly. 'I'm sorry I was so long in answering the door, but I was lying down — '

'I'm sorry to have disturbed you,' said Mr. Budd apologetically, as she led the way into the sitting-room, 'but I want to get as much information as I can, and I thought — '

'What information can I give you?' said the girl. 'I've already told the police I know nothing. Questions — questions — questions! What's the good of them? Why don't you find Harold? It's only a waste of time to keep on questioning me. If I knew anything, do you think I wouldn't have said so?'

Her voice choked in a sob.

'I'm goin' ter do my best to find your husband, ma'am,' said Mr. Budd gently. 'But I'm new to the case, an' I've got to start at the beginnin' . I've read all the reports, of course, but there's nothin' like gettin' things first-hand, so if you'll be a bit patient, ma'am, an' go over it all again with me, it'll be best in the long run, I assure you.'

'I — I'm sorry.' She blinked away the tears that had gathered in her eyes. 'But it's all been so dreadful — like a nightmare — '

'It must have been very distressin' for you, ma'am,' agreed the big man sympathetically. 'But maybe it'll all come right. Now, if you'll just tell me what I want to know — '

She answered his questions to the best of her ability, but the total result was not very helpful.

Harold Walbrook had left the flat on the morning following the presentation of his cheque, with the intention of going as usual to his office. He had also intended visiting his bank and paying in Smallwood's cheque. They had planned a small dinner and a theatre trip to celebrate their good luck for that evening, and he had promised to be home early.

She had waited, ready dressed for their outing, until midnight, but there had been no sign or word from him. At last she had gone to bed, a little uneasy and wondering what had happened to detain him. It had crossed her mind that he might have met with an accident, but since he was rather methodical and always carried his name and address on him, she concluded that if such had been the case she would have been notified.

When the morning came, however, and he had not returned, she was really alarmed, and telephoned to the office. They informed her that her husband had not put in an appearance at all on the previous day, nor had there been any message from him. Another telephone call to the bank manager elicited the fact that he had not been there, either, to pay in the cheque. She had informed the police at once, and they had instituted inquiries, but no trace of the missing man could be found. When Harold Walbrook had walked out of his flat that Friday morning he had, apparently, walked off the earth.

Mr. Budd tactfully questioned her about his private affairs, but here there was nothing to help him, either. He definitely established one thing, however.

Neither Harold Walbrook nor his wife had ever heard of Alfred Gummidge or Louisa Mote until they had met them as fellow-prizewinners.

A little disappointed, for he had expected to add something to the meagre information already in his possession, the stout superintendent had risen to take his leave, when there was a ring at the front door bell. While the girl went to answer it, he waited in the sitting-room, staring gloomily out of the window at the flats opposite.

He heard the front door opened, and then a familiar voice brought him round with a muttered ejaculation of annoyance.

'Mrs. Walbrook?' inquired the voice. 'My name is Ashton. I'm a reporter on the *Morning Mail* — '

Mr. Budd jerked open the sitting-room door, and stepped out into the little hall.

'Good-bye, Mrs. Walbrook!' he said, firmly interposing his huge bulk between the girl and the freckled-faced man in the shabby mackintosh who stood on the threshold. 'I'll be seein' you again soon, I expect.'

'Budd!' exclaimed Peter Ashton. 'Budd! Twice as large as life, and completely unnatural; so there is something in this rumour — '

'There's nothin' in anythin' for you!' said Mr. Budd, gripping his arm and swinging him round. 'Come along, Leek. We'll be going.'

'Here, I say — ' began the reporter indignantly, as he was firmly escorted to the staircase.

'The less you say the better!' snarled Mr. Budd. 'You just come along with me, an' shut up!'

'That's all very well,' protested Peter, 'but I want to see Mrs. Walbrook.'

'Well, you've seen her!' said the big man. 'An' you've seen all you're goin' to see of her, so get that in yer head!'

For a second Peter looked rebellious, and then his face cleared and he grinned.

'All right,' he remarked cheerfully. 'I'd just as soon see you. I can always go back to Mrs. Walbrook. Look here, what's all this about the first dividend winners of Smallwood's Pools disappearing?'

'I don't know anythin' about it!'

grunted Mr. Budd shortly.

'Of course you don't!' retorted the reporter. 'That's why I found you at Mrs. Walbrook's. Now, come on' — his tone was conciliatory — 'you might just as well tell me all about it.'

'I'm tellin' you nothin', Ashton,' asserted Mr. Budd bluntly.

'You'll be making a mistake if you don't,' said Peter. 'If there's any truth in this story that's going round, it's a big thing, and I could help you.'

There was some truth in this. Peter Ashton was one of the cleverest crime reporters in Fleet Street, and he might be useful. The stout superintendent made up his mind.

'I tell ye what I'll do,' he said. 'I'm goin' back to the Yard now, but if you like to meet me at six o'clock in that tea-shop in Whitehall, we might 'ave a cup o' tea an' a chat. But you've got to promise that you won't go trying ter interview Mrs. Walbrook in the meanwhile.'

'Done!' said Peter instantly. 'You are fat but comely! At six, I'll be there!'

He left them with a wave of his hand,

and climbed into the open sports car which had brought him to Balham.

Mr. Budd was silent during the journey back to Scotland Yard, and his thoughts were not pleasant ones. A tough job, he had said, and the Assistant Commissioner had agreed. And a tough job it certainly looked as if it was going to be. His visit to Mrs. Walbrook had brought him no nearer a solution. Perhaps he would have better luck with Mrs. Gummidge when he saw her. At the back of his mind he scarcely thought so. The motive for their disappearance was not to be found in the lives of these people. It was outside them — in some way connected with their luck in Smallwood's Pools.

The house telephone was burring when he reached his cheerless little office, and lifting the receiver, he spoke, breathless from his ascent of the stairs. It was the Assistant Commissioner.

'I've just had a message through from the Gravesend police,' said Colonel Blair. 'Louisa Mote has come back.'

'Come back, has she?' said Mr. Budd. 'Did she explain where she'd been?'

42

'She didn't explain anything,' broke in the Assistant Commissioner. 'She wasn't in a position to explain anything. She was found dead in her cottage, and she'd been strangled!'

4

Mr. Budd is Uneasy

There was dust on the old furniture in Miss Mote's little cottage; dust on the ornaments, and on the ledges, and on the pieces of brass and china ranged so neatly on the Victorian sideboard. And on the bed, upstairs, lay Miss Mote, shortly to be dust, too.

At the round, mahogany table in the small, overcrowded sitting-room sat Mr. Budd, sleepily regarding a collection of objects spread out under the lamp before him. Near the window, staring mournfully into the dark garden, stood the ungainly Leek, his long, thin face wearing an expression of the deepest gloom. Side by side, on an uncomfortable-looking horse-hair sofa, sat Peter Ashton and Inspector Shodhorn, of the Gravesend police.

'It's a queer business, isn't it?' remarked Shodhorn in a flat voice, breaking a long silence.

'Um-m-m!' grunted Mr. Budd, pursing his lips and completely closing his eyes. 'Um-m-m, very queer!'

'I can't understand why anyone should have wanted to kill the old lady,' said Peter, frowning. 'It seems such a meaningless murder.'

'You're right there!' muttered the inspector. 'She was a harmless old soul, with no relations living, and practically no friends.'

'She won this money in the football pool,' murmured Mr. Budd, pinching a roll of fat under his chin between a finger and thumb. 'That's why she was killed. But don't ask me what for, or why they brought her back here, an' sat her up in 'er chair, an' tore up the cheque an' scattered it in 'er lap, because I can't tell yer.'

'There must be a reason,' said the reporter, 'unless the person responsible is mad.'

'That 'ud be all right,' answered the stout superintendent, 'if one person could o' done it. But that's impossible. You've got to take into consideration what happened to that feller Gummidge, an' young Walbrook. It's all connected, an' you'll never get me to believe that there's a whole bunch o' lunatics runnin' about the country kidnappin' an' murderin' people because they've won prizes in football pools.'

'It doesn't seem possible,' agreed Shodhorn.

'It ain't possible,' said Mr. Budd. 'You'd 'ave ter be clean crazy yerself to believe it. No. There's somethin' deep at the back of it.'

'Well, there's certainly nothing here to help us,' said the inspector, shaking his head. 'Whoever killed the poor old lady didn't leave any traces behind.'

'What did they bring her back for?' said Peter, nibbling at his thumb-nail. 'It was taking an infernal, and apparently useless, risk.'

'That's what's puzzlin' me,' replied Mr. Budd. 'She wasn't killed 'ere. The doctor said she'd been dead for over thirty-six hours, an' it was only the day before she was found that the police 'ad been here, makin' a further search ter see if they could find anything that 'ud explain 'er disappearance.'

'Yes, I was here myself,' put in Shodhorn.

'So,' continued Mr. Budd, 'she was brought here dead, an' that was a pretty risky thin' ter do.'

'There's no sense in it,' declared Peter irritably.

'Maybe there's too much sense in it,' grunted the big man paradoxically. 'What I'm worried about is them other two. Is the same thin' goin' to happen with them?'

Peter Ashton had been wondering the same thing, ever since Mr. Budd had hastily told him about Miss Mote, in the little tea-shop in Whitehall where they had arranged to meet.

'If it does,' he said seriously, 'then there must be a motive — '

'There's a motive, all right,' interrupted the fat detective. 'I'm pretty sure of that. The trouble is, how are we goin' ter find it? We've got nothin' ter go on at present. There's nothin' at all to point to the people behind it. The only people who

47

could help us are the people who've vanished, an' one of them's dead. Most likely the other two are by now,' he ended pessimistically.

'They must have brought the body here by car,' said Peter. 'Isn't it possible somebody may have seen it and — '

'My sergeant's attendin' to that now!' broke in Inspector Shodhorn. 'If anybody did see it, he'll find 'em.'

'It's about one chance in a million that anybody saw it,' grunted Mr. Budd — 'to reco'nise it as having anything to do with the murder, I mean. I expect scores o' people saw it, but they wouldn't notice any difference between it an' any other car.'

He sighed wearily, and stifled a yawn.

'The thing we've got ter do,' he went on, leaning back gingerly in the fragile chair on which he was seated, 'is ter find some sort o' kickin' off place. That's what we've got to do, an' I don't mind tellin' you that I can't think of anythin' at the moment. I've come up against some queer cases in me time, but this is the queerest, bar none.'

He shook his head slowly, and a silence fell on the little room. Peter Ashton stared at the ceiling with wrinkled forehead, vainly racking his brains to find some suggestion to offer. Inspector Shodhorn, his fingers loosely clasped between his knees, gazed steadily at the floor, equally vainly trying to seek inspiration. Sergeant Leek continued to look blankly out of the window.

As Mr. Budd had said, there was no 'kicking off' place; nowhere to begin. Although an almost microscopic search had been made of the cottage, the road outside, and the garden, nothing that by the wildest stretch of the imagination could be called a clue had been found.

Miss Mote had been found by the police sitting stiffly and unnaturally in her easy-chair, the cheque which had been presented to her by Sir Hector Blatherwaite torn into minute fragments and scattered in her lap. Her latchkey was on the table beside her, together with her shabby little handbag. And that was all. There was nothing to indicate where she had come from, or who was responsible

49

for the marks on her thin neck, or why those cruel fingers had choked her inoffensive life.

Mr. Budd roused himself at last, and got ponderously to his feet.

'Well,' he growled, 'it ain't no good stoppin' here. We've done all we can, an' that's nothin' .'

He collected the torn pieces of the cheque, which had been tested for finger-prints without result, put them into an envelope, and stowed them away with the key and the handbag in his own worn attaché-case.

Sergeant Leek came to life as he did so, and looked around.

'Are we goin'?' he asked.

'Well, you didn't s'pose we were goin' ter stop 'ere for ever, did you?' snarled Mr. Budd. 'I'm sorry ter wake you up, but we're goin' back to the Yard.' He turned to Shodhorn, who had risen, too. 'You'll look after the removal of the body, will yer?' he said, and the inspector nodded.

'Yes,' he replied. 'And if there's any information about that car, I'll telephone you through at once.'

'I don't suppose you'll hear anythin' ter-night,' said Mr. Budd. 'Maybe you won't hear anythin' at all.'

He went out into the narrow passage and opened the front door. A constable, who was on duty outside, straightened to attention as they passed down the little garden path to the gate, in front of which stood the police car that had brought them from London. The big superintendent took his leave of Shodhorn, growled a word of instruction to the driver and climbed heavily into the back, followed by Peter. Leek took his place beside the driver, and the car moved off.

During the journey back, Mr. Budd huddled himself in the corner, and with his hands folded over his capacious stomach and his chin sunk on his breast appeared to sleep.

Peter, who knew him rather well, guessed that he was probably never more wide awake than he was then. But since he obviously desired not to talk, the reporter refrained from disturbing him.

Mr. Budd remained oblivious to his surroundings until the car was on the point of turning into the arched entrance to Scotland Yard from the Embankment, and then he sat up.

'You'd better come in,' he grunted, preparing to get out as the car slowed down. 'I know you're burstin' ter get ter the office o' that rag of yours an' spread the glad news, but a minute or so won't make any difference.'

Peter thought quickly. In ordinary circumstances, a 'minute or so' might make all the difference, but it was doubtful if any of the other papers had anything but the bare news of the murder as yet, and there would be still time to catch the edition with his exclusive story, even if he waited another hour. And there was the chance that he might learn something that would add to the knowledge he already possessed.

'All right,' he said.

When they reached his cheerless little office, Mr. Budd sat down in the chair behind his desk without bothering to remove either his hat or his overcoat. Pulling open a drawer, he took out a box of his thin, black cigars, stuck one in the corner of his mouth, and lighted it.

'That's better,' he muttered, blowing out a cloud of rank smoke. 'I fergot to take any away with me. Now, look here, Ashton. It's impossible ter keep this out o' the newspapers, an' they're goin' ter make the dickins of a song and dance about it.'

'I'll say they are!' agreed Peter. 'It's the biggest thing that's 'broken' for months. A bigger sensation than any recent crime, because it's closer to the 'man in the street'. Everybody's interested in football pools, and it's got a human interest, too. Why — '

'All right; I know, without your tellin' me,' broke in the big man impatiently. 'It's goin' ter be News with a cap'tal 'n' . An' if these other two are killed it's goin' to be bigger news. I know all that. Now, what I'm proposin' to do is ter let you in on the inside — '

'Come to my arms, my beamish boy!' quoted Peter delightedly. 'You ought to get a knighthood for this — '

'Don't fool!' snapped Mr. Budd crossly. 'I'm doin' this because I think you may be useful. I'm worried about this business, Ashton. I don't like it. There's somethin' that isn't wholesome about it. It's nasty.'

'I know what you mean,' said Peter, becoming instantly serious. 'And you're right — it is nasty.'

'It's not what you might call straight-forward crime,' went on Mr. Budd, 'an' I don't mind tellin' you that I'm uneasy.'

Peter looked at him in surprise. During the many years he had known this man he had never seen him so grave.

'Why do you feel like that?' he asked.

'Because I don't know where it's-goin' ter stop!' replied the stout superinten-dent. 'If we could be sure that it was goin' to end with these three people that 'ave vanished it 'ud be bad enough. But we can't be sure. It may go on. There'll be other people winnin' big dividends, an' what's goin' ter happen to them? Are they goin' the same way?'

'Good lor'!' exclaimed Peter, aghast at the idea. 'You don't think — '

'I don't think nothin' ,' interrupted Mr. Budd. 'I haven't got to the thinkin' stage yet. I'm just supposin' , that's all. An' what I'm supposin' may quite easily 'appen — unless we can find out who, an' why, an' what for.'

'But — surely — ' began the reporter jerkily, and again Mr. Budd interrupted him.

'There's no connection between these three, Gummidge, Mote, an' Walbrook,' he said, 'except that they all won large prizes in Smallwood's Pools, so it must 'ave been because o' that, that whatever happened to 'em happened. An' there'll be others winning large prizes.'

'You're not suggesting that — ' Peter stopped as the telephone buzzer broke into the middle of his sentence.

Mr. Budd stretched out a fat arm and lifted the receiver off its rest.

'Hallo!' he said. And Peter heard a faint chattering from the telephone.

'When was this?' asked the stout man, rolling his cigar from one side of his mouth to the other.

'I see — just a minute.' Mr. Budd picked up a pencil and began to scribble on a pad at his elbow. 'All right.'

He took the receiver from his ear and held it in front of him, without making any effort to put it back on its rest.

'What was it?' asked Peter.

'A call from the Information Room,' answered Mr. Budd slowly. 'They've just 'ad a message from Darlington — '

'That's where Gummidge lives, isn't it?' said Peter quickly, as he paused.

'Where he *lived*,' corrected Mr. Budd. 'He was found dead on his doorstep an hour ago — '

'Dead?" breathed the reporter. And Mr. Budd nodded.

'Strangled!' he replied.

5

The Letter

In the early hours of a wet spring morning Darlington is not the most cheerful place in the world, and possibly the most cheerless part of it was Reed Street. At any rate, Mr. Budd thought so when he caught his first glimpse of that narrow, dingy thoroughfare through a curtain of driving rain at a little after six o'clock that morning.

In spite of the hour and the rain there were knots of people gathered on their front doorsteps, talking eagerly to their immediate neighbours, for the residents of Reed Street are normally early risers, in order to get their menfolk off to work, and this exciting event, which had exploded like a bombshell amid the drabness of their lives, was something that warranted discussion.

There was a craning of necks and a

staring of curious eyes as the taxi containing Mr. Budd, Leek, and Peter Ashton drew up before the door of No. 9. A constable, who regardless of the stares and whispers had been standing stolidly on guard in front of Mr. Gummidge's little house, came forward and opened the door of the cab. Mr. Budd got gingerly out and stood on the wet pavement, looking sleepily about him. On this occasion his sleepy appearance was no mere characteristic, for he was in truth a very tired man indeed.

It had been just on midnight when the telephone-call had come through from the Information Room, notifying him of the discovery in Darlington, and he had already spent an anxious and tiring day. There had just been time for Peter to rush to the office of the *Morning Mail*, turn in a hasty account of the murder of Miss Mote, draw some money, telephone his wife, and meet Mr. Budd and Leek at the station. They had snatched a little sleep on the train, but it had been broken and restless, and as a restorative was not very successful.

'The inspector's inside, sir,' said the constable, when Mr. Budd had introduced himself. 'He's been waiting for you.'

The inspector, a grizzled man, with a great beak of a nose, and thin lips that drooped at the corners, had evidently been listening, too, for he appeared at that moment on the threshold.

'Glad t' meet you,' he said, extending a bony hand and gripping Mr. Budd's podgy fingers. 'Come inside.'

They trooped into the dark passage, after Peter Ashton had settled with the taximan, and were ushered by the inspector into a small, musty-smelling room on the right. It was cluttered up with old-fashioned furniture; worn plush-covered chairs, antimacassars, waxen fruit, and flowers covered with glass, and several aspidistras on bamboo stands in the window.

'Mrs. Gummidge has given me the use of this room,' said the inspector. 'You haven't been long getting here.'

'We left as soon as we got the news,' said Mr. Budd. 'You didn't take long notifying the Yard, either.'

'Put through a trunk call at once,' answered Inspector Chinn. 'Thought it best to lose no time in the circumstances.'

The stout man nodded approvingly.

'I wish all the provincial police were as sensible,' he said, and the inspector smiled. The smile changed the whole aspect of his face completely. Before he had looked rather dour and disagreeable, now there was a twinkle of amusement in his eyes, and the drooping lips curved humorously.

'I expect you do,' he said. 'In this case, you see, the Yard had already been called in. I won't waste time about that, though. You want to hear the details of how the discovery was made. Well — '

The inspector cleared his throat and began. He was evidently a stickler for saving time, and he compressed his story into the fewest possible words.

The people of Reed Street, due to their having to get up so early in the morning, were, with the exception of Saturdays and Sundays, usually in bed and asleep by ten o'clock. At that hour the narrow street was quiet and deserted. Constable Piler had, therefore, been rather surprised when he turned into Reed Street at half-past ten on the preceding night, to see a car drawing away from the kerb about two-thirds of the way down on the right-hand side. It was a big car, with dim lights, and it passed him at a fair speed. He had stopped to look after it, rather curious that such an obviously expensive machine should be connected in any way with the residents of this poor neighbourhood. Unfortunately, he had failed to see the number, for the plate was so spattered with mud that it was indistinguishable.

The car continued round the corner, and he had continued on his beat, still a little curious. Nearing the place where the car had been standing he caught sight of a dark object sprawling in one of the doorways, and discovered when he reached it that it was the body of a man. It was not only the body of a man but it was the body of the man who had so mysteriously disappeared — Alfred Gummidge.

A quick examination had assured

Constable Piler that he was quite dead, and that he had been murdered. He knocked up Mrs. Gummidge, who had been reduced to a state of screaming hysterics by the news, and had despatched her eldest son to the nearest call-box to ring up the police station.

Inspector Chinn himself had gone round at once to Reed Street, verified the information, and immediately telephoned the Yard.

'And that's really all there is,' concluded the inspector. 'Except that we found the cheque Gummidge had won from Smallwood's torn up and stuffed into one of his waistcoat pockets.'

Mr. Budd who had been listening with closed eyes, opened them.

'It's a pity that feller o' yours didn't get the number o' that car,' he said regretfully. 'Can he describe it?'

'Not good enough to be of much use, I'm afraid,' said Chinn, shaking his head. 'He says it was a big saloon, and he thinks it was painted black, but he can't be sure. I've already sent out that description, but — '

'There are about umpteen hundred cars which it 'ud fit,' finished Mr. Budd. 'Um! No, I don't think it's going to help much.' He yawned. 'Well, that's two of 'em come back dead. I wonder when Walbrook 'ull turn up?'

Chinn shot him a quick glance.

'Two of them?' he repeated questioningly, and the big man nodded.

'Yes,' he answered. 'Louisa Mote was found in 'er cottage yesterday — strangled.'

'The same as Gummidge!' exclaimed the inspector, and then with a face that had suddenly gone very grave: 'What's at the back of it all?'

'Now yer askin' me somethin' ,' said Mr. Budd. 'I've no idea. No more than the man in the moon. But I'm going ter find out,' he added obstinately. 'What did you do with the body?'

'It's upstairs,' answered Chinn. 'I didn't order it to be removed until after you'd seen it.'

'I'd like ter take a look at it,' murmured the stout superintendent. 'There might be somethin' — '

He followed the inspector out into the

passage and up the narrow stairs. Peter Ashton, as he accompanied them, caught a glimpse of a woman's face peering at them from a half-open door at the back and concluded that it must belong to Mrs. Gummidge. It was terribly tragic, he thought, this trick which fate had played. These poor people had been lifted to the heights, and then flung mercilessly into the lowest depths. It was worse for the Gummidges than for Miss Mote. She had had no relations to suffer. And if anything happened to Walbrook — The white strained face of Molly Walbrook, with its swollen eyes, floated for a moment before him, and he suddenly felt a wave of anger break over him against the unknown people who had been responsible for so much misery. It was inhuman — devilish!

The others had gone into a bedroom opening off a passage that was the counterpart of the one downstairs, and when Peter joined them, they were looking down at the sheeted figure on the bed.

Inspector Chinn removed the sheet, and Mr. Budd bent over the body. It looked very frail. Not a great deal of strength had been necessary to break the thread of life. Hard work and years of undernourishment were stamped on the grey, rather flabby face, with its deeply graven lines.

The fat detective made a careful examination of the body and the clothing, but he found nothing. On the cheap dressing-table were the things which had been taken from the pockets, and among these was the torn cheque.

'I wonder what the idea of that was?' murmured Mr. Budd thoughtfully, as he looked at it. 'It was the same in the other case. But why tear it up?'

'Spite, I should think,' said the inspector. 'They knew it was no good to them — '

'They, whoever they are, must 'ave known that from the start,' said Mr. Budd, rubbing his fat chin. 'They must 'ave realised that these cheques would've bin stopped directly these people was found to 'ave been missin' . That's what makes the 'ole thin' so queer.' He came back to the body and stood looking down at it through half-closed eyes. If only by some miraculous power Alfred Gummidge could be given the sense of speech for five minutes. He could clear up this tangle, for he had known —

With a sigh Mr. Budd turned away.

'There's nothin' more to see here,' he said wearily, and the inspector replaced the sheet.

'I s'pose you've questioned the wife?' continued the stout superintendent, as they returned slowly down the stairs.

Chinn nodded.

'She knows nothing,' he answered.

'Well,' said Mr. Budd, 'for the moment it seems ter be a deadlock, don't it? I tell yer candidly I don't know what line of investigation to adopt.'

'These people — Gummidge, Mote, and Walbrook, must have been taken somewhere,' said Peter. 'If the place could be found — '

'If it could be found,' broke in Mr. Budd. 'But 'ow are yer goin' to find it? There's the whole of England to choose from. We can't search every house from Land's End ter John o' Groats. That's the trouble about this business. We don't know enough. All we've got is a couple of dead bodies an' two torn-up cheques. We don't know where these people was taken to when they disappeared; we don't know where they've come from. In fact, we don't know nothin' ,' he ended disgustedly.

Peter frowned and ran his thumb-nail between his teeth. The big man had stated no more than the truth. They did know nothing. Unless Walbrook —

Walbrook! A sudden idea occurred to him.

'Listen!' he said excitedly. 'I've thought of something. Gummidge and Miss Mote were murdered, and their bodies brought back to their homes, weren't they?'

'Well, what about it?' grunted Mr. Budd. 'We know that — '

'Wait until I've finished,' broke in Peter, impatiently. 'If Walbrook's murdered, too, it's ten chances to one that his body will be returned to the flat. There's no reason why an exception should be made in his case. The same method will more than probably be adopted.'

'Well — ' began the stout man.

'Will you wait!' snapped Peter. 'This is my idea, and I think it's a good one. Why not have the flat watched from now on, day and night. Then if they bring back Walbrook, as they did Gummidge and Mote, you'll catch 'em.'

Mr. Budd's sleepy eyes opened, and the weariness left his face.

'It's a good idea,' he declared. 'It's a very good idea, Ashton. I wonder I didn't think of it meself. I'll do it!' He turned to Leek. 'You might as well do somethin' fer yer livin' ,' he went on. 'Go down to the station, an' put through a call ter the Yard. Tell Inspector Halford to put two men on to watch Brockvale Mansions right away. The watch is ter be kept up night an' day till further notice. You can explain what they're lookin' fer, can't yer?'

The lean sergeant nodded lugubriously.

''Ow do I get ter the police station?' he asked.

'On yer feet!' snarled Mr. Budd.

'I mean where is it?' explained Leek.

'You've got a tongue in yer head, ain't you?' demanded his superior. 'You must 'ave got somethin' .'

Inspector Chinn intervened with directions for finding the police station, and Leek took his departure.

'That's that,' remarked the big man when the sergeant had gone. 'If we're lucky somethin' might come o' this idea o' yours, Ashton. It's certainly the best we've struck up ter now.'

''Praise from Sir Hubert is praise indeed,'' murmured Peter. 'If you had a few reporters at the Yard there wouldn't be so many unsolved crimes — '

'Because you've 'appened ter hit on somethin' sensible fer once,' interrupted Mr. Budd, 'there's no need ter go on gettin' a swelled 'ead. An' 'oo's this feller Sir Hubert you're talkin' about?'

'A quotation only,' replied Peter.

'Oh, I see!' grunted the stout superintendent. 'Well, now. I suppose you'll be makin' all the arrangements fer the inquest, Chinn?'

The inspector nodded.

'I think,' continued Mr. Budd, 'you'd better try an' get an adjournment pendin' — '

He broke off as there came a sharp rat-tat at the front door.

'It's only the postman,' said Peter, who was standing by the small window. There was a shuffling step in the passage outside, and then, as Mr. Budd was in the act of opening his mouth to continue his remarks to the inspector, a gasping cry.

'That's Mrs. Gummidge!' muttered Chinn. 'What's happened?'

He pulled open the door and peered out, Mr. Budd and Peter looking over his shoulder. Mrs. Gummidge, a thin woman, with streaks of grey in her hair, and a lined face that was ravaged by grief, leaned against the wall, staring blankly at a sheet of paper in one work-worn hand, and moaning to herself. At her feet lay an envelope.

'What's the matter?' asked the inspector.

Without answering she thrust the sheet of paper into his hand, and began to sob jerkily. Chinn looked at it, uttered an exclamation, and passed it to Mr. Budd.

It was one of Smallwood's coupons,

and scrawled across it in red ink was the message:

'THE WAGES OF SIN IS DEATH! ALFRED GUMMIDGE R.I.P.'

Mr. Budd stooped and picked up the envelope. It bore a Darlington postmark, and it had been posted in time to catch the last collection on the previous night.

6

The Third Cheque

When Mr. Budd told Peter Ashton that the football pool mystery would be news with a capital 'N,' he had not exaggerated. The newspapers vied with each other to produce the most startling headlines, and if, as was only natural in the circumstances, the *Morning Mail* was the first with the full story, the others ran it a close second.

Photographs of poor Miss Mote's little cottage taken from every conceivable angle, appeared on the front pages of most of the 'dailies', side by side with similar photographs of Alfred Gummidge's small house in Reed Street. Reporters besieged the village of Meopham, and descended in train loads on Darlington. The distracted Mrs. Gummidge and her family were questioned and interviewed and photographed until they became dizzy through constant repetition of the same story. The headquarters of Smallwood's Pools were diligently bombarded for news and opinions, but they maintained an attitude of discreet silence and refused to supply the Press with any information whatsoever. So persistent did this thirst for knowledge become in the case of Molly Walbrook, that she had to shut herself up in her flat, refusing either to go out or to answer the door, lest she should encounter one of the hoard of newspaper men who lurked continuously about the vestibule and staircase.

It was without any doubt the greatest sensation that a jaded public had experienced for many a long day. The mystery surrounding the disappearance, and the subsequent deaths, of two of the principal persons concerned, combined with the tremendous attraction of the football pool interest, gripped the imagination of the man in the street, and sent his hand hastily fumbling in his pocket whenever a fresh edition came out that might contain further news.

But although the newspapers kept the pot boiling with all kinds of theories, suggestions, interviews, and photographs, of real, authentic, further news there was none.

A duplicate of the message received by Mrs. Gummidge had arrived at Miss Mote's cottage on the afternoon of the same day. In this case it had been posted in London, too late for the last collection. It differed only from the 'Gummidge' message in that the name of Louisa Mote had been substituted for that of Alfred Gummidge.

Mr. Budd had passed both on to the finger-print department for test, but the result had been comparatively negative. There seemed little doubt, however, that the person responsible for the sending of the messages was a fanatic of some kind. The wording hinted at religious mania, and unless the whole thing had been done for a blind, this constituted a step forward. Before the arrival of the messages there had been no clue at all concerning the motive of the murders. But now it appeared possible that they were the work of someone with a strong anti-gambling obsession.

With this possibility in mind, Mr. Budd had, immediately on his return to Scotland Yard, set in motion a vast network of inquiry, with the object of listing all the known people in the country whose views were opposed to gambling in general, and football pools in particular. When this had been done, they could then be weeeded out for those who were definitely 'queer'. In this way he hoped to eventually find the person he was looking for. Always supposing, of course, that he wasn't on the wrong track altogether.

Of necessity the inquiry would take time, and in the meanwhile there was the chance of a short cut to the same end in Peter Ashton's idea of having Brockvale Mansions watched. So far the two men who had been on duty day and night had seen nothing to report, but there was no saying what they might.

Hunched in the chair behind his desk, chewing the butt of a cigar that had long since gone out, the big man turned over in his mind for the hundredth time all the aspects of this queerest of queer cases. It was late, and by rights he should have long since gone home, but he couldn't summon up enough physical energy to move. It was on record that he had once spent the entire night dozing and thinking in his office, for no other reason than that he lacked the initial effort necessary to get up and walk down the stairs.

Twelve o'clock sounded sonorously from Big Ben near by, and Sergeant Leek, who had been perched on his usual chair, frowningly studying some papers on his thin knee, looked across at his superior.

Mr. Budd appeared to be asleep. His podgy hands were clasped loosely over his capacious stomach, and his eyes were closed; but his lean sergeant knew that this attitude was deceptive.

'It's gone twelve,' he ventured, and his information was received with a grunt.

A little discouraged by this lack of enthusiasm, he remained silent for a minute or two, and then tried a fresh opening.

'If there's nuthin' you want me for,' he said, 'I think I'll be gettin' along 'ome.'

Mr. Budd opened his eyes slowly.

'What's the hurry?' he growled.

'Well,' said Leek rather plaintively, 'it's gettin' late, an' there doesn't seem much sense in sittin' 'ere when one could be relaxin' the mind an' body in sleep — '

'You ain't got any mind, an' precious little body!' broke in Mr. Budd rudely. 'An' anyway, you couldn't relax either of 'em any more than you do all day! Where did yer get hold of all that stuff about relaxin'?'

'I read it in a book,' answered the sergeant mournfully. 'It said that the sleep you get before twelve is worth all you get after — '

'Well, you ought ter be all right,' grunted Mr. Budd. 'You're thirty years to the good! Is that what you've bin readin' all the evenin'?'

Leek looked guiltily at the papers on his knee, and shook his head.

'Then what 'ave yer bin so busy at?' demanded Mr. Budd.

'I've jest bin 'avin' a look at these coupons,' said the sergeant sheepishly.

'Coupons? What coupons?' asked the big man, heaving himself into a more

77

upright position.

'I got 'em from Smallwood's this morning,' explained Leek. 'This football pool scheme seems ter be a good idea. All yer 'ave ter do is ter forecast what fourteen teams 'ull do, an' yer get a dividend o' thousands.'

'An' you think that's easy?' said Mr. Budd sarcastically.

'Well, it ain't exac'ly easy,' said the sergeant. 'I mightn't get it right the first time — '

'Oh, I see!' The stout superintendent took the stub of cigar from his mouth, looked at it with distaste, and dropped it into the waste-paper basket at his side. 'You don't expect to win a few thousands first go off, eh?'

'That's right,' said Leek. 'It ain't no good bein' too optimistic over these things. But I should think I might pick up a nice bit o' money in a week or two. I'm workin' out a system.'

'Like yer racin' system, I s'pose?' remarked Mr. Budd, producing a fresh cigar and biting off the end. 'That was a pathetic effort, if yer like!'

The sergeant reddened.

'That would 'ave bin all right if the 'orses 'adn't let me down by not running ter form,' he mumbled. 'But this's different. There's a lot of funny stuff goes on in racin' , but football's straight. Yer 'aven't got ter wonder whether a team is tryin' , f'rinstance. All yer've got ter do with this 'ere coupon is ter make up yer mind whether it's an 'ome win or an away or a draw, and — '

'An' after you've made up yer mind, they go an' do somethin' different!' said Mr. Budd. 'When we was tacklin' that 'Jockey' business an' the 'Horseshoe' job you tried to make a fortune outer backin' 'orses. That nearly made yer bankrupt. Now yer goin' ter try to get easy money outer football pools. I only 'ope we never come up against a murder in the Stock Exchange!'

Leek sighed and rose to his feet.

'Well, I don't see why I shouldn't 'ave a shot at it!' he said defensively. 'There ain't much money ter be got 'ere. If they paid yer what yer was worth — '

'You'd owe 'em a bit!' snapped Mr.

Budd. 'Well,' he added, 'I think I'll clear off home an' do some o' this relaxin' you was talkin' about.'

The sergeant brightened visibly.

'There don't seem much point in stopping 'ere,' he agreed hastily, in case Mr. Budd should change his mind. 'What about the mornin' — '

Before he could finish what he had to say, the telephone uttered a subdued buzz, and the big man picked up the receiver.

'Hallo! Yes, I'm here, but you were lucky ter catch me, I was just goin' .' His face changed as he listened. 'Put 'em through ter me, will yer?' There was a pause, then he continued: 'That you, Reeves? What is it? Right. I'll be along in twenty minutes.'

He hung up the receiver and turned to the thin sergeant.

'There'll be no relaxin' fer either of us yet,' he announced. 'We're goin' ter Balham. Get on ter 'transport', will yer, an' ask them ter have a car ready in two minutes.'

'Why are we — ' began Leek; and Mr.

Budd interrupted him.

'Don't go wastin' time askin' questions!' he snarled irritably. 'Get that car!'

More or less resigned to the loss of a complete night's sleep, the melancholy sergeant obeyed.

By the time the stout superintendent had pulled on his coat, and they had made their way down the stairs to the entrance, the order for the car had been carried out. A fast police tender was waiting for them, and, with a word to the driver, Mr. Budd climbed inside, followed by the tired Leek. The car swung through the arch on to the Embankment, and sped away in the direction of Balham.

'Now,' said Mr. Budd, ensconcing himself comfortably in a corner of the seat, 'I'll answer them questions that you didn't ask! That was Reeves who rang up. He and Salter 'ave bin watchin' the block o' flats where Walbrook lives, an' a few minutes ago they saw a man staggerin' along the street looking as though 'e was drunk. He got as far as the entrance ter Brockvale Mansions, an' then collapsed. They found that he wasn't drunk, but was half-starved an' sufferin' from a pretty bad wound in the 'ead. His clothes were in rags, an' he looked like a tramp, and when they searched 'im ter see if they could find anythin' that would show his identity, they found a Smallwood's cheque for ten thousand four hundred pounds, made out to 'Arold Walbrook.'

In the dim interior of the car Leek gaped stupidly.

'Yer don't mean ter say,' he gaped, 'that this feller's Walbrook?'

'I don't mean ter say nothin',' answered the big man. 'He may be Walbrook, an' he may not be Walbrook. We're goin' ter find out.'

7

The Unknown

Harold Walbrook left his flat on the morning following the presentation of his cheque at the Astoria Hotel, full of plans for the future, both pleasant and practical. This unexpected good fortune that had come to him should form the basis of a useful and successful career. He had for a long time cherished a secret ambition to become a playwright — an ambition fostered by certain complimentary remarks passed about two sketches he had written for the revue performed at Christmas by the office dramatic society. This small success had imbued him with a desire to do something bigger. The plot for a full length play had slowly taken shape in his mind, though at the time he had seen very little hope of ever finding time to write it.

But his luck with Smallwood's Pools had put the opportunity within his reach.

If he invested ten thousand pounds in something solid and substantial, it should bring him in enough to live comfortably for the rest of his life, and enable him to devote all his time to the furtherance of his ambition. And there would still be four hundred to spend on the things that he and Molly had planned to buy . . .

'Excuse me, Mr. Walbrook!'

A voice snapped the thread of his thoughts, and, startled, he stopped and looked round. A large car had come smoothly to a stop at the kerb, and a man was leaning out of the window.

'I was on my way to call on you,' said the stranger. 'It is Mr. Walbrook, isn't it?'

Puzzled and wondering, Harold nodded.

'I thought I recognised you,' went on the other. 'I'm from Messrs. Smallwood's. There has been a slight mistake made over the cheques that we issued yesterday. A certain secret mark, known only to our bankers, was unfortunately omitted, but if you will come along with me to the Astoria Hotel, the matter can very easily and quickly be put right.'

Harold gave a quick breath of relief. At

the mention of a mistake his heart had for a moment given an unpleasant leap.

'Certainly I'll come,' he said.

The pleasant-faced man opened the door of the car, and he stepped inside.

'I'm very sorry to inconvenience you like this, Mr. Walbrook,' he said apologetically, as the car moved off. 'But our bankers have instructions not to cash any cheques of ours unless they bear the mark I mentioned. You have your cheque with you, of course?'

'Yes,' replied Harold, without any suspicion that the man beside him was other than he had said. 'I was taking it to my bank this morning.'

'What a stroke of luck that I was in time to catch you!' murmured the other, and it was not until some time later that Harold realised the exact meaning of that remark. 'This will save a lot of unnecessary delay.'

He produced a large cigarette-case and offered it. Harold took one, waited while his companion helped himself, and struck a match.

'Thank you.' The man dipped the end

of his cigarette in the flame, and blew out a cloud of fragrant smoke. 'I have these specially imported from Egypt,' he said. 'Perhaps you prefer Virginia tobacco?'

Harold did. He thought there was something extremely unpleasant about the flavour of the cigarette he was smoking, but he was too polite to say so. His companion began to chat about a variety of subjects as the car sped on, and presently Harold found that his voice was growing fainter and fainter, as though he were slowly receding out of earshot. That, of course, was ridiculous. The man was sitting within inches of him. It was queer how tired he felt, and what a nasty sensation had suddenly come to the pit of his stomach. His head felt very stuffy and heavy. The cigarette must have disagreed with him. He hoped he wasn't going to be sick. And then he no longer hoped anything . . .

★   ★   ★

His first impression on slowly recovering his senses was that in some extraordinary and unaccountable way he had got very tight. On one never-to-be-forgotten occasion he had gone out on a binge with several of his friends at the office, and had been deposited at his flat in a state that could only be described as paralytic. His sensations on that following morning were so exactly like his present ones that his conclusion was understandable.

His eyes smarted and his head ached. There was an unpleasant taste in his mouth, and he felt that at any moment he might be violently sick. Opening his eyes made his head worse, and it was too dark to see anything, anyway, so he closed them again. How in the world had he got in this state? Celebrating with some of the fellows at the office? But he hadn't *been* to the office! He'd started to go and met that chap from Smallwood's. Memory came back with a rush. The car — the cigarette — He'd been drugged!

He opened his eyes quickly as this appalling conviction seized him, and tried to sit up. But he couldn't move! The effort made his head throb terribly, and he tried to lift his hand to his forehead, but he found that this was impossible, too. He was bound — bound hand and foot, and helpless!

With a groan he relaxed and lay still, forcing himself to think. He was still feeling desperately ill, and his mind was cloudy and uncertain. He couldn't concentrate. The drug which had made him unconscious was still partially stupefying his brain. Its soporific effects had not entirely worn off, and presently these reasserted themselves, and he drifted into a state that was midway between sleep and coma.

A bright light shining full on his face brought him out of this semi-trance, and he blinked up resentfully at its source. It came from a lamp held in the hand of a man who was bending over him and peering down at him through the holes in a baglike mask that covered his head. The eyes glittered unnaturally, and Harold Walbrook felt a clammy little shiver run down his back.

'So you're awake.' The man spoke in a soft, slurred voice, slightly muffled by the material of the mask.

'What's the idea? Who are you?'

croaked Harold with difficulty, for his throat was dry. 'What's the meaning of bringing me here — '

'Gently, gently!' interrupted the other. 'You want to know too much all at once, Mr. Walbrook. Be patient.'

'Damn your patience!' said Harold angrily. 'What d'you think you're playing at? Bringing me here and tying me up — '

'You are suffering in a good cause,' broke in the man with the lamp. 'You might be compared to the early Christian martyrs, only they suffered voluntarily, and you, I'm afraid, will have no choice in the matter.'

Again Harold experienced a cold sensation creep down his back.

'I don't know what you're talking about,' he said. 'You'll get into serious trouble for this, I can tell you — '

'Don't be ridiculous!' snapped the other curtly. 'There will be no trouble for me. For that matter, there will be very little trouble for you or your companions in sin. It will soon be over.'

Harold stared up at him in blank astonishment.

'What the devil are you talking about?' he demanded. 'What do you mean by 'my companions in sin'?'

'The man, Gummidge, and the woman, Mote,' was the reply.

'Good Lord!' breathed Harold incredulously. 'Have you got hold of them, too?'

'They will be here soon,' said the unknown. 'Their bodies, and yours, will be sent back to serve as a warning to others.'

He spoke calmly and without raising his voice above its original low, husky whisper, but there was a deadly certainty about it that filled Harold Walbrook with terror.

'Do you mean — that you're going to — kill us?' he whispered hoarsely.

The other nodded.

'That is my intention,' he replied. 'You will have the satisfaction of knowing that your death will show to others the dangers of the curse of gambling — '

'You're mad!' gasped Harold. 'Stark, staring, raving mad!'

He might have touched a spring, so sudden was the change in the man beside him. His calmness slid off him like a dropped cloak, and the lamp in his hand shook, as though he had been stricken with an ague.

'You lie!' he almost screamed, the words tumbling over themselves in a slobbering, slurring torrent. 'You lie! I'm not mad, I'm not mad, I tell you! I am the only sane person in a mad world — a world of corruption and death. My mission is to purify mankind, and purge the earth of its sins. For this I have been chosen by the Fates — appointed an apostle of righteous wrath to wreak vengeance on you, and such as you, who have polluted the very air with the lust of greed. Gambling is the root of all evil — a creeping growth that is strangling the goodness of the world, and making of mankind a race of avaricious creatures whose one aim in life is the quest of gold. Mad! Instead of hurling such an insult at one, who by prayer and meditation has been permitted to see the chaos and destruction to which this goal is leading, you should be humbly thankful that you have been chosen as an unworthy example to bring back rectitude to your fellow sinners.'

The outburst ceased as abruptly as it had begun, the shaking hand became steady, and the unknown drew a long breath.

'I'm afraid I have allowed my enthusiasm to get the better of me,' went on the muffled voice, once more soft, and almost apologetic. 'But you angered me with your absurd accusation. I should have accepted it from whence it came. It has always been the lot of a pioneer to be misunderstood.'

Harold could only stare, speechless. That half-hysterical flood of rhetorical nonsense would, in different circumstances, have been merely pathetic. As it was, it was rather terrible. The man was as mad as a hatter. A crazy idealist labouring under the delusion that he was the chosen instrument of Providence to rid the world of sin. The thing was grotesque, unreal, horrible, and — dangerous.

'I shall leave you now,' said the other, setting down the lamp he had been holding on a small table. 'Ponder well over your iniquities, for your days among the living are numbered, and the hour of atonement is at hand.'

Without another word he walked over to the door and went out, closing it and locking it behind him.

For nearly a minute after he had gone, Harold lay still, staring up at the dim ceiling above him, scarcely able to believe that he was really awake. This was the stuff of dreams and nightmares, not of ordinary, everyday life. And yet there was no doubt that it was real. If he required any assurance of this he found it in his aching head and cramped limbs. He was helpless in the power of a madman!

The knowledge was anything but pleasant, and the prospect was decidedly worse. Unless he could get out of this awful situation it looked as if it would mean his finish. The question was, how could he get out of it?

He tried to discover if there was any chance of loosening the cords which bound his wrists, and quickly found there was not. They had been very thoroughly and securely tied, and were unshiftable. With an effort, he managed, at the second attempt, to hoist himself up into a sitting position. The movement made his head throb wildly, and resulted in a wave of dizziness that for the moment almost blinded him. In a little while, however, this passed off, and he began to look about him.

He was in a large, bare room, that was nearly empty of furniture. A curtainless window faced him, over the panes of which had been pasted brown paper. There was a large marble fireplace on his right, with a rusty iron grate full of rubbish. On his left was the door. He was sitting on a heap of very old and very dirty blankets, which had been piled on the bare boards, and the only article of furniture in the room was a rickety table on which the lamp stood.

The silence was complete. Although he listened intently, he could hear no sound at all, either from within or without. This utter silence suggested that the house, of which this bare and dismal room formed a part, was somewhere in the country. By what he could see, it looked as though it was an empty house, but any other characteristics about it were shut off from him by those four blank and dingy walls.

His inspection had not proved very helpful, as he realised, with a sinking heart. Edging himself backwards on the blankets, he managed to prop his back against the wall, and, thus supported, found sitting up a little easier.

The after-effects of the drug were beginning to wear off, and although he still felt far from well, his mind was clearer. As calmly as he could, he proceeded to review the situation. He was in a nasty mess, and he had to find some way out of it, and find it quickly. There was no knowing how soon that crazy lunatic would return to carry out his threat, and speed was, therefore, essential. But what could he do?

Summoning up every ounce of mental energy that he possessed, he worried at this problem. There must be some way out. It was impossible that this could be the end —

Man finds it very difficult to imagine his own complete extinction, just as he finds it impossible to imagine limitless space, and Harold Walbrook found the visualisation of his own death at the hands of the unknown too incredible to contemplate. Something was bound to happen to prevent such a thing. It must happen. Such things had no place in real life. One read about murders in the newspapers, of course, but they had happened to somebody else. Lots of things happened to other people which it was impossible to imagine could happen to one's self —

In the midst of his thoughts came a sound, breaking clearly through the silence. A thin, plaintive sound, that first froze his blood, and then filled him with a sudden rush of hot anger. The sound of a woman sobbing.

8

The Escape

The sound came from the other side of the wall against which he leant, and he guessed that it must be Miss Mote who was crying. That timid, grey-haired little woman, whom he had met at the Astoria on the previous day. Was it only the previous day? It seemed as if years had passed since that pleasant function.

The sobbing continued, interspersed with faint moans, and Harold clenched his hands. To have to remain here helpless while that was going on was almost unendurable, but he could do nothing. Presently the sobbing ceased and there was silence once more. He wondered how long he had been a prisoner in this house, but there was no means of telling. His watch was on his wrist, and his hands had been tied behind his back. It couldn't have been very long. The unconsciousness induced by the drug would have worn off in an hour or so at the most. Now that he was feeling better, he was beginning to feel hungry. Would they bring him any food, or was starvation part of the programme?

His mind was set at rest concerning this, for at the end of a long interval — it must have been several hours — he heard footsteps outside the door, there was the rasp of a key in the lock, and the man who had stopped him in the car came in carrying a glass of water and a thick slice of bread.

He was still smiling cheerfully, and looked almost benevolent as he came over to where Harold sat.

'How are you feeling?' he asked, rather in the manner of a doctor visiting a patient. 'Not too good, I'll bet. That dope is grand stuff for the job, but it makes you feel like nothing on earth after, so I'm told.'

'It's filthy stuff!' grunted Harold, glaring at him. 'But very appropriate to the people who use it.'

The other grinned broadly.

'You can say what you like,' he replied,

amiably, 'you won't rattle me. I'm not like his nibs — easily upset. You touched him up all right, didn't you?'

'I told him he was mad, if that's what you mean,' said Harold. 'And so he is. He ought to be shut up.'

'We won't argue about that,' said the pleasant-faced man. 'I've brought you your supper, and you'd best make the most of it. You won't get any more till to-morrow night.'

He stooped and held the glass to Harold's lips.

'I'm sorry I can't untie your hands,' he said. 'You'll have to manage this way.'

Harold drank greedily and then ate the bread, as the other fed it to him.

'There,' said the man when it was gone. 'That'll keep you going, if it won't exactly fatten you up.' He straightened and turned towards the door.

'Look here,' said Harold. 'What is all this about? What do you intend to do with me?'

'I'm afraid you're booked,' said the other, pausing on the threshold. 'He told you, didn't he?'

'But he's mad!' cried Harold. 'He was talking utter nonsense. Surely you're not going to stand by and allow us to be murdered by a lunatic?'

'I'm doing as I'm told!' retorted the man coolly. 'I'm being well paid, and so far as I'm concerned you can be hung, drawn, and quartered!'

He turned on his heel and went out, pulling the door shut behind him and turning the key.

During all the rest of his life, Harold Walbrook never forgot the days that followed. He was given nothing but bread and water, and very little of that, and the lack of proper nourishment reduced him to a state of weakness that brought with it periods of mental apathy during which he cared very little what happened to him. These were interspersed with fits of furious rage against the people who were responsible, and prolonged endeavours to find a way of escape.

During most of the time the silence in the house was profound, but occasionally he could hear sounds of activity, and once during the night he woke from a fitful sleep, with the perspiration streaming down his forehead and a thin gurgling scream ringing in his ears. It stopped almost before he was fully awake, and he was undecided whether it had been real or a nightmare. There were movements going on in the house, however, and the murmur of voices reached him, so he concluded that the scream had not been a figment of his imagination. Shortly afterwards the engine of a car started up, and a few minutes later faded away in the distance. Somebody had left, and Harold wondered grimly if the first 'example' had been sent to its destination.

Of the madman, he had seen nothing since that first interview, but the other man came at irregular intervals to bring him the bread and water. It was during one of these visits that accident supplied him with a slender chance of escape. He had finished his frugal meal, and the man was turning away to leave him, when his foot caught in the pile of blankets and he stumbled. In saving himself from falling, the empty glass dropped from his hand and smashed on the bare floor. The man cursed loudly and collected the broken pieces, with the exception of a large splinter that had jumped on to the blankets and which he overlooked. The sight of this gave Harold an idea, and when the other had gone he proceeded without delay to put it into practice. With difficulty he succeeded in getting hold of that scrap of glass between his fingers, and laboriously began to rub its sharp edge against the cords at his wrists. To accomplish this, he had to twist his hand up at a painful angle, and but for the fact that his wrists had been bound several inches above the joint, it would have been impossible. As it was, it took him hours before he made any impression on the thick cord, and then, with a thrill of delight, he felt them give —

After that it was easy. In less than an hour he was free and rubbing his cramped limbs to restore the circulation. There was little likelihood of his being disturbed. His gaoler had paid his visit. He would not appear again for many hours, unless some other and more sinister reason than food brought him.

Harold scrambled to his feet, and stood for a moment, swaying shakily, supporting himself by the wall. In a little while he attempted to walk a few steps, and succeeded, although his legs shook under him. Presently his weakness passed, and he made an inspection of the window. To his joy, he discovered that it was not secured in any way except by the usual hasp. His captors had relied on his helpless state, and taken few other precautions.

Cautiously, he undid the hasp and attempted to raise the lower sash. It was very stiff and defied his efforts at first, but with a little coaxing, he eventually succeeded in pushing it up eighteen inches, where it stuck, and definitely refused to budge.

He thrust out his head into the darkness gulping in great draughts of cool, sweet-smelling air, that tasted good after the mustiness of the room. It was not very far to the ground, and there was a drainpipe running down beside the window. He listened, but he could hear nothing in the house, and deciding that he might as well get away while the going was good, hoisted himself on to the sill, gripped the pipe, and slithered to the ground. He landed in a clump of bushes which scratched his face and hands, but since that was the only casualty, it didn't trouble him much. In front of him stretched a neglected garden, waist-high in weeds and brambles, and far beyond that, the dark mass of trees.

Stumbling now and again over the stones and rubble, which he could not see for the weeds, he made his way towards the shelter of the belt of trees. They were farther off than they had looked. He crossed a lawn, now only an expanse of rank grass, and came to a sunken garden, with sundial and a small lily pond. Beyond this was the remains of a rose garden, the pergolas broken down and the climbing roses rioting over the paths in tangled confusion. Here he paused for a second and looked back at the house he had left.

It loomed up mistily against the night sky, black and forbidding; a huge, rambling mansion, apparently standing by itself in a considerable acreage of ground. There were no lights in any of the many windows, and no sign that the place was in occupation. It struck Harold that his first conjecture had been right, and that it was an empty house which the crazy unknown had appropriated for his own purposes.

He plunged on through a shrubbery into a strip of parkland. The trees were nearer now, a little wood that ran thinly along the edge of the estate. He came to a barbed-wire fence and was climbing it when disaster overtook him. Catching his foot in one of the strands, he went sprawling into the undergrowth beyond. His head came in violent contact with something jagged and hard, there was a momentary twinge of excruciating pain, and then — nothing —

★　★　★

He came to his senses, shivering with cold, and with a head that was aching violently. Staggering to his feet, he remembered what had happened, and discovered that he had fallen on a large stone, half-buried in the undergrowth. One side of his face was stiff, and he found that it was caused by the blood from the wound in his head, which had dried. How long he had lain on the fringe of the little wood he had no idea, but it was dangerous to linger. His escape might be discovered at any moment and his captors come to look for him.

As quickly as he could, he hurried away through the trees and presently came to a rough road. Without any idea where he was, he turned to the left and followed it. It branched, after a little while, into a wider thoroughfare and, walking along this for half a mile, he came to a fork and a signpost. It bore a double arm and Harold read, in faded black letters, the directions: 'Brimley ¼ Miles — Fallingham ¼ Mile.' Fallingham lay in the direction he was already going, and it seemed the nearest, so he continued.

It proved, when he reached it, to be a small village, but there was a railway station, and inquiry at the tiny booking-office elicited the fact that he was in the county of Hampshire, and that there was a train in a few minutes that would take him to Basingstoke, where he would be able to get a connection for London. Luckily, his money had not been taken from him, and he bought a ticket. Weak and thoroughly weary, he at last reached Waterloo and took a bus to Balham, but on the threshold of his own home his strength gave out and he collapsed, to be found by the watchful detectives whom Mr. Budd had put on to keep the block of flats under observation, and taken by ambulance to the police station.

* * *

This was the story to which the stout superintendent and the melancholy and sleepy Leek listened in the early hours of the morning, seated in the small charge-room at Balham police station. A doctor had been summoned and, under the powerful restorative that he had administered, Harold Walbrook had recovered sufficiently to give an account of his adventures.

'H'm!' commented Mr. Budd, when he had finished. 'This man who stopped you in the car — can you describe him?'

To the best of his ability Harold did so.

'We'll 'ave a description circulated at once,' murmured the big man. 'Now, what about the car? Did yer notice the make or the number?'

Harold had to confess that he had noticed neither of these things.

'Well,' said Harold, 'I s'pose you'd be able to find this house again, wouldn't yer?'

To this Harold could reply with a truthful affirmative.

'I could take you there quite easily from the station at Fallingham,' he said. 'It's only a mile away.'

'In the meanwhile, perhaps the Hampshire police can do something. Get me the Yard, sergeant, will yer?'

The grey-haired desk sergeant complied, and Mr. Budd spoke rapidly to the night officer in charge.

'That may save us a bit o' time,' he announced, when he had finished. 'I've given instructions for the Hampshire police to locate this 'ouse at once an' arrest anybody they find on the premises. Now what about this lunatic? Could you recognise 'im again?'

Harold started to shake his head, was reminded of his wound, and winced.

'I never saw his face at all,' he replied, 'and his voice was soft and muffled on account of the mask which was drawn over his head. But he shouldn't be difficult to find. He was undoubtedly as mad as a coot.'

Mr. Budd pursed his lips dubiously.

'He may not be mad at all, an' all this ravin' about the sins o' the world was jest put on ter make you think so.'

'I don't see what object there would be in that,' said Harold. 'There was no need to try to bamboozle me. He had no intention of my ever leaving that house alive — I'm convinced of that.'

'I'm pretty certain o' that, too,' agreed Mr. Budd, 'but he may have taken inter account the possibility of somethin' goin' wrong. He took the precaution of wearin' a mask so that you couldn't see 'is face, didn't 'e, an' he may 'ave taken other precautions. Anyway, we're a little nearer than we were — not much, but a little. I think, Mr. Walbrook, you'd better go home to yer wife an' have a good sleep. To-morrer, I'll come an' fetch you an' we'll go an' find this house near Fallingham. Maybe we'll find this crazy killer, too.'

9

The Empty House

The morning was wet and unpleasant, and Mr. Budd, reacting to the sombre greyness of the sky, and the dripping trees and hedges, huddled himself up in his overcoat, and stared silently through the window of the car at the depressing country road.

Wedged in between the stout superintendent and Peter Ashton, sat the thin and melancholy Leek, gazing without expression at the back of Harold Walbrook's head, which was the only part of him visible above the back of the front seat.

The gloomy atmosphere of the dreary morning seemed to have affected them all, for they had scarcely spoken since leaving London. In Mr. Budd's case, however, his depression was directly attributable to the message which he had found waiting for him on his arrival at the Yard after his brief rest. The police in Hampshire had nobly carried out the instructions issued by their London colleagues and located the house where Harold Walbrook had been imprisoned, but its occupants had gone. They must have discovered that Walbrook had escaped, and cleared out at once. Although the big man had been prepared for this, it had, nevertheless, come as a disappointment. He had hoped that by quick action he would be able to secure the whole bunch, but luck was against him, and all that remained to hope for now, was that in their necessarily hurried flight, these people had left behind them something that would give a lead to their identity.

Mr. Budd had slept very little on the previous night. Although he had gone to bed to snatch what few hours' rest he could, he had lain wakeful and restless until it was time to get up. One of those unaccountable hunches that had contributed so much to his success, had begun to gnaw and worry at his brain like a mouse at the wainscot. He tried to ignore it but it continued to make itself heard, much as an unexplainable background noise will be audible on the wireless, even through the loudest music.

And the burden of the hunch was that he just did not believe it!

This crazy man, who was filled with a conviction that he was the chosen instrument of Providence to punish humanity for its sinful love of gambling, did not ring true. It was all too easy and neat. It covered all the facts, left no loose ends, and made everything shipshape. It offered a plausible explanation for the unexplainable, and left no worrying discrepancies regarding motive. It was, in fact, completely satisfying, but it did not satisfy Mr. Budd. Something which he could not have explained, persistently kept telling him that it was all wrong — that there was a great deal more behind it than this. A lunatic there might be; but his lunacy was directed to a purpose — and a purpose that was not a wish to improve the world. Why, if this were the explanation, had he confined his murderous activities only to those who had won dividends in a football pool? There were other forms of gambling a great deal more heinous than that — even if football pools could be classed in the category of gambling at all. Surely a person with an anti-gambling kink would have been more likely to devote his attention to racing, cards, and the greyhound tracks, than to the football pools?

It was, of course, impossible to tell what a deranged mind would do, but Mr. Budd felt convinced that whatever it did would be less cool and calculating than was evident in this particular case. There were signs of careful planning — of a thorough and well-thought-out organisation — that were not entirely consistent with the acts of a madman.

He had said nothing of this steadily growing conviction, however, to anybody. Preferring to keep it to himself until such time, if ever, as he was able to produce some sort of proof to back it up.

The car slowed and stopped, and, peering through the rain-smeared window, the stout superintendent saw the entrance to a wide drive, weed-covered and neglected, with the ruins of a lodge on the right.

'Is this the right place?' he grunted.

The driver turned his head.

'This is Fallingham Place, sir,' he answered. 'The name's on that estate agent's board there. Can you see it, sir?'

Mr. Budd twisted himself until he could get a glimpse of the large, square board that announced that the 'property known as the Fallingham Place Estate' was for sale.

'Um! Yes, this is the place!' he growled. 'All right, go on.'

The driver turned the car in between the broken stone pillars, and proceeded slowly up the tree-lined drive. In the grey wetness of that unpleasant morning, it was anything but prepossessing. A tangled shrubbery sprawled in unkempt confusion on each side of them, from which the shining trunks of the gaunt trees reared themselves to spread their interlacing branches overhead. The swish of the wheels on the soaking gravel was accompanied by the continual patter of the drippings from the trees on the car's roof — an irritating and curiously melancholy sound.

'It ain't a very cheerful lookin' place, is it?' remarked Sergeant Leek mournfully.

'What did you expect — a fun-fair?' snapped Mr. Budd. 'It ain't any worse than most o' these old houses that 'ave bin empty fer a long time.'

'It looks ideal for the purpose to which it was put,' said Peter Ashton. 'Away from any other house, and a good distance from the village. I shouldn't think anybody came near it from one week's end to another.'

The car rounded a bend as he finished speaking, and they saw ahead of them the rambling old mansion, with its blank, staring windows, and great pillared portico. On the top of the steps in the shelter of this, stood a caped policeman. As the car drew up, he came forward and opened the door.

'Superintendent Budd, sir?' he inquired, his eyes travelling questioningly from one to the other.

'That's me,' said the stout man, hoisting himself out of his corner.

The constable saluted.

'Superintendent Collis is inside, sir,' he said.

'That's where we'll be in a minute,' grunted Mr. Budd, as he got ponderously out of the car. 'What an infernal day!'

He pulled the collar of his coat higher round his fat neck and lumbered up the steps. The others joined him, and the constable opened the door. Their footsteps echoed through the huge hall, as they followed the policeman across bare boards to a room near the foot of the massive staircase where Superintendent Collis was awaiting them.

He greeted Mr. Budd warmly.

'Glad to meet you,' he said, his shrewd eyes flickering over the rest of the little party. 'I'm afraid we were too late to catch these birds.'

'So I gathered from the message,' said the big man sadly. 'Pity, but it can't be helped. Maybe there's somethin' they've left behind that'll help us get on to 'em.'

Collis shook his neat grey head.

'I think you'll be disappointed there,' he replied. 'There is nothing at all. From what I can see, it doesn't look as though they used the place much.'

'That 'ud bear out what you said, Mr. Walbrook,' murmured the stout superintendent. 'About the place bein' so silent. Like as not there was nobody 'ere half the time except you an' the other two.'

'That suggests that the real headquarters of these people is somewhere in the neighbourhood,' put in Peter quickly. 'I mean they wouldn't have chosen a place to keep their prisoners very far away from where they hung out themselves, would they?'

'Um,' remarked Mr. Budd, scratching his chin thoughtfully. 'There's somethin' in that idea, Ashton. There'd be no point in choosin' this partic'lar place unless it was easily accessible for 'em. We'll look into that matter. Meantime, I'd like to go over this house.'

It took him some time, for the place was a great barracks, with many rooms and staircases and odd corners, and he insisted on examining every square inch thoroughly. His patience and energy were, unfortunately, unrewarded. The people behind the murders of Mr. Gummidge and Miss Mote had left nothing incriminating. In the big room on the first floor, from which Harold Walbrook had made his escape, they found the heap of old blankets on which he had lain. But they offered no clue. Neither did the remains of the cords which lay near them. It was very ordinary cord, and might have been bought at any shop which catered for such things.

Crumbs and marks in the dust on the floor of two of the other rooms were the only traces of where Miss Mote and Mr. Gummidge had been put, and in these instances no blankets were found. Mr. Budd remarked on this.

'It looks as if you were the favoured one, Mr. Walbrook,' he muttered. 'The other two 'ad ter be content with bare boards fer a bed. I wonder why that was?'

'Perhaps the blankets were already in the house?' suggested Superintendent Collis. 'They're old enough, and dirty enough.'

'Maybe that's it,' said the big man sleepily, and yawned. 'Well, I think we've seen all there is ter be seen, an' that ain't sayin' much. Let's go back downstairs.'

They returned to the hall, and, seating himself on the bottom stair of the staircase, Mr. Budd produced a cigar and carefully lighted it.

'Now,' he said slowly, when it was well alight and he had taken one or two preliminary puffs. 'What about this idea of Mr. Ashton's? You know all the people livin' in the district. Can you suggest anybody who might fit? We're lookin' fer a man who's got a kink, remember.'

Collis smiled.

'I can think of so many people who have got kinks of one sort or another,' he said, with a humorous twinkle in his eyes.

'I dare say yer can,' answered Mr. Budd. 'Most people 'ave; but the sort o' kink we're lookin' for isn't so common. We want ter find a man who's a fanatic on the subjec' o' gamblin' . One o' these queer people who think that because the workin' classes 'as an occasional bet on an 'orse, or spends an hour or two a week in fillin' up football coupons, that the whole world's goin' ter the devil. You know the type I mean?' Collis nodded.

'Well,' continued Mr. Budd, 'that's the type we're after. Only in his case he's got it a bit more badly.'

The local superintendent pursed his lips and gently smoothed his closely-clipped moustache.

'There's one person I can think of straight away,' he replied. 'He fits your description to a 't.' Unfortunately, he happens to be the Vicar of Brimley, so he can't come into the list of possible suspects.'

'I'm not so sure o' that,' retorted Mr. Budd. 'If he's mad he wouldn't be accountable fer his actions, any more'n what anyone else 'ud be.'

'Oh, he isn't as mad as all that,' said Collis. 'But he's a queer old chap. Very old-fashioned in his views, and certainly dead nuts on gambling in every form, and the football pools in particular. He thinks that the money that is spent on them should be put to a better purpose. He doesn't realise, and neither do all these other cranks, that if the working man didn't spend his bob or two a week on the pools, he'd possibly spend it in a local pub on beer — '

'Without the possibility of gettin' anythin' to show fer it,' interrupted Mr. Budd, nodding. 'That's true enough. This feller's like that, is he? What's his name?'

'The Reverend Clement Rockforth,' said the superintendent. 'He's a queer old bird. Very thin, with a great beak of a nose, and a mop of thick grey hair streaked with black, and eyes that peer out at you from very deep sockets — '

'He sounds like Boris Karloff,' said Peter. 'He's the Vicar of Brimley, you say? That's not very far, is it?'

'The next village,' answered Collis. 'But, seriously, I don't think you need waste time over him. He's eccentric, but he wouldn't hurt a fly.'

'You never can tell what a person with an obsession 'ull do,' said Mr. Budd sagely, blowing out a great cloud of evil-smelling smoke. 'Any'ow, leaving him out of it, can you think of anyone else?'

Collis shook his head.

'Not offhand, I can't,' he replied. 'But then, I don't pretend to know everybody round these parts. The person who'd be able to tell you better than me, would be Sir Mathew Franklin. He knows everybody.'

'Who is he?' demanded Mr. Budd.

'He's practically a millionaire,' answered Collis. 'Owns most of the property in and around Brimley, and lives at Brimley Court with his sister. He's the nicest, pleasantest gentleman you'd meet in a day's march, though he has had a lot of trouble in his time.'

'What sort o' trouble?' asked Mr. Budd.

'Domestic,' said the superintendent. 'That's why his sister's looking after the house for him. He married some flighty bit of goods, and there was trouble. I don't know what it was all about exactly, but I believe she ran off with somebody or other. Sir Mathew was very ill for some time, and people say that he wasn't expected to live. Anyway, he's the fellow who could tell you of any queer people about the neighbourhood.'

'Um!' said the fat detective thoughtfully. 'I think maybe I'd like a word with him. How long would it take us to get from 'ere to — What did you say the place was called?'

'Brimley Court,' replied Collis. 'It's on the outskirts of the village — about seven miles away.'

'Would 'e be in, d'yer think?' asked Mr. Budd, and the local superintendent nodded.

'Yes, he'll be in,' he replied. 'He seldom goes out these days. Spends most of his time in his study with his books.'

'Well, let's go,' said Mr. Budd.

He rose with difficulty, twitching his shoulders to shake his overcoat into position, and made for the front door.

The constable was standing at the side of the car, talking to the police driver, and turned towards them as they came out on to the steps.

'Have you got the key, sir?' he asked, as Collis was about to close the door behind them. 'Because — '

A sharp crack, like the flick of a whip-lash, made him stop abruptly, and with a muttered exclamation, Peter Ashton felt his hat jerked from his head. Two more reports followed quickly, and the bullets thudded dully into the wood of the massive front door behind them.

'What the hell — ' began Superinten-dent Collis, but Mr. Budd broke in quickly.

'Get inside!' he snapped. 'Go on, jump for it! There's somebody over among them trees with a repeatin' rifle, an' I don't think it's very healthy where we are!'

10

The Man in Black

In their hurry to escape from the hail of bullets that were smacking around them, they almost fell into the hall.

'Tell your man an' the driver to make a dash for it,' panted Mr. Budd. 'If they stop out there, they'll be hit.'

Superintendent Collis called urgently through the partly open door, and the two came hastily.

'Lumme!' exclaimed the astonished driver, as Collis shut the door. 'What's the idea, eh?'

'Somebody doesn't like us!' grunted Mr. Budd. 'Did any of you see anyone?'

There was a concerted shaking of heads.

'The thing was so sudden,' said Peter, 'and unexpected. The shots came from among those trees.'

'I know that!' snarled the big man

irritably. 'Come upstairs. Maybe we'll get a glimpse of this sniper from one o' the windows.'

He led the way, the others following close on his heels. The firing had stopped, now they were no longer available for targets, and from the window of a room overlooking the front of the house, they peered cautiously out in the hope of seeing something of the sniper.

'There he is!' cried Peter excitedly. 'Look! In the fork of that tree!'

'Be careful!' said Mr. Budd warningly, as the reporter, in his eagerness, moved close to the window. The warning was not unjustified. From the man perched in the branches of the tree came a flash of flame and a puff of smoke, and the upper pane of the window splintered. The watchers drew quickly back.

'He's a pretty good shot, whoever he is,' said Peter. 'That tree must be a good hundred and fifty yards away.'

'You go on admiring his marksman-ship!' growled Mr. Budd. 'I'm not so interested. I s'pose nobody 'ere 'as got a gun?'

Nobody had.

'I thought not,' muttered the stout superintendent. 'That's p'lice regulations. They expect yer to go out after thugs an' armed gangsters, an' knock 'em down with a feather!' He frowned and rubbed his fat chin. 'Well, I don't see what we can do,' he went on, after a pause. 'If we had a gun with us, we might slip out by the back an' work round to this feller an' pick him off; but as it is, it 'ud be suicide ter attempt anythin' o' the sort. We can only stop 'ere until 'e gets tired, an' goes away.'

'How long 'ull that be?' said Leek mournfully.

'It may be for years, and it may be for ever,' sang Peter softly. 'I wish this place was on the telephone,' he added, with visions of a 'scoop' for the *Morning Mail*.

'We ought to do something,' said Collis, scratching his head. 'This chap may bottle us up here for hours.'

'How about trying to get away by the back?' suggested. Walbrook. 'The same way as I did.'

'Perhaps there's another gent waiting for us there,' said the reporter. 'However, we can but try. What do you say, Budd?'

'There's no harm in 'avin' a shot at it,' agreed the big man. 'Though I'd like ter get me hands on that feller — '

'There's no hope of doing that while he's cuddling that rifle,' broke in Peter. 'Let's have a look at the back.'

They made their way down the stairs again and through to the back of the house. There was a door, which was bolted, that led out into a kitchen-garden, and opening this, they peered cautiously out. No fusillade of shots greeted them, and they stepped out into the open.

'We'll have to leave the car,' said Mr. Budd. 'I s'pose they thought the feller at the front 'ud do all the damage that was necessary, an' didn't bother to plant anyone at the back.'

'What do you think the idea was?' asked Peter, as they walked down a little path between a row of unkempt currant-bushes.

'Pretty obvious, I should think!' grunted Mr. Budd. 'The idea was to bump us off as we came out. And if that feller 'ad waited a few seconds longer before 'e

129

opened fire, 'e'd 'ave done it. He was too impatient — that was 'is trouble. We 'ad time ter get back inter the house before 'e prop'ly got 'is range.'

'I know that part of it,' said Peter impatiently. 'What I mean is, what good would it have done? If we'd all been killed somebody else would have taken over the inquiry, so what was the object?'

'What's the object in any of it?' replied Mr. Budd. 'Why was Gummidge an' Louisa Mote killed an' their bodies brought back? Don't start askin' me questions, Ashton. I'm askin' meself enough that I can't find the answers to, without you addin' to 'em.'

He relapsed into gloomy silence, the stump of his cigar, which had gone out, wedged in one corner of his capacious mouth.

The kitchen-garden came to an end, and after wading waist-high through a tangle of weeds, they found themselves by a brick wall covered in ivy that appeared to be a boundary wall to the grounds.

'I think this runs along by the road,' said Collis, halting, and Mr. Budd eyed it dubiously.

''Ow d'yer s'pose I'm goin' ter get over that?' he demanded. 'It's all right fer you skinny-gutted lot, but what about me?'

'I'll give you a leg up,' said Peter. 'Then you can get your hands on the top and pull yourself the rest of the way.'

It was not quite as easy as that, but eventually, after a lot of puffing and grunting, Mr. Budd succeeded in scrambling over the wall and falling ungracefully into the road on the other side.

'Where are we now?' he grunted, brushing himself down.

'This is the road we came along in the car,' answered Peter. 'Look! There's the entrance to the house.'

He pointed ahead to where the ruined lodge and the stone pillars showed clearly in a curve of the road.

'Um!' grunted the stout superintendent. 'Well, what do we do now? We can't go back an' pick up the car, or we'll run inter that feller with the gun. Is there any chance o' gettin' a lift ter the police station? If we could get there we might send out an armed detachment to try to pull that feller in.'

131

Superintendent Collis did not seem to think that there was much chance of getting a lift.

'There's very little traffic along this road,' he said.

'I can hear a car, all the same,' said Peter suddenly. 'Listen!'

They all heard it, and presently saw it. It was speeding towards them along the road they had previously travelled when they came to Fallingham Place.

'Let's stop it,' said Peter, 'and ask for a lift.'

But there was no need. The car skidded to a halt as it drew level with them, and a familiar, husky voice roared a greeting.

'Hallo, cock!' it said. 'What a bit o' luck! We was jest on our way ter find yer!'

'Bellamy! Jacob Bellamy!' cried the astonished Peter. 'What in the world are you doing here?'

'Lookin' fer you, boy,' replied the bookmaker, thrusting his big, ugly face out of the window. 'Your rag told us where you'd gone, an' we was comin' ter find yer.'

Peter Ashton, looking past the old man,

132

saw his wife sitting beside him.

'What's the idea, Marjorie?' he asked. 'Why are you and Jacob chasing me all over England?'

'For your own good, darling,' replied Marjorie Ashton. 'I had a message from Mr. Sorbett, just after you left this morning. He wanted you to go to the office at once. I said you weren't in, and could I do anything? He said that a letter had arrived for you which you ought to see at once. I thought quickly, and said that I might be able to find you if it was important, and should I come to the office and collect the letter? He said yes, so I rang up Jacob, our car not being available because the garage people hadn't finished repairing it, and asked him if he would drive me to the office — '

'And 'ere we are, cock!' broke in Jacob Bellamy, with a broad grin. 'Hallo, Budd! I ain't seen you since that business of the Horseshoe racket. 'Ow are yer, cock?'

'I'm all right,' said Mr. Budd, 'but you wouldn't have bin, if you 'adn't met us.'

'Wotcher mean?' asked the bookmaker, in surprise.

'If you'd driven up to that 'ouse,' said the big man, 'you'd have got a warm reception from an unpleasant feller with a gun who's sittin' up in a tree watchin' the front door.'

He explained more fully what had happened, and old Jacob Bellamy's eyes glistened.

'Blimey! I wish I'd bin there, cock!' he exclaimed. 'I was only thinkin' last night how tame things 'as bin since that Horse-shoe gang was rounded up, an' pinin' fer a bit of excitement.'

'That was a queer business, too,' murmured Mr. Budd. 'It looked just a plain, straight-forward racket until yer got at the truth. I wonder if this 'ull turn out the same?'

'I bin readin' about it,' said Bellamy, frowning, 'an' yer right about it bein' queer, cock. I can't see any sense in it meself, unless it's somebody who's got a grudge against the pools.'

'Let's have a look at this letter that old Sorbett thought was so important,' interrupted Peter, and Marjorie fumbled in her bag and gave it to him. It was addressed in an illiterate hand, and marked 'Private,' but that had not, apparently, stopped the news editor of the *Morning Mail* from opening it.

'Just like his cheek!' grumbled Peter. 'Nothing's sacred to that man! Phew!' He had extracted the contents — a single sheet of paper — while he had been speaking, and when he saw what was written on it he broke off and whistled softly.

'You've read this, Marjorie, of course?' he said, and his wife nodded.

'Of course, darling,' she said; 'and, like a dutiful wife, knowing where you were, I brought it to you at once.'

'Look at this, Budd!' said Peter, turning to the big man. 'No wonder Sorbett thought it important.'

Mr. Budd took the cheap sheet of paper in a podgy hand, and read the ill-written scrawl:

'Dear Mister Ashton, — I have read your writtings in the morning mail about the murders of the people what wun the football pools and I can give

you some exclusif infermashun about them if you will make it worth my wile as I understand a newspaper will pay a lot of muney for exclusif stuf. don't bring the perlise into this but come and see me tomorrow nite at the abov adress and ask for mister james stacker that's my name, it ort to be worth five hundred quid what I can tel you.'

There was no signature.

'To-morrow night must mean to-night,' commented Mr. Budd, looking at the envelope. 'This was posted yesterday evenin' . Where does this feller hang out? No. 8, Cecil Street, New Cut. Um, I know that well. Nice bunch o' crooks live round that way. I wonder if this feller really knows anythin' or if 'e's jest tryin' ter get hold of some easy money.'

'He's struck the wrong horse, if that's his game,' said Peter. 'I'm too old a hand to be caught. If his information is worth anything the *Mail* 'ull pay him; if it isn't they won't. Anyhow, I shall call and see Mr. James Stacker to-night.'

'In the meanwhile,' said Mr. Budd,

'would you drive us ter the p'lice station, Bellamy? There's jest a chance, if we can get some men up there in time, of catchin' this gunman.'

'Drive yer anywhere yer like cock,' replied Jacob Bellamy obligingly. 'Jump in!'

'You'd better stop 'ere,' said Mr. Budd to the police driver. 'You an' the constable. Don't take any risks, but try an' see if yer can get within sight of that feller up the tree, without bein' seen. We'll rush up reinforcements as soon as possible.'

Neither the driver nor the constable looked too happy about these orders, but they obeyed, and, when the others had climbed into the car, Bellamy drove off.

Brimley proved to be a more imposing village than they had anticipated. The police station was a new building, of fair size, and the local superintendent, whose real headquarters were at Basingstoke, quickly collected three men, armed them with a rather mixed bunch of revolvers, and sent them off in an ancient Ford to try to pull in the sniper.

'Now,' said Mr. Budd, when this had

137

been attended to, 'what about payin' a visit to this feller, what's-his-name?'

'Sir Mathew Franklin?' asked Collis, and the big man nodded. 'All right, come on!'

They returned to Bellamy and Marjorie, who had waited in the car outside, with Leek and Harold Walbrook. Mr. Budd explained where they wanted to go and Collis gave the necessary directions. As the car turned into a secondary road, they passed a gaunt man in black, who was hurrying along the sidewalk, talking rapidly and gesticulating to himself.

'Bats in the belfry,' said Bellamy.

'That's the man I was telling you about,' remarked Collis to Mr. Budd. 'The Reverend Clement Rockforth.'

The stout superintendent twisted round with difficulty, for it was a tight squeeze in the car, and looked back. The gaunt man had stopped, and was staring after them intently.

'So that's the feller, is it?' he murmured. 'He seems very interested in us, don't he?'

'Strangers are few in Brimley,' answered

Collis. 'That's probably — Why, what's the matter, Mr. Walbrook? You look as if you'd seen a ghost!'

'His hands!' muttered Harold Walbrook. 'Did you see his hands?'

'What's the matter with his hands?' snapped Mr. Budd quickly.

Walbrook passed his tongue over his suddenly dry lips before he answered.

'I'll swear they were the hands of the man who raved at me in that room at Fallingham Place,' he said.

11

The Recluse

Walbrook's statement so startled the occupants of the car that for a moment nobody spoke. And then Collis, Peter, and Marjorie all began together.

'You must be mistaken, sir — '

'Are you certain — '

'How can you be sure — '

They each stopped politely to let the other continue and Mr. Budd took advantage of the pause to intervene.

'Jest a minute,' he said. 'It's no good everybody speakin' at once. Why are you so sure about this, Mr. Walbrook?'

Harold Walbrook, who had recovered from his first shock, shifted round in his seat and rested his arms along the back.

'You couldn't mistake those hands,' he replied. 'Didn't you notice them? All covered over with large orange sort of freckles — '

'And this crazy man's hands were marked like that, too?' interrupted the stout superintendent.

Walbrook nodded.

'I'm sure you must have made a mistake, sir!' broke in Collis, shaking his head. 'That gentleman was the Reverend Clement Rockfort, the Vicar of Brimley. He's a bit queer and eccentric, I'll admit, but he wouldn't go murdering people. That's absurd.'

'When a man's loony, cock,' put in Jacob Bellamy, without taking his eyes off the road, 'there's no knowin' what he'll get up to. And that chap what passed us just now's as potty as a coot. I'll take me dyin' oath on that.'

'But — ' began the local superintendent, and Mr. Budd interrupted him.

'It's no good arguin' that he did or 'e didn't,' he said irritably. 'That isn't goin' ter get us anywhere. The only thing to do is ter note the facts an' act on 'em. Now, Mr. Walbrook says that this feller's got the same sort o' hands as what the man had who kept 'im prisoner at Fallingham Place. That's fact No. 1. Fact No. 2, is that this feller Rockforth lives in the district. Fact No. 3, is that he's got an obsession against gamblin' , an' in particular against the football pools. Fact No. 4, is that he's queer in the head. So far he fits exactly the man we're lookin' for, an' all you can put up against it, is that he's the Vicar o' Brimley, an' therefore can't have had anythin' ter do with it.'

'It's ridiculous to even suggest such a thing!' grunted Collis.

'I'll agree that it's a bit far-fetched,' admitted Mr. Budd amiably. 'But then, the whole of this case is abnormal. There ain't ever been anythin' like it before, an' I shouldn't think there'd be again. That's why we've got to take everythin' inter consideration, however impossible it seems. An' Mr. Walbrook is sure that that feller's hands are the same as those he saw at the empty 'ouse.'

'I'm absolutely positive!' declared Walbrook emphatically.

'You can't be sure that they are the same,' said Peter. 'You can only say that they are very similar. Those queer freckles are not common, but they are by no means unique. Don't forget that.'

'It 'ud be a very big coincidence, though,' remarked Mr. Budd, 'if, as well as possessin' all the other characteristics of the feller we're lookin' for, this man Rockforth has the same sort o' hands. What I can't understand, Mr. Walbrook,' he added, 'is why you didn't say anythin' about these freckles before.'

'I forgot all about them,' said Walbrook quickly. 'It was only when I happened to see that man's hands just now that I remembered.'

'This the place, cock?' called out old Jacob suddenly, and slowed the car before the entrance to an imposing drive.

'That's it,' said Collis, and with a wrench at the wheel, Bellamy swung the car between the mellow, red-brick pillars.

The drive was straight and well-kept, running between neatly trimmed hedges of yew, backed by beech-trees. They saw the house long before they reached it, framed like a picture at the end of the avenue. It was smaller than Fallingham Place, and more compact; a lovely Georgian building, set among shaven lawns and glowing flower-beds. There were many beautiful examples of topiary art in box and yew, and Marjorie's eyes sparkled with delight as she looked about her.

The car circled a wide expanse of gravel and came to a stop before the front of the house.

'Now, look here,' said Mr. Budd, as he prepared to get out. 'We can't all go in. You'd better come with me, Collis, an' the rest o' you can stay 'ere — '

'What about me?' demanded Peter. 'You can't leave me out of it — '

'I can, an' I'm goin' to,' retorted Mr. Budd. 'We're callin' on a gentleman, an' therefore, you'd be out o' place. Come on, Collis.'

He walked away before Peter could think of a suitable retort, with Collis at his heels.

In answer to their ring the front door was opened by a wrinkled old man in the black garb of an upper servant. He listened doubtfully while Collis put his request.

'I'm afraid the master won't see you,

sir,' he said, shaking his grey head. 'He sees very few people these days. But I'll take up your card. Perhaps if the master won't see you, Miss Mathilde would be able to help you, sir?'

'We would rather see Sir Mathew,' replied Collis, and the old man bowed and hurried away. There was a long interval, and then, down the big staircase came the figure of a woman. She was small and delicate, with snow-white hair that she wore brushed away from her forehead. Mr. Budd, regarding her through sleepy eyes, was reminded of an exquisite piece of Dresden china. It was only when she came nearer that he was able to distinguish the lines of age about eyes and mouth. But they were slight, and the face that turned inquiringly from one to the other was still very beautiful.

'My brother regrets that he is too busy to see you,' she said, in a rich contralto that was surprising from such a tiny woman. 'No doubt, if you tell me your business, I can deal with it equally as well.'

Collis hesitated, and Mr. Budd interposed.

'Well, miss,' he said, 'that's very kind of you, but if we could see Sir Mathew for a few minutes it would be very helpful. We shouldn't keep him long. It's jest a matter of askin' one or two questions — '

'Concerning what?' interrupted the little woman sharply, and for a second the stout superintendent could have sworn that there was fear in the large blue eyes. It was gone in an instant, and he wondered if he hadn't been mistaken.

Rapidly he explained the situation, and she listened without comment until he had finished.

'I doubt if my brother would be able to help you,' she remarked. 'However, I will try to persuade him to see you for a minute or two. If you will wait here, I will not be long.'

She walked daintily across to the staircase, and they watched her slight figure disappear round the bend.

'Like a little doll, isn't she?' murmured Collis, and Mr. Budd nodded.

'Yes,' he answered. 'But there's nothin' doll-like about 'er mind. I wouldn't like ter come up against 'er, not if she was

146

really roused. I'll bet she's got a temper.'

They had to wait a long time before she returned; but when she did she announced that her brother would see them for a few minutes.

They followed her up the stairs to a broad landing and along a corridor. At a door near the end she stopped, turned the handle, and ushered them into a large, book-lined room, with long windows opening on to a balcony. A man who was seated at a big, flat-topped table, covered with books and papers, looked up as they entered.

'Come in!' he said, a little querulously. 'My sister has told me the reason you wish to see me. I hope you won't think me rude if I ask you to make this interview as short as possible. I seldom receive visitors, and I am very busy.'

He leaned back in his chair, and clasping his hands, rested his chin on them, peering up at them over his glasses. In appearance, he was very like his sister, who had quietly seated herself in a chair by one of the windows and, with her hands folded in her lap, was staring out into the garden. There was the same snow-white hair and blue eyes, the same delicate features. In his case, the lines of age were more pronounced, but the relationship was unmistakable.

'Well, sir,' began Mr. Budd, clearing his throat, 'as the lady 'as already explained what we've come about, that'll save a lot o' time. What we want ter know, sir, is this . . . ' He explained at some length, and Sir Mathew Franklin listened, his large, light-blue eyes fixed on the fat detective with a rather embarrassing stare. When Mr. Budd had finished he pursed his lips and shook his head.

'I'm afraid I can't help you — er — superintendent. My life during recent years has been one of almost complete seclusion. I seldom go out beyond the confines of these grounds. Perhaps my sister — ' He paused, and turned to the woman by the window: 'Mathilde, my dear. Can you suggest anyone who would fit the — er — the requirements of these gentlemen?'

She did not answer at once, and when she did her reply was accompanied by a slow shake of the white head.

'No,' she said. 'I'm afraid I cannot.'

'You see?' said Sir Mathew. 'We cannot help you.'

He leaned forward in his chair and began to fidget with the papers on his desk, as a hint that the interview was over. But Mr. Budd refused to take the hint.

'You are, of course, acquainted with the Reverend Clement Rockforth, sir?' he said gently.

Sir Mathew Franklin looked up quickly, and his brows drew down over his eyes.

'I know him slightly,' he replied. 'Why? Surely you can't have any suspicion that *he's* the man you are after?'

'Well, I'm given to understand, sir, that he's a little queer in the head,' said Mr. Budd. And Sir Mathew made an impatient gesture.

'He's eccentric,' he answered. 'But then, so are a great many people. If, however, you are under the impression that he would be capable of carrying out a series of cold-blooded murders, you are entirely mistaken.'

'That's what I said, sir,' put in Collis, looking rather pleased at this confirmation of his championship of the vicar.

'Of course — of course!' said Sir Mathew testily. 'Anyone would say so who knew him. A lot of ridiculous nonsense!'

'You must understand, sir,' murmured Mr. Budd, 'that I'm not accusin' him or anybody else. All I'm doin' is ter collect information — '

'Yes, yes — I quite understand that, superintendent,' broke in Sir Mathew, nodding quickly. 'But you'll be wasting your time over Rockforth, I assure you. He's a fanatic over some things, and — well, perhaps a little queer in his habits, but he wouldn't harm a fly.'

'Well, I'm glad to have your opinion, sir,' said the big man, 'an' if you — ' He stopped suddenly, stammered a few words that were inaudible, and then went on: 'If you can't help us we won't waste any more of your time.'

Sir Mathew was frankly relieved. Almost before they had left the room he was once more immersed in his papers.

The old butler was waiting in the hall to let them out, and when they were outside and the big door had closed

150

behind them, Superintendent Collis gave vent to his opinion of the interview.

'Well, that wasn't very helpful,' he remarked disappointedly. 'We didn't learn a lot, did we?'

'*I* learned a lot,' answered Mr. Budd thoughtfully.

Collis gave him a surprised glance.

'What did you learn?' he demanded.

The stout man moved ponderously down the steps towards the waiting car.

'I learned enough to make me curious ter learn more,' he said. 'A lot more. Did you notice the fireplace in that room?'

The surprise on Collis' face changed to blank astonishment.

'The fireplace?' he repeated, and Mr. Budd nodded. 'No, I can't say that I noticed it particularly. Why?'

'You should've done,' said the stout superintendent. 'It was very interestin' — and informative.'

'I don't know what you're talking about,' said Collis, in bewilderment. 'How was the fireplace interesting and informative?'

'You should use your eyes,' replied Mr.

Budd. 'There's two people in this district I want ter know a lot more about. One of 'em's that crazy parson feller, Rockforth, an' the other's Sir Mathew Franklin.'

'Sir Mathew Franklin?' echoed the local superintendent. 'What's he got to do with it?'

'A lot,' answered Mr. Budd. 'A lot, Collis. I'm very glad we paid that visit. If we hadn't I shouldn't 'ave — ' He stopped to yawn widely.

'Shouldn't have what?' asked Collis.

'Seen what I did see,' replied Mr. Budd gravely, and opened the door of the car.

12

A Broken Appointment

He definitely refused to discuss the matter further, and the curious and disgusted Collis had to try to puzzle out what he meant for himself. Leek could have told him how exasperating this little habit of Mr. Budd's was, for the lean sergeant was used to it. At the beginning of an inquiry, Mr. Budd was ready enough to talk about it, but as fresh facts came to light, and he began to weave theories in that alert brain of his, which was in such violent contrast to his outward appearance, he became more and more reticent. When he did speak, his utterances were so cryptic as to be unintelligible to those who were not in a position to follow the train of thought which had given rise to them. There was a strong element of the dramatic in him, which loved to spring a surprise, and, although his heavy face never showed it, he thoroughly enjoyed mystifying the people around him.

Collis, who had not known him long enough to be aware of this characteristic, could hardly be expected to appreciate it. And he certainly did not. Quite errone-ously, he concluded that the big man was merely trying to be clever, and that his reason for refusing to say what he had seen was simply that he hadn't seen anything.

His attitude, in consequence, became a trifle cold and distant.

At the police station, where they stopped on their way back to London, a disappointment awaited them. The men who had been sent up to Fallingham Place to pull in the gunman had failed to find him. The constable and the driver of the police car reported that by the time they had got within sight of the tree there had been no sign of the man with the rifle.

'Most likely he guessed we'd gone by the back way,' said Mr. Budd, 'an' sheered off. It's a pity, but it can't be helped. Well, I don't think we shall do any good in this district for the moment, so we'll be gettin' along back to the Yard. Are you comin' with us, Ashton, or are yer goin' with yer wife an' Bellamy?'

'I'll go with Marjorie, I think,' said Peter. 'It'll give you more room. I want to see you later, though, about this appointment with Stacker.'

'You'll find me at the Yard durin' the afternoon,' said Mr. Budd. 'Well, so long fer the present, Collis. I shall be seein' you very soon again. In the meantime, get somebody to keep an eye on Rockforth. I'll tell yer now, that in my opinion the hub o' the whole business of these murders lies within a five-mile radius of this police station, so don't forget that.'

'Did yer mean that?' asked the melancholy Leek, as he walked with Mr. Budd to the waiting police car, which the driver had brought to the station.

'Have you ever known me say what I don't mean?' grunted the big man.

Leek could have truthfully answered 'Yes' to this, but he contented himself with a further question.

'Who's at the bottom of it, then?' he asked.

'What do yer take me for — a clair-thingummy-jig?' said Mr. Budd. 'How should I know?'

'Well, you said the whole business lay round 'ere,' protested the sergeant, 'so I thought you knew somethin' — '

'I do know somethin' ,' retorted his superior. 'But I don't know everythin' , an' that's one of the thin's I don't know.'

He resumed his old position in the corner during the journey back, his eyes closed, but his mind busily active, sorting and cataloguing the information he had acquired.

They dropped Harold Walbrook at his flat, and went on to the Yard. Here a number of reports awaited the stout superintendent. The first list of the people known to have anti-gambling views had come in, and although Mr. Budd was pretty sure that these could be narrowed down to someone in the immediate vicinity of Fallingham and Brimley, it was necessary that this should be proved before other possibilities could be discarded. The list was formidable, and he spent a long time reading it through and marking certain names that might be worth further investigation. During the afternoon he was called to the Assistant Commissioner's room, and went, to find that Colonel Blair had news.

'Smallwood's are distributing another lot of cheques to first-dividend winners at the Astoria Hotel, on Thursday,' said the dapper man, 'and naturally, in view of what happened before, they are a little worried. They suggest that we should arrange with the local police in the various districts where these people come from to keep them under observation. Their own men will look after them while they are brought to London and taken back again, but Messrs. Smallwood's think, and I agree with them, that some sort of precautions should be taken after that. I have the list of winners here. There are nine this time, each receiving two thousand three hundred and forty pounds. What do you think?'

'I think it's a good idea, sir,' said Mr. Budd. 'Though I'm doubtful if these people 'ull be in any danger.'

Colonel Blair looked at him shrewdly.

'What makes you say that?' he asked.

'Only one of my hunches, sir,' answered the big man slowly. 'I've got nothin' really definite ter go on, but it's my opinion that there's a plan behind this that was confined to these first three — Gummidge, Walbrook, an' Mote. I didn't think so at first, an' I don't mind sayin' that I was uneasy about these other winners, but I'm not now.'

'Well, I'm glad to hear you say so,' said the Assistant Commissioner. 'All the same, we can't neglect these precautions unless you've got some kind of proof to back up what you think.'

'No, sir. I quite realise that,' said Mr. Budd. 'I wouldn't suggest that we did, sir.'

Colonel Blair regarded him curiously.

'I suppose you've got something in your mind,' he remarked with a smile, 'and I suppose you're not going to tell me, eh?'

'Well, sir' — Mr. Budd gently rubbed his fleshy chin — 'I'd rather wait until it's a bit more concrete, if you don't mind. Of course, if you insist — '

'I don't,' interrupted the Assistant Commisioner. 'I know your method of working, Budd, and although it's distinctly unorthodox, it is usually justified by the results.'

'Thank you, sir.' The stout superintendent's face flushed with pleasure.

'There is one other item of information that may be of assistance to you,' went on Colonel Blair, 'though I don't know in what way exactly. It is this. Messrs. Smallwood's have paid the ten thousand four hundred pounds that would have gone to Alfred Gummidge to his widow. Walbrook, of course, still has his cheque, and now that he has returned, the order to stop payment has been cancelled.'

'What about the money that would have gone to Louisa Mote?' asked Mr. Budd. 'What's happening to that, sir?'

'Smallwood's are waiting to see if any relatives claim it,' answered the Assistant Commissioner. 'They have advertised for any relatives of Louisa Mote to communicate with their solicitors. In the event of nobody coming forward, the money will go to the Crown.'

'I see, sir,' murmured the big man thoughtfully. That ended the interview, and he returned to his own cheerless little office, to find Leek busily engaged filling up a football-pool coupon.

'Started wastin' yer time on that now, 'ave yer?' growled Mr. Budd. 'You'll do anythin' sooner than yer proper job.'

'If there's anythin' ter do, I'll do it,' said Leek. 'I'm no shirker. But there wasn't nothin' to do, so I thought I might as well fill in the time with this. If I could win one o' them big prizes it 'ud make a nice nest-egg fer me old age.'

Mr. Budd sniffed disparagingly.

'The nearest to a nest-egg you'll get,' he said, 'is to hear the first cuckoo. Is this goin' ter be like your racin'?'

'Racin's a mug's game,' replied the sergeant. 'You can't rely on them 'orses at all. Even with my system, I lost money.'

'Even!' echoed Mr. Budd scornfully. 'It was that what did it! If you'd bin content to 'ave a bet like any normal 'uman bein' you might have won a bit.'

Leek looked a little aggrieved.

'Well, you'll see,' he said. 'I'll bet I win a good packet over this football. I feel I got a flame for it, as the sayin' is.'

'I s'pose you mean 'flair' — but that don't matter,' grunted his superior, lighting a cigar carefully. 'Well, mind you don't go up in smoke, that's all!'

The arrival of Peter Ashton put an end to the argument, and Mr. Budd transferred his attention to a discussion of the letter which the reporter had received from James Stacker.

'He may know somethin' , an' he may not,' he said, when he had read it again. 'Whenever there's a sensational crime committed we get scores of letters like this to deal with, an' mostly there's nothin' in 'em. This one's a bit different, though. This feller's after money, not notoriety, like the rest of 'em. What time are you goin' ter see 'im? He don't state no time in his letter.'

'Round about nine o'clock, I thought,' answered Peter.

'D'yer want me to do anythin'?' asked the big man, eyeing him sleepily through a cloud of smoke.

161

Peter shook his head.

'I don't think it 'ud be wise,' he said. 'If this chap got an inkling that I'd brought the police into it he'd probably shut up like an oyster. There'll be time enough for you to interfere after we find out what he knows.'

'I rather agree with you,' said Mr. Budd. 'But,' he added warningly, 'don't you go keepin' back information fer that paper o' yours, or there'll be trouble.'

'Have you ever known me do a thing like that?' demanded the reporter indignantly.

'Yes,' retorted Mr. Budd calmly. 'That's why I'm warn-in' yer!' He looked at the clock on the wall. 'Let's go an' 'ave a cup o' tea,' he said. 'I ain't had any lunch yet.'

It was still raining when Peter Ashton arrived in the New Cut and searched for Cecil Street. It was difficult to find, but he discovered it at last; a narrow, ill-lighted cul-de-sac, with a double line of drab houses, all exactly alike, whose front doors opened directly on to the pavement.

No. 8 was near the end on the

right-hand side, and he surveyed the exterior without enthusiasm. It was a dirty-looking house, with torn lace curtains in the windows, and no light visible anywhere. Peter approached the front door and gripped the rusty iron knocker. There was no reply to his first knock, but the second brought a shuffling step, and a blowsy woman appeared on the threshold and peered suspiciously out at him.

'Wotcher want?' she demanded, perfuming the immediate atmosphere with a generous odour of gin.

'I want to see Mr. James Stacker,' said Peter.

'Well, yer can't!' snapped the woman, and made to close the door. The reporter deftly inserted a foot and prevented this.

'Why?' he asked. 'Doesn't he live here?'

'He lives 'ere, but 'e ain't in,' answered the woman crossly. 'Take yer foot away from my door, will yer?'

'Mr. Stacker asked me to call and see him,' said Peter. 'What time do you think he'll be in?'

'I don't know, an' I don't care,' she

replied. 'Maybe if yer hang about long enough yer'll see.'

Peter diplomatically produced a ten-shilling note.

'It's rather an unpleasant night for 'hanging about' outside,' he said pleasantly. 'Perhaps you wouldn't mind if I came in and waited?'

She eyed the slip of paper between his fingers greedily.

'You ain't the police, are yer?' she said; and nothing could have been more illuminating regarding Mr. James Stacker.

Peter assured her that he was not, and she grudgingly admitted him.

'This way,' she said; and he stumbled after her up a dark and narrow staircase. At the top she threw open the door of a room and ushered him in.

'Wait a minute while I gets a light,' she said. He heard her fumbling about, and then a match was struck and she lit the gas.

'There yer are,' she said. 'Yer can wait as long as yer like.'

'Thank you,' said Peter, and held out the ten-shilling note. She grabbed it with a dirty hand and departed. The reporter looked round the uninviting abode of Mr. James Stacker. It was a bed-sitting-room, filthy and dingy. The furniture was old and falling to pieces, and comprised a bedstead, a deal table, a washstand, a broken chair, and a dilapitated easy-chair of wickerwork.

After one glance at his surroundings, Peter decided to remain standing during his wait. There was less risk that way of carrying away any of the livestock which might be plentiful. How anyone could live in such a hole was beyond him, although he had seen many such places. Mr. Stacker's finer feelings must be practically non-existent.

There was nothing in the room to give him any idea of the character of the man he had come to meet; no articles belonging to him lying around. But he required none to form his judgment. The room itself was sufficient — the room and that remark of the woman's.

He glanced at his watch. Half-past nine. How long would he have to wait?

It was longer than he expected. Ten

o'clock came and went. Eleven. And no sign of Mr. Stacker. At half-past eleven he heard the woman coming in, singing drunkenly, and guessed that she had expended her unexpected windfall at the nearest pub on more gin. She must have forgotten all about him, for she did not come near, and presently he heard her go stumbling and singing to bed.

He frowned. Mr. Stacker seemed to have forgotten him, too. It was nearly half-past twelve. The sound of a car reached his ears. Perhaps the man he was waiting for had come in a taxi, though it seemed scarcely likely. He went over to the window and peered out into the wet street; but the glass was grimy, and he could see nothing, except the dim light of a car which had stopped farther down the street.

At one o'clock he decided to give it up. The unmusical snores of the landlady were making the house hideous as he crept down the stairs to let himself out. The front door was unbolted, and he cautiously pulled back the catch. Opening the door, he stepped out on to the step

166

— and nearly fell sprawling over the thing that lay there.

With a thumping heart, he pulled a box of matches from his pocket, struck one, and stared down at the obstacle. It was the body of a man. He was quite dead, and the dreadful face which showed in the flickering light of the match told Peter that he had been strangled.

13

The Next of Kin

The deadness of Cecil Street had changed. The dingy little cul-de-sac was full of life and activity. A crowd of hastily attired and partially dressed people had gathered round No. 8, and were staring with morbid curiosity at the police cars drawn up at the kerb, oblivious of the repeated demands of a harassed constable to 'move along there!'

Mr. Budd, sleepy-eyed and weary from the sudden disturbance of his rest, remembered Reed Street in Darlington in the early hours of that wet and dismal morning when he had gone to inquire into the murder of Alfred Gummidge, and was struck by the resemblance. And this resemblance was not only in the environment, but in the crime itself. James Stacker's life had been choked out of his frail body in the same way as had

Gummidge's and little Miss Mote's. And also, as in the other two cases, the body had been brought back to the place where he had lived, with nothing to even hint at the identity of his murderer.

There was no doubt now that Stacker's letter to Peter Ashton had been genuine. He had known something about the murderer and had been killed before he could talk.

His reputation, according to the local police inspector, was bad. He had been mixed up with a number of undesirables, was believed to have been a member of the 'Borough Boys,' a notorious race-gang, and had definitely served five sentences of varying lengths.

'An habitual criminal,' was the inspector's description. 'He was out for anything that would bring him in a bit of money.'

'So are most people,' grunted Mr. Budd. 'Well, he won't bother you any more. Let's 'ave that woman in, an' see if she can tell us anythin' .'

Accompanied by a strong odour of gin, the slatternly woman who had admitted

Peter was brought into the sitting-room which the stout superintendent had commandeered for his use. In the white light from the incandescent gas mantle she looked even less prepossessing than she had looked before. Her wispy hair was lank and dirty, and her bloated face grey. She had been crying, and the tears had left white rivulets in the grime of her cheeks.

'My 'ouse 'as always been respectable,' she whined. 'I don't know — '

'Never mind about that!' interrupted Mr. Budd curtly. 'It ain't no good you tryin' to tell us that you didn't know the character of yer lodger, because I'm sure you did — '

'If I never move from this spot — ' began the woman indignantly.

'Yes, I know!' snapped the big man. 'You're as innocent as a new-born babe. I've 'eard it all before, an' so many times that I'm sick o' hearin' it. What I want ter know is who used ter come an' see Stacker?'

The landlady shot him a malignant glance.

"E didn't 'ave many visitors,' she answered sullenly:

'But 'e had some,' said Mr. Budd. 'Who were they?'

'There was two fellers called Ted an' Joe wot come once or twice,' she said. 'That's all.'

'Ted Dillon and Joe Binns, d'yer mean?' interposed the local inspector, and the woman nodded.

'You know them?' asked Mr. Budd.

'Yes. They're two of the Borough Boys,' replied the inspector. 'An' two thorough bad lots.'

'Didn't anyone else ever come to see 'im?' inquired the fat detective.

'No; only them two,' said the landlady. 'An' they didn't come orfen. Last time they was 'ere was over a month ago.'

Mr. Budd gently massaged the bridge of his broad nose. He wasn't particularly interested in Ted Dillon and Joe Binns. Neither of them was likely to be the person he was seeking. He described the man who had accosted Harold Walbrook in the car on the morning of his disappearance, but the woman affirmed that he had

171

never been to the house. She might be lying, but Mr. Budd rather thought she wasn't.

'Did a man ever come 'ere to see Stacker with big freckles on the backs of his hands?' he asked.

'I've told yer,' said the landlady, 'that no one come 'ere ter see 'im, 'cept them two — Ted an' Joe.'

She stuck to this in spite of every attempt to shake her, and the stout superintendent finally dismissed her.

'I've got an idea she was speakin' the truth,' he said. 'The man we're after never came 'ere at all. Stacker must 'ave got in touch with 'im outside. It's my opinion that 'e was hired by this man to 'elp with the disappearance o' them three pool winners. We know that 'e must have 'ad some help, and a feller like Stacker is just the sort 'e'd choose.'

'And Stacker thought he could make a bit of easy money by giving his employer away to me,' said Peter Ashton, and Mr. Budd nodded.

'That's about it,' he answered. 'He thought he could sell 'is information ter you an' no questions 'ud be asked. Poor devil!'

'I wonder how the man who killed him found out what he intended doing?' remarked Peter, after a short silence.

Mr. Budd nipped the lobe of his right ear between a fat forefinger and thumb and waggled it thoughtfully.

'Can't say,' he replied. 'But he did find out. Stacker wouldn't be dead now if 'e hadn't.'

'Whoever this chap is, he's a pretty cool customer,' said the local man. 'It wanted some nerve to bring the body back.'

'It's gettin' a habit with 'em,' grunted Mr. Budd. ''E's got plenty of nerve — '

'Madmen always have,' put in Peter, and the big man looked at him queerly.

'I'm wonderin' if he *is* so mad,' he murmured softly.

'He can't be sane!' protested the reporter. 'There's certainly a motive for killing Stacker, if what we think is right, but there's no motive for the other murders — '

'Not that we know of, Mr. Ashton,' interrupted the stout superintendent.

'Not that we know of.'

Peter looked at the fat, sleepy-eyed man before him shrewdly.

'I believe you're on to something,' he said. 'What is it?'

Mr. Budd's heavy lids lifted slightly.

'What makes yer think that, Mr. Ashton?' he asked innocently.

'Because I know you so well!' retorted Peter. 'You've started being mysterious, and that's always a sign that you know something.'

'Well, it's not a very good sign in this case,' murmured the big man, 'because I don't know nothin' . I've got an idea buzzin' round in me head, but that ain't knowin' .'

'What is the idea?' demanded the reporter quickly.

'I don't think I'm goin' ter tell you that,' said Mr. Budd, yawning. 'No. I think I'll keep it ter meself for a bit, until I've got somethin' more to back it up. This business is pretty complicated, as it is, without me goin' an' makin' it worse with ideas that there may be nothin' in.'

He ended the subject on this, to Peter,

unsatisfactory note, and devoted himself to the exhaustive routine work which an inquiry into wilful murder necessitates.

It was dawn when he and the reporter left Cecil Street, Peter to make his way to Fleet Street and Mr. Budd to return in one of the police cars to Scotland Yard.

★ ★ ★

The *Morning Mail* made a sensational 'splash' of the killing of James Stacker, printing the letter which Peter Ashton had received, and rehashing all the circumstances surrounding the other murders.

Among the millions who read the account was the man responsible for the events which it so graphically described. He read it with interest, a smile curling the corners of his tight-lipped mouth, and when he had finished he laid aside the paper and stared thoughtfully into the fire. The first stage of his campaign was over, and, with the exception of Harold Walbrook, had been thoroughly successful. And Walbrook mattered very little. In one way it might be all to the good that he had

175

managed to get away from the house at Fallingham. It would mean greater publicity, and that was what he wanted. The more publicity the better. There would have to be one more murder, which, so far as he was concerned, would not be a murder at all, and then — He chuckled and rubbed his thin hands together as his imagination conjured up the pleasant prospect which lay before him . . .

The man who had offered Harold Walbrook that drugged cigarette on the morning of his disappearance, read the news of Mr. Stacker's murder with less enthusiasm. This orgy of killing was scaring him. The five hundred pounds which his unknown employer had paid him to take part in what he had called 'a purity campaign' was all very nice. It was quite a respectable sum. But it was insignificant compared to the value he put upon his life. Mr. Montague Lucas was not in the least bit squeamish where other people's lives were concerned, so long as there was a profit to be made, but he was very particular regarding his own safety.

And by getting mixed up in this business, he had seriously jeopardised that safety. In the eyes of the law he was an accessory both before and after the fact, and, as such, equally responsible. It was true that he had known this before he had agreed to the unknown's proposal, but then he had not foreseen that Walbrook would succeed in escaping. That was what was worrying him and frightening him.

Walbrook knew him. He had taken no pains to alter his appearance, believing that Walbrook would share the same fate as the others, and therefore, never be in a position to indentify him. But now Walbrook *was* in a position to identify him. Even now his description was probably circulated throughout the country, and every policeman would be looking for him. A verbal description was, certainly, very unsatisfactory, but all the same it might lead to his arrest, and then he wouldn't stand a hope. Walbrook would see to that. He had only to say 'that is the man,' and the game was up.

Mr. Lucas took out his spotless handkerchief and wiped the beads of sweat from his forehead. The thought was very alarming.

For the hundredth time since he had discovered that Walbrook had gone from that room in Fallingham Place, he cursed the greed which had made him accept the unknown's tempting offer. At the time there had seemed very little risk, and five hundred pounds was five hundred pounds. He had been crazy — almost as crazy as the lunatic fanatic who had got him into this mess through his mad idea of making an example of the people who had won money by gambling on football pools.

There was no doubt about it, his position was a dangerous one. It would be better to get out of the country while there was a chance. He had close on four hundred left, and in another country, where the cost of living was cheap and the rate of exchange favourable, that ought to last him long enough to look round for some means of replenishing the exchequer.

It was a pity he couldn't squeeze a bit more out of his employer, but unfortunately, he had no idea who he was. He had never seen him without the mask, and, except that he was definitely 'batty,' had never got an inkling of his identity.

The trouble in leaving the country was Walbrook. The ports would all be watched — that was a certainty — but that wouldn't matter so much if Walbrook wasn't waiting to identify him if he were stopped. Without that danger, the police would have nothing to go on. Even if they arrested him they would have to let him go for lack of supporting evidence. Stacker, the only other person who might have been dangerous, was dead. There was absolutely nothing to connect him with the murders — except Walbrook!

With Walbrook out of the way there would be no need to leave the country . . . With Walbrook out of the way . . .

Mr. Lucas toyed with this sentence, turning it over and over in his mind, as a gourmet might have savoured a tasty dish. Well, why not? It shouldn't be very difficult, and it would have the effect of making him safe.

He lighted a fresh cigarette, and settled himself more comfortably in his chair, letting his mind play with ways and means of achieving this desirable end.

The murder of James Stacker had taken place in the early hours of the Tuesday morning, and on the Thursday following, Messrs. Smallwood's presented a further batch of cheques to the lucky winners in their football pool. Rigid precautions were adopted, and vigilant police officers in plain clothes watched throughout the proceedings, and kept the people who had been brought from their homes to the Astoria for the presentation, under a close guard. But nothing unusual happened. There was no attempt to interfere with the dividend winners, either during their journeys or when they returned to their various homes. Their houses were kept under observation, however, in case any belated effort might be made to spirit them away, as in the case of the others. The winners themselves had no knowledge of this care. It had been thought better not to acquaint them with the precautions that had been taken, and they went about their lawful occasions unconscious of the keen-eyed men who watched over their safety.

Mr. Budd, during this interval of quiescence, was a very busy man indeed. He had started a string of inquiries, and as the reports concerning these began to trickle in, he dealt with them methodically. Most of his time was, in consequence, spent in his office.

Peter Ashton calling in for news on the Saturday morning, found the fat man surrounded with papers, immersed in a flood of reports from all parts of the country.

'Routine work,' grunted Mr. Budd, in answer to his question. 'Nothin' spectacular — nothin' sensational. That's nine-tenths o' police work, Mr. Ashton — jest sheer ploddin' through. It's not very exhilaratin' but it's got ter be done!'

He took off his spectacles, rubbed his eyes, and yawned.

'I was hoping you'd have some news,' said Peter. 'Old Sorbett wants a follow up.'

'I'm afraid 'e'll have ter want,' grunted the big man. 'I've got nothin' ter give yer at the moment.'

'I thought you were concentrating your

inquiries in the neighbourhood of Brimley?' said Peter, lighting a cigarette.

'I'm not concentratin' my inquiries anywhere,' retorted the superintendent. 'So far as this case is concerned the world is me oyster. But Brimley's being looked after. Leek's there keepin' an eye on things.'

'What was it you saw in that room at Sir Mathew Franklin's?' asked the reporter suddenly. 'I've been meaning to ask you before.'

Mr. Budd produced a cigar from his waistcoat pocket and looked at it with great interest.

'I saw a photograph,' he answered slowly. 'That's all — jest a photograph. It was standin' on the mantelpiece — '

'Whose photograph?' demanded Peter with interest.

Mr. Budd shook his head as he peeled the band carefully off the cigar.

'I'm not tellin' you that,' he replied, 'partly because I only think I know whose photograph it was, an' partly because — well, because I'm not goin' to.'

Peter gave a snort of disgust.

'You're the most exasperating beggar I know!' he declared.

Mr. Budd's big face broke into a smile.

'Lots o' people 'ave told me that,' he said gently. 'I can't help it — it's jest me way!'

'You're like a miser with a hoard of gold so far as information is concerned,' growled Peter crossly. 'You hate parting.'

'I don't mind partin' with real information,' said the stout superintendent. 'What I 'ate doin' is ter tell what I only think. It's a form o' vanity, I s'pose. I'm scared I might be wrong an' look foolish. We've all got our little pecul — '

The telephone broke into the middle of the word, and he reached out an arm for the instrument.

'Hallo, yes?' he called, and then: 'It's from Liverpool. There may be somethin' — yes! Oh, that's interestin' — very interestin'. What? There's no doubt about that, I s'pose? Yes, I'm very glad ter have the information. Yes. Thank you!'

He slammed the receiver back on its rest, and leaned forward.

'That call was from the solicitors who

act for Smallwood's he said. 'They've bin searchin' fer Louisa Mote's next-o'-kin, so as ter be able ter know who to pay the cheque to.'

'Well?' prompted Peter impatiently, as he paused.

'Well, they've found 'im,' went on the big man. 'An' who d'yer think he is?'

'I've no idea,' snapped the reporter. 'Who is he?'

'The Reverend Clement Rockforth, vicar of Brimley,' answered Mr. Budd.

14

Leek's Luck

The vicarage in Brimley stands opposite the small square-towered church, facing a road which is a continuation of the High Street. It is a fairly large house, built of red brick, and more modern than the church which it serves. The original building was burned down in the early '90's, and the present one erected on its site, and although ivy has done much to soften its hard lines, the architecture still faintly clashes with the Norman period of the church across the way.

It is a pleasant house, however, with smooth lawns and old-fashioned borders, and a rose garden enclosed by trim hedges of box. There is a great cedar-tree before the front door, whose plate-like branches throw a welcome shade in the heat of summer, and around whose massive trunk a rustic seat has been built to give rest to the weary.

The Reverend Clement Rockforth, pacing up and down his study, paused at the window to glance at this tree. It fascinated him; it had fascinated him when he had first come to Brimley as a young man, thirty-five years previously, and it had never lost its fascination. There was something beautiful and at the same time oddly sinister about it. When he stood beneath its dark, spreading branches he experienced a fear that was unaccountable, but very real. The tree seemed to exude a menace.

With working face and twitching fingers, he stood for several minutes staring at it, and then his attention was distracted by the sight of a car turning in at the wide gate and circling the gravel drive. He frowned. Who had come to disturb his peace? The car belonged to nobody in Brimley. He muttered angrily to himself as he watched a large and bulky man get ponderously out, followed by a slimmer and younger man in a soiled macintosh. They disappeared from his view as they passed under the porch, but a moment later he heard the bell ring softly below. There was an interval, then a rumble of voices, and presently a tap on his study door.

'Come in!' he called in his high voice that sometimes had a disconcerting habit of cracking.

His elderly housekeeper entered with a card on a tray.

'If you please, sir,' she said, holding out the brass salver, 'there's a man from the police wants to see you.'

'A man from the police?' muttered Rockforth, raising his bushy eyebrows. 'What does he want, Mrs. Sparrow?'

'He didn't say, sir,' replied the house-keeper.

'Superintendent Budd, of New Scotland Yard,' read Rockforth, and passed a gaunt hand over his thick, untidy grey hair. 'What can he want with me? Unless he states his business, I'm afraid I can't see him. I am very busy composing my sermon for to-morrow, and — '

'I shan't keep you long, sir,' interrupted a husky voice from the doorway; and Rockforth jerked up his head quickly. The big man he had seen get out of the car was standing on the threshold.

'Really!' he cried, his white face flushing angrily. 'This is an unwarrantable intrusion.'

'I thought I'd save your servant the trouble o' comin' all the way down them stairs again,' said Mr. Budd, not in the least disconcerted. 'I jest want a word with you about your sister.'

The flush faded from the face of the man before him, and the lines deepened. The lean jaw set harshly, and the thin-lipped mouth was compressed into an implacable line.

'I don't know what you mean,' he whispered hoarsely. 'I have no sister.'

His voice cracked and was silent.

'But you had a sister, sir,' murmured Mr. Budd gently.

'I tell you I have no sister!' The thin voice was shrilly harsh. 'Do you not understand plain English? I have no sister.'

'I'm sorry to contradict you, sir,' said Mr. Budd, 'but I'm afraid I must. You had a sister, and her name was Louisa. For some reason or other — that's one of the things I've come 'ere ter find out — she dropped her own name, an' was livin' under the name of Louisa Mote when she was killed — '

'Louisa Mote?' interrupted Rockforth. 'Louisa Mote? That was the woman who was murdered.' His lean hands worked, the ugly, reddish-brown freckles on their backs showing up vividly. 'The woman who was murdered,' he muttered again. 'She sinned, and it is written that the 'wages of sin is death.''

Peter Ashton, watching and listening, felt his flesh creep. The words which had been scrawled across the coupon sent to the addresses of the two murdered people! Was it possible that this gaunt man had been responsible for those atrocious crimes? That he was mentally unbalanced was obvious. There was a glitter in his dark, sunken eyes, and his whole thin body was in a constant state of movement. Mr. Budd's slow, unemotional voice broke in on the reporter's thoughts.

'In what way did your sister sin, sir?' he inquired.

Rockforth seemed to come out of a daze. His restless hands moved up, and the fingers slid up and down the lapels of his worn jacket.

'That is of no consequence to you,' he said at length. 'It was many years ago. I shall not discuss it. It is a private matter entirely.'

Mr. Budd pinched his fat chin. He couldn't force this man to answer questions against his will.

'I'm sorry you should adopt this attitude, sir,' he said, a little sadly. 'I was hopin' that you'd help me. There is, as you probably know, a large sum o' money due from Messrs. Smallwood's to your sister's next-of-kin, which apparently, is you, and — '

'I know nothing about it,' broke in Rockforth curtly. 'I have no wish to know anything about it. Money acquired by gambling is tainted money. These football pools should be stopped by law. Perhaps the fate which has overtaken these misguided people will serve as a lesson and a warning. If any suggestion is made to me that I should accept this money I shall refuse. Good morning!'

There was nothing for it but to accept his rather curt dismissal, and with as good grace as possible Mr. Budd took his departure. He had come to Brimley immediately after receiving the message from Liverpool, and he was not in possession of all the facts. He had hoped that by breaking the news to Rockforth in the abrupt way he had, that eccentric man would talk; but this hope had not been realised. He had, however, learned that there was some unpleasant secret in the man's past, which also concerned his sister. Why if her name had been Rockforth had she called herself Miss Mote? In conjunction with Rockforth's attitude this seemed to suggest that she had done something that had estranged her from her family. But whatever it was, it was scarcely likely that it had anything to do with the mystery of her death. That was more recent, and was definitely connected with her luck in the pool — unless Rockforth was at the bottom of it.

So quickly does the brain work that all

this had run through his mind before he had reached the waiting car.

'Where do we go from here?' asked Peter.

'The nearest pub,' answered Mr. Budd promptly. 'A nice drop o' beer is what I want after that.'

'Well, what do you make of the Reverend Clement Rockforth?' said the reporter, when they were seated in the car and it had moved away.

'He's as mad as a hatter!' declared Mr. Budd.

'Did you notice what he said — about 'the wages of sin'?' asked Peter; and Mr. Budd nodded.

'It's queer that he should have used the same words as the messages, isn't it?' went on the reporter.

'It might easily be a coincidence,' said the big man. 'The expression's pretty common. I s'pose you know that I've got enough evidence to 'ave him arrested?'

'Is that what you're going to do?' asked Peter quickly.

Mr. Budd frowned uncertainly.

'I don't know,' he answered candidly. 'I

ain't made up me mind yet. I don't want to act in a 'asty way, but when yer come to think it over the evidence is pretty strong against him, ain't it? An' 'e's got a motive, which is more'n can be said of anyone else.'

'You mean the ten thousand four hundred pounds?' interjected Peter.

'I do,' said Mr. Budd. 'That's a pretty good motive ter my way o' thinkin'. That money comes to 'im, now his sister's dead.'

Peter was unconvinced.

'I can imagine him killing for the sake of an ideal,' he said, 'but not for gain.'

'Well, anyway, I'm goin' ter see that he's kept under observation,' replied Mr. Budd. 'That feller's dangerous.'

The car slowed and came to a stop outside a white-washed inn, and they got out.

In the bar, thoughtfully eyeing a lime-juice-and-soda, they discovered the melancholy Leek. Mr. Budd ordered beer, and they joined the sergeant.

'Well,' said the big man, 'what 'ave you been doin'?'

'I posted me coupon last night,' answered Leek; and his superior uttered a snort of disgust.

'Never mind the coupon,' he said. 'You came down 'ere on a job o' work. What 'ave you done?'

'I've been gettin' acquainted with people,' said the sergeant mournfully — 'makin' meself popular-like.'

'I see,' said Mr. Budd. 'The life an' soul of the funeral! Well, 'ave yer got hold of anythin'? Or 'ave yer forgotten about the case we're on?'

'I'm doin' what you told me to,' protested the sergeant. 'I'm 'ere an' I'm startin' the inquiries you suggested. But you've got ter go tactful with country people. It ain't no good rushin' things.'

'I can't imagine you rushin' if it was,' growled Mr. Budd. 'Well, don't forget what you're 'ere for, that's all, an' report ter me d'rec'ly yer get anythin'.'

He finished his beer, accepted another from Peter, and when this had been consumed they said good-bye to Leek and set off for London.

It was at a quarter to seven that

evening, and Mr. Budd had just reached the stage of considering going home, when the telephone-bell rang insistently. Putting the receiver to his ear, the big man called a gruff 'Hallo!' and was answered by the voice of Leek.

'I've got it,' said the sergeant, with unusual excitement. 'I've got it!'

'Got what?' demanded Mr. Budd irritably. 'Don't shout so! Speak — '

But Leek took no notice and went rushing on.

'I've got a line correct in the penny points pool,' he said, the words tumbling over each other in his eagerness to impart the news. 'I told yer I'd do it!'

'Thank goodness for that,' snarled Mr. Budd. 'Maybe you'll disappear now an' come back strangled. If yer do, my sympathies 'ull be with the feller what does it!'

15

Mr. Lucas Meets With Disaster

Mr. Montague Lucas, having weighed the matter carefully up, decided to make his getaway on the Sunday. Ever since he had concluded that his personal safety was in danger, he had been preparing for this move. A friend of his, for a small sum, had prepared a very creditable passport, bearing a photograph of Mr. Lucas, plus a small moustache, and made out in the name of one 'George Brigham,' which Mr. Lucas considered was both unassuming and suggestive of the right degree of dullness and respectability to avoid question.

He had also converted all his available assets into cash — not a very large sum, it was true, but sufficient to give him a start in a fresh country. His own wits would, he hoped, find a means of replenishing the coffers when that had gone. There was a seat booked in the Paris plane, and it was his intention to steal, if not silently, at least quickly, away from his native land in the morning. Once he reached France, he could make his way at his leisure, and by easy stages, to some obscure country, where all traces of him would be lost.

He had no particular desire to leave England, but he considered that it was safer. He had, through greed, allowed himself to become very seriously involved in a case of wholesale murder, and the thought of what would happen to him if he were caught was a constant source of terror. Mr. Montague Lucas was not of the stock from which heroes are born. His career had been full of a number of crimes, both large and petty, but he had always been extremely careful to ensure that there was nothing to connect him with any of them. Certainly his reputation had become a little tarnished in the process, but a tarnished reputation was not an indictable offence, and there was nothing that could have been proved against him. Until now! This was a different matter. If he could have foreseen the outcome, he would never have got mixed up with that crazy lunatic and his wild and ridiculous scheme for the redemption of the world. But who could have foreseen that Walbrook would escape? Except for that piece of consummate bad luck, he would have been safe. And now he was anything but safe — at any rate, so long as Walbrook was in a position to talk.

That would have to be put right before he left. After that there was nothing to worry about. His unknown employer could give him away, certainly, but the evidence of a madman would carry little weight with a jury. It was only Walbrook who was the danger, and before morning he would be a danger no longer.

He went over his plans for the twentieth time as he prepared for his departure. Brockvale Mansions possessed neither a porter nor an outer door. At any hour it was possible to walk in and up the stairs to any particular flat. The difficulty was after that. Walbrook was a married man, and his wife would be there. The problem that had given him so much trouble to solve was how to deal with Walbrook without his wife having a chance to give the alarm. And, after a lot of thought, he had found a way. It was an ingenious solution, and he congratulated himself on his cleverness when he thought of it. That it meant the deaths of two people instead of one never troubled him at all. He would have cheerfully sacrificed a dozen to ensure his own safety. Mr. Montague Lucas had been born with one idea, and that was the welfare of Mr. Montague Lucas. Given an enlarged sense of one's own importance in the scheme of things, and a total lack of conscience, everything is possible, from murder downwards. It is such stuff as this that dictators are made of.

Mr. Lucas lived in a small, but comfortable, flat in a side street in Bloomsbury. It was a monthly tenancy, and he had already informed the landlord that business necessitated his going up North. His rent was paid in advance, and he had taken the flat furnished, so his departure would be a simple matter. All he had to do was to walk out with his luggage, step into the car which he had hired for the occasion, and be driven to Croydon. As simple as that.

He ate his frugal meal with satisfaction, drank a final glass of beer, and looked at the clock. It was only ten. There was plenty of time. If he started for Balham at twelve, it would be soon enough. Lighting a cigarette, he began to while away the time with his plans for the future. He would make for some warm country, where there was always plenty of sunshine. Mr. Montague Lucas detested the cold. The Argentine! He had always had a hankering for the Argentine. Living was cheap, and the attractions were many. Lying back in his chair, he let the smoke curl round his head, and allowed his imagination full play. Nobody seeing him at that moment would have guessed that he was contemplating a double murder within the next few hours. He looked a rather stout, pleasant-faced business man, thinking over a profitable deal. There was nothing about him at all to suggest the criminal, unless it were the eyes of a peculiar shade of pale blue.

At ten minutes to twelve he roused himself, went into the bathroom, and had a wash. Returning to the sitting-room, he put on his overcoat, took from the drawer of a desk in one corner a small cardboard cylinder and a leather case, which he put in his pocket, and, pulling on a soft felt hat, left the flat and made his way down the street.

At Theobalds Road he boarded a tram, which set him down on the Embankment. After a short wait a Balham tram came along, and he swung himself on to it.

There was not a soul about when he reached Brockvale Mansions, and the ugly block of flats was in complete darkness.

He walked briskly in at the arched entrance, and slipped silently up the stairs. At the door of Flat No. 7 he paused, and, bending down, listened at the letter-slit. There was not a sound from within. Straightening up, he examined the lock. As he had expected, it was a Yale. But during his life Mr. Lucas had acquired much out-of-the-way knowledge, and there were few locks that offered any serious barrier to him. In this respect only, he resembled Love. The leather case came out of his pocket, and he rapidly screwed together a small brace and bit. Near the round, shining brass of the Yale lock, he noiselessly drilled a hole, half an inch in diameter, and then another beside it, until a circle sufficiently large to admit his hand had been cut through the panel of the door. This he carefully removed, put in his hand, and felt about for the catch. At the third attempt he succeeded and gave it a twist. The door swung inward under the pressure of his hand.

Mr. Lucas stepped into the tiny hall, produced a torch from his pocket, over the lens of which he had taken the precaution to stick a piece of thin paper to dim the light, and in its faint beam took stock of his surroundings. On the right was the sitting-room. The door was half open, and he could see in. The door at the end of the passage would be the kitchen. That other door, which was shut, must be the bedroom.

Mr. Lucas tip-toed towards it, his

breath coming a little quicker. Pausing outside, he took from his pocket the cardboard cylinder, pulled up an inch of fuse, and, setting it on the floor, produced his lighter and ignited the wick. It fizzled, dully red, and opening the door cautiously, he picked up the cylinder, set it inside and pulled the door to again noiselessly.

The thing was done! When the fuse burned down to the contents of the cylinder, enough cyanide gas would be liberated to kill any living thing in that room. Walbrook and his wife would die in their sleep without knowing what had killed them.

Trembling from the nervous reaction that set in now that he had carried out his scheme, Mr. Lucas turned and went back to the front door. His hand was on the catch when he heard the sound of someone coming up the stairs outside, and he paused. One of the tenants of the flats, who had been out late, coming home, he thought. Better wait until they had gone by.

But they did not go by!

The footsteps stopped on the landing outside the door behind which he stood. He heard the jingle of keys, and then a clink as the key was thrust into the lock. His hand flew to his pocket, and his fingers closed round the torch, the only weapon he possessed.

The door was pushed open and somebody came into the tiny lobby. Mr. Lucas struck with his torch as hard as he could, and tried to make a dash for it. There was a grunted oath, and his arm was gripped tightly. He tried to break away, but the fingers that dug into his flesh were like steel. There was a snap of a switch and the light came on.

'Now then, cock! Let's 'ave a look at yer!' said a deep, husky voice; and Mr. Lucas stared with panic-stricken eyes at a huge, rugged-faced man, who held him as easily as though he'd been a tailor's dummy.

'What's the idea, eh, cock?' said Jacob Bellamy. 'Bit o' burglary, eh? You're unlucky, ain't yer. I just got back in time.'

Into Mr. Lucas's dazed brain came the conviction that in some extraordinary way he had made an awful mistake. This was the right flat, but who was this huge man with the face like a battered prize-fighter?

'Got a bit of a shock, eh, cock?' said old Jacob. 'Thought everyone was in bed an' sleepin', I'll bet. Hey! What's the queer smell?'

He sniffed the air like a bulldog. Mr. Lucas tried a last desperate effort to break free.

'Here, you keep still!' growled the bookmaker. 'Yer'll break yer arm if yer don't. What 'ave you bin up to, eh?'

Still sniffing, he dragged his captive towards the door of the bedroom.

'Don't open that!' whispered Mr. Lucas huskily. 'For God's sake don't open it!'

Bellamy looked at his terror-stricken face, and his own hardened.

'I'm beginnin' ter think I made a mistake when I took you fer a burglar, cock,' he said grimly. 'What 'ave you bin up to, eh?'

The wretched man he was holding said nothing, and the bookmaker shook him.

'Come on!' he snarled. 'Spill it! I'll beat yer against the wall till you're a mass o' pulp if yer don't!'

He looked so threatening that Mr. Lucas's last remaining shred of nerve gave way.

'Let me go!' he muttered fearfully. 'Let me go! I — I — I — '

'Not so much of the I — I — I!' snapped Bellamy. 'Are yer goin' ter talk, or am I going ter start on yer?'

Mr. Lucas began to mutter an incoherent story.

'I don't want to listen ter any fairy tales,' said the bookmaker roughly. 'I want the truth! What 'ave yer put in that room, eh?'

Mr. Lucas stammered and spluttered, his flabby face the colour of chalk. He hadn't meant any harm, he was just playing a joke. He scarcely knew what he was saying in his terror.

'Now I'm just goin' ter play a joke,' said Bellamy. 'I'm goin' ter take you round ter the nearest police station. I've got an idea they'll be pleased ter welcome you, cock. When I tell 'em your joke of puttin' cyanide stink-bombs in people's bedrooms they'll laugh like hell!'

They didn't laugh, but they were interested.

'I think we've been looking for this man, sir,' said the sergeant in charge. 'He answers the description of a man wanted in connection with them football pool murders.'

'I thought he might,' said Jacob Bellamy, with great satisfaction. 'You 'ang on to 'im, sergeant; 'e's a nasty piece of work. Mr. Walbrook 'ull be able to identify 'im if 'e is the feller who whisked 'im away in that car.'

'Where is Mr. Walbrook, sir?' asked the sergeant curiously. 'How was it he wasn't in his flat?'

''E's taken 'is wife down ter the country,' answered the bookmaker. 'She went through a pretty rough time worryin' over his disappearance, an' the doctor ordered her a complete change. I 'appened ter mention that my 'ouse was being redecorated, an' that I was goin' ter stay at an 'otel while the painters was in, an' Walbrook offered me 'is flat. That's 'ow I 'appened ter be there.'

'It's a lucky thing you were, sir,' said

207

the sergeant gravely. 'If them two had been asleep — ' He shook his grizzled head. 'What 'ave you got to say for yerself?' he added sternly to his prisoner.

But Mr. Lucas was beyond speech. All his carefully laid plans had crumbled about his head in ruins.

'You'll be charged with attempted murder,' said the sergeant, 'an' if Walbrook identifies you there'll be other charges.'

Mr. Lucas was led away and locked up in an uncomfortable cell. Sitting dejectedly on his hard pallet-bed, he remembered his dreams of a warmer climate.

It looked very much as if they were coming true, though not quite in the way he had intended.

16

Lucas Speaks

Mr. Budd was busy in his little garden, pruning his beloved roses in the still peace of a Sunday morning, when he was notified of the arrest of Mr. Montague Lucas. Reluctantly, he dragged himself away from his pleasant labours, exchanged the old stained suit he had been working in for one of more suitable appearance, and departed for Balham police station.

He found Jacob Bellamy and Peter Ashton awaiting him in the charge-room.

'How did you get on to this?' he asked the reporter, and Peter smiled.

'I could say a little bird told me, but you wouldn't believe me,' he answered. 'So I'll tell you the truth. Jacob rang me up.'

'H'm!' grunted the big man. 'Well, let's hear all about it.'

The bookmaker told him.

'This Lucas seems an amiable sort o'

feller,' said Mr. Budd, when he had finished. 'Has anybody thought o' sendin' fer Walbrook?'

'Yes,' replied old Jacob. 'I wired for 'im this mornin'.'

'Bein' a Sunday, an' him in the country, it's ten chances ter one 'e won't get it,' remarked Mr. Budd pessimistically.

'I telephoned to the nearest police station, sir,' put in the sergeant. 'They are sending a message to Mr. Walbrook.'

'Oh, well, then, he probably *will* get it,' said the stout superintendent. 'When was these messages sent?'

The sergeant glanced up at the clock on the charge-room wall.

'Two hours ago, sir,' he answered.

'It shouldn't be long before 'e's here, then,' murmured Mr. Budd. 'Let's have this feller up while we're waitin'.'

'You'd better come into my office,' said the divisional-inspector. 'It'll be more private there.'

He led the way into a small room opening into the charge-room and sent for Mr. Lucas.

He was brought by a stolid constable, a

210

pathetic and contemptible figure. His fat face was white and drawn, and there were unhealthy bags beneath his light eyes. He had had time to think during the long night, and had come to the conclusion that the only way of saving his own skin was to make a clean breast of his share in the murders.

'If I do all I can to help you, it'll go in my favour, won't it?' he asked anxiously. 'You'll put in a good word for me, won't you? I had nothing to do with the actual killing of these people. When I realised what was going to happen to them, I was horrified, gentlemen, horrified!'

Mr. Budd looked at him distastefully.

'An' I s'pose yer goin' ter try an' tell us that you were 'orrified at this attempt ter kill Mr. and Mrs. Walbrook, too?' he said sarcastically.

'I was mad!' declared Mr. Lucas. 'I didn't realise what I was doing. I've been through a very great mental strain during the last few days. The appalling result of my getting mixed up with this dreadful man was weighing on my mind. Imagine — '

'You're doin' all the imaginin' at the

moment,' interrupted the big man. 'Let's hear about this feller. Do you know 'is name?'

Mr. Lucas shook his head.

'I neither know his name, nor anything about him,' he answered, 'except that he's completely crazy — a dangerous lunatic. It was partly through fear of what he would do to me if I refused his demands that made me a party to this dreadful business — '

'Let's stick ter the truth,' said Mr. Budd wearily.

'I swear that that is the truth,' declared Mr. Lucas. 'I've no more idea who this man is than you have.'

'How did you come in contact with him?' asked the stout superintendent.

'He wrote to me in the first instance,' answered Lucas promptly, 'and made an appointment. His letter said that he could put something in my way that would be profitable. I was hard up at the time, and I thought the letter meant that he could give me some kind of a job. I met him that night — a Monday it was — in a car. He'd told me to look for a car with a

212

green light on the radiator, in a country road near Fallingham. He said he was determined to put a stop to gambling in all forms, and he was going to start with the football pools.'

'An' did he tell you this precious scheme of his?' said Mr. Budd, opening his eyes.

'He didn't say anything about killing these people,' replied Lucas untruthfully. 'He told me that he was going to keep them shut up for a time, just to frighten them, and then let them go. His object was to create a panic, that was all.'

'H'm,' remarked Mr. Budd sceptically. 'An' what were you goin' ter get out of all this?'

'I was to get five hundred pounds,' confessed Mr. Lucas, after a momentary hesitation. 'It was paid to me in one pound notes.'

'An' was you responsible fer the abduction of Louisa Mote?' asked Mr. Budd.

Lucas nodded.

'Yes. I took her on the Thursday night,' he said. 'This crazy man had it all planned.'

'An' what about Gummidge?' inquired

the stout superintendent. 'You couldn't 'ave done that, too.'

'He did that himself,' answered Mr. Lucas quickly.

'How did this man Stacker come into it?' asked Mr. Budd. 'What was 'is job?'

Mr. Lucas had brought the unfortunate Stacker into it, but he thought it was better not to say so.

'I suppose this man found him, the same as he did me,' he replied. 'He just did as he was told.'

'H'm,' grunted Mr. Budd non-committally. 'Well, do yer know anythin' about this lunatic feller that would enable us ter find 'im?'

'The only thing about him that was at all distinctive,' said Mr. Lucas, 'was his hands. They were queer-looking hands, thin and bony, and covered with large brownish-coloured freckles.'

The big man shot a quick glance at Peter. The evidence against the Reverend Clement Rockforth was piling up thick and fast.

'You'd know 'em again if yer saw 'em?' he said.

214

'I'd know them anywhere,' declared Mr. Lucas. 'It was the only thing I do remember about him. I never saw his face. He always wore a sort of silk bag over his head.'

Mr. Budd questioned him closely concerning the make of the car in which he had first met the unknown, what sort of voice he had, and a hundred and one details, going over the same ground again and again. But Mr. Lucas had supplied all the information of which he was capable.

'All right. Take him away,' said the fat detective. 'We'll have 'im back when Walbrook arrives, so as he can identify 'im.' And the abject Mr. Lucas was taken back to his cell.

'A thoroughly nasty piece o' work,' remarked the big man. 'But I think 'e's told all he knows. He's in such a state of funk at the moment that if he could give this feller who employed 'im away he would.'

'It's beginning to look bad for Rock-forth, isn't it?' said the reporter.

'It certainly is,' agreed Mr. Budd thoughtfully — 'very bad indeed, Ashton.

He fits in perfectly — and he's got the motive. Yes, I'm afraid it looks very bad for 'im!'

He rubbed his chin and stared at the ceiling.

'There's one thing I can't fathom,' he went on — 'how did Rockforth, or anyone, know who'd won those dividends? That's the puzzle. The names could only 'ave bin known to Smallwood's, an' yet this feller, whoever 'e was, knew 'em, too. I can't see how.'

'Did he?' questioned Bellamy. 'He may not have known the names of the winners — he may just 'ave been goin' ter carry out this idea on anybody.'

'In that case, the motive which we've given ter Rockforth goes west,' grunted Mr. Budd. 'If 'e didn't know it was 'is sister who won, 'e couldn't 'ave bin after the money.'

'It might have been a coincidence,' suggested Peter; but Mr. Budd shook his head.

'I don't believe in them sort o' coincidences,' he said. 'If this feller Rockforth's guilty, an' 'e hadn't been

216

found out, 'e would 'ave got ten thousand pounds out of it. That sort o' coincidence don't 'appen, Mr. Ashton.'

'But he said he wouldn't touch the money,' said Peter.

'I know what 'e said!' snapped Mr. Budd irritably, 'but 'e may not 'ave meant it. People say a lot o' things they don't mean. Look at the things I say ter Leek.' The use of the melancholy sergeant's name touched a chord of memory, and he smiled. 'I 'spect he'll be retirin' soon now,' he said. 'Livin' in luxury an' lookin' on the poor policemen who're still workin' with pity.'

'Why?' demanded the astonished Peter.

'He's got an all correct in 'is penny pool,' said Mr. Budd. 'He rang me up last night ter tell me. Bit o' luck fer 'im, ain't it?'

'Beginner's luck, cock,' said Jacob Bellamy. 'There's somethin' in it, after all.'

'Fancy Leek with money,' said Peter. 'Perhaps he'll forget himself an' smile!'

The arrival of Harold Walbrook put an end to the discussion of the lean sergeant's amazing luck. Mr. Lucas was brought once more from his cell, and Walbrook identified him without hesitation.

'Well, that's that,' said Mr. Budd. 'It was only a matter o' form, o' course. He'd already admitted that he was the man.'

Walbrook wanted to know how they had caught him, and listened with growing horror and astonishment, when they told him.

'What a fiendish idea!' he exclaimed. 'If Molly and I had been sleeping in that room we'd have been dead by now.'

'That was the intention,' said Mr. Budd. 'You were the only witness against him, Mr. Walbrook; without you he could have defied us to prove anything.'

He rose ponderously to his feet.

'Well, Sunday ought ter be a day o' rest,' he remarked wearily, 'but that don't apply to the police force. I'm goin' ter take this feller down to Brimley and confront 'im with Rockforth.'

A police car was secured, and with Mr. Lucas in the charge of a constable, Peter and Mr. Budd set off for Brimley.

They reached the little village just after lunch-time, and as they were passing the inn Mr. Budd stopped the car.

'We'll just call in an' congratulate Leek,' he said. 'Maybe 'e'll have some news, too.'

But there was no sign of the mournful sergeant.

'I don't know where he is, sir,' said the landlord, in answer to Mr. Budd's inquiry. ''E ain't bin in all night.'

'Not bin in all night?' repeated the big man, and there was a sudden edge to his usually slow and gentle voice.

'No, sir.' The landlord shook his head. 'I was gettin' a bit worried. He went out just afore seven last evenin', an' 'e ain't bin back since.'

The stout superintendent looked at Peter.

'I wonder what's happened to him?' he muttered anxiously.

'What could have happened to him?' demanded Peter.

'I don't know, Mr. Ashton, but I'm worried,' said Mr. Budd. 'He won that football pool last night, an' now 'e's disappeared. I don't know what can 'ave 'appened to 'im, but I'm worried — very worried indeed.'

17

Leek Meets With Adventure

Sergeant Leek came out of the little post office in Brimley's narrow High Street, after telephoning the news of his success to Mr. Budd, with a feeling of complacency.

To say that he was elated would be an exaggeration. He was neither elated nor surprised. What had happened had only been what he had expected. It did not strike him as anything at all remarkable that he should have got a correct line in Smallwood's Penny Points Pool. The fact that the odds were several millions to one against such a thing never occurred to him. He would have been more surprised if he had failed, for deep down in his subconscious mind was an enormous belief in his own capabilities. He was given to dreams wherein he performed the most remarkable and amazing feats with effortless ease, and although few people suspected it, was convinced that, given the opportunity, these achievements could be as readily translated into the realm of fact.

It was this supreme egotism that enabled him to put up with Mr. Budd's pawky and sometimes caustic humour and treat it with a kind of resigned tolerance. It was merely the big man's way of expressing himself and was not for a moment to be regarded seriously. Leek was entirely satisfied with himself, and this being the case, was quite incapable of seeing why anyone else should be dissatisfied. And in this lay both his strength and his weakness. To most people he presented the appearance of a man with a strong inferiority complex, but this was due entirely to an inherent shyness and nervousness which he had never been able to eradicate, and not to any uncertainty concerning his own infallibility.

His immediate reaction to the discovery that he had been successful, therefore, was one of satisfaction that his prophecy had proved correct. He had said that he would win and he *had* won. Budd had, of course, received the information with a characteristic remark, but he couldn't fail to be impressed, all the same.

As he walked slowly up the High Street the sergeant considered what he would do with the money. It was bound to be a respectable sum — probably it would run into many thousands. A good sound investment was the sensible thing. Something that would bring him in a steady income for the rest of his life. He could, of course, retire if he wished. That was a pleasant thought to toy with. His own master and a life of leisure — a very pleasant thought indeed.

He came in sight of the square tower of the little church, looming darkly against the deepening blue of the sky, and it switched his mind fom the contemplation of his good fortune to the reason for his presence in Brimley. It would be nice if he could, in addition to having won the first dividend in the penny points pool, bring the mystery which was baffling Budd to a successful conclusion. His imagination pictured a triumphal return to Scotland Yard and the complete stupefaction of the stout superintendent when he announced that he had arrested the murderer and the case was over. He would be congratulated by the Assistant Commissioner and most probably promoted. His long, thin legs moved more slowly and presently he came to a stop in the shadow of a tall hedge that enclosed the churchyard. From here he could see the vicarage, or rather part of it, for the cedar tree prevented an absolutely clear view, and he eyed the building speculatively. Through the thick, plate-like branches of the great tree he could see a light in an upper window. It was the only light in the house, but he knew from what Mr. Budd had told him concerning the layout of the house that it came from Rockforth's study. Rockforth was apparently at home.

The lean sergeant watched the faint yellow gleam that filtered through the tree and wondered whether it was worth while remaining. His instructions had been to pick up all the information he could concerning Rockforth and Sir Mathew

Franklin, but up to now this had been surprisingly little. The villagers were a reticent lot and apt to regard a curious stranger with suspicion. His tentative inquiries about the two people he was interested in had been met with blank faces and shaking heads. That Rockforth was 'queer' nobody denied, but beyond that they refused to go. Neither were they any more informative about Sir Mathew. There had been a very tragic episode in his life, which had been connected with his marriage, but no one seemed to be able to supply any details. This much they already knew from Superintendent Collis, and, anyway, Leek couldn't see how Sir Mathew Franklin could come into it at all. But Rockforth was different. He was definitely queer in the head and Walbrook had recognised his hands. In his own mind, the lean sergeant was pretty sure that Rockforth was the man they wanted. He fitted too well not to be. If only some concrete evidence could be found — At that moment the light went out and Leek's musings stopped abruptly.

The putting out of the light in his study

looked as though Rockforth intended going out. It was too early for him to be going to bed yet, surely.

Leek drew closer into the shadow of the hedge and waited, his eyes fixed on the house. It was very quiet and presently he heard the click of a latch. The front door of the vicarage opened, an oblong of blackness, for there was no light in the hall, and the tall, thin figure of Rockforth emerged. He shut the door behind him and walked quickly towards the gate giving admittance to the road. Leek thought that he might be coming across to the church, but he turned to the left and strode rapidly away along the open country road, without even a glance in that direction.

Leek watched the tall figure until it reached the bend and then he followed, keeping as much as possible in the shadow.

Rockforth was covering the ground at a brisk pace, moving with the curiously jerky stride that was characteristic of him. Once he stopped and looked back and Leek had to dodge quickly behind a convenient tree trunk to avoid detection. Apparently he was not observed, for the man in front went on again. The sergeant's rubber-soled boots made no sound on the muddy surface of the road but Rockforth's footsteps were clearly audible. Leek wondered where he was making for. The likeliest suggestion seemed to be that he was going to visit a parishioner, and yet there was an air of secrecy about him that was out of keeping with this. Every now and again he would stop abruptly and search the road behind him suspiciously, as though to assure himself that he was unobserved, and each time he did this the sergeant managed to take cover.

They must have been walking for nearly two miles, according to Leek's calculations, before Rockforth stopped at a gate set in the hedge, and after a sharp glance round, climbed it and disappeared on the other side.

Leek cautiously approached the gate and peered through. A narrow path cut across the corner of a field and along this Rockforth was hurrying. The sergeant hesitated. If he followed and the other took it into his head to look back, nothing could save him from discovery. There was not a vestige of cover, and although the night was dark, it was not sufficiently dark to prevent him being seen. But if he didn't follow, there was a pretty good chance of losing Rockforth altogether. He made up his mind quickly. The only thing he could do was to take advantage of the shelter offered by the hedge and hurry round the angle of the field in the hope that he would see where the other made his exit. It would take him just twice as long as Rockforth to reach the other end of the path, but he would have the man in sight all the time. He climbed the gate, fervently praying that Rockforth would not choose that moment for one of his periodical halts of inspection, and dropped on the other side. He was only just in time, for he had barely reached the shelter of the hedge before the other stopped and looked round. But Leek was crouching in the deep shadow and could not be seen.

When Rockforth moved on again, satisfied, the sergeant stumbled forward as quickly as he could. The ground near the roots of the hedge was uneven, and he almost fell in his eagerness to skirt the field and reach the outlet of the path before Rockforth vanished from view. He came to the angle which formed the corner of the field, and ran along the other side. He was near enough to be able to distinguish that the outlet to the footpath was a stile, when Rockforth reached it, and climbed over.

Beyond, as Leek presently found, was a lane. It was little more than a cart-track and very dark, because of the thickly growing trees on either side, whose branches interlaced overhead. He couldn't see any sign of Rockforth here, but he could hear him, as he stumbled over the rough ground.

It certainly looked as though he might be on the verge of making an important discovery. Rockforth was behaving very suspiciously over this mysterious excursion.

The trees began to thin, and the lane to widen, and then, suddenly, the footsteps in front of him ceased.

Leek stopped, too, and listened. There

was no sound at all from the man ahead. The unbroken silence seemed to the sergeant to continue for a long time, and then there came the squeak of a hinge, and the thud of a closing gate, followed by the scrunch of feet on gravel.

Leek could see nothing, but he concluded from the sounds that there was a house somewhere near at hand. After allowing a minute to elapse, he moved forward cautiously. A few yards farther on, the lane took a bend to the right, and just round this bend was the white gate of a house. It was set between two neatly-trimmed hedges of golden privet, and beyond it he could glimpse a well-kept gravel path, bordered by flower beds and smooth strips of grass. The house itself was dimly visible, glimmering a whitish-grey in the darkness, and showing a strip of light, that shone from between the closed curtains of a down-stairs room.

It all looked very respectable, and Leek began to have misgivings that he had been wasting his time. Had Rockforth, after all, only come to visit a friend? It appeared very much like it, but why had he made such a parade of secrecy? Perhaps that was his normal way of proceeding. After all, he was queer.

Leek stood in the darkness by the little gate, debating what he should do next. Rockforth had certainly called on the person or persons who lived in the house. The lean sergeant had heard the door open and close. The question was, was this an innocent proceeding, or not?

The only way Leek could see of finding this out was to try to learn what was going on in the house, and this was easier to decide than to do.

It might be possible to see into the room with the light, he thought. The curtains had been drawn carelessly, and there was a slit an inch wide between them. If he could get close enough he might be able to see, and perhaps hear what was going on in the room beyond.

He made up his mind to try. Remembering the squeaking hinge on the gate, he climbed it, and keeping to the grass moved as silently as he could towards the house. It was larger than it had looked, he saw as he drew closer; a white, half-timbered house with many gables. It didn't look the kind of place where one would have expected to find anything in the nature of a conspiracy taking place. It was the sort of house that might belong to a fairly prosperous, retired business man. There were neat flower-beds, and rows of standard roses. At one side was a rustic screen covered with climbing roses, in the centre of which was an arch that evidently led to the back of the premises. The more Leek saw, the more he became sure that his adventure of the evening was going to end in dismal disappointment. It was more than likely that behind the curtains of that window, some stout and elderly gentleman was entertaining Rockforth with a whisky-and-soda, and listening to some business connected with the parish. Probably one of the church wardens lived here.

With a feeling that he was not only wasting his time, but that he was laying himself open to a very unpleasant reprimand if he were discovered, the sergeant carefully approached the window.

A narrow flower-bed ran beneath it,

and to avoid this, for he had no desire to leave any traces of his presence, Leek had to lean forward, supporting himself by gripping the sill. It was an uncomfortable position, and at first he could see nothing. By shifting a little, however, he managed to get a partial sight of the room.

It was a large room, furnished comfortably as a lounge, and lighted by several lamps which stood on tables and cabinets. He could see Rockforth plainly, but the person to whom the vicar was speaking was hidden from his view by the back of a large armchair. One glance at the clergyman told him that this was no social call. Rockforth was talking rapidly, accompanying his torrent of words with violent gestures, his thin, lined face twitching spasmodically. Every now and again, he flung back his head, and raising a clenched hand, shook it at the ceiling. Except for the expression on his face, he might have been preaching. But that expression was terrible; an indescribable mixture of anger, sorrow, fear, and despair.

The person to whom he was speaking

was apparently saying very little, for Rockforth scarcely paused in his flood of rhetoric. Leek could hear the harsh tones of his voice, but that was all. Not one single word was distinguishable.

The hysterical excitement which had marked his every movement, suddenly died out of Rockforth. He drooped like a wilting flower in the sun, his long arms fell to his sides, and his chin sank on to his breast. The faint deep tones of another voice reached the listening Leek. It spoke slowly and quietly. When it ceased, Rockforth raised his head. But now his attitude was weary and pleading. All the fire seemed to have gone out of the man. His dark cavernous eyes had sunk farther into the drawn, white mask of his face. He looked like a man defeated.

With a gesture of despair, he picked up his wide-brimmed hat and turned towards the door. Leek fixed his eyes on the back of the chair, hoping that the man who sat in it would get up, but his hope was not realised.

Rockforth paused at the door and appeared to make a final appeal, then with another hopeless gesture, he turned and disappeared in the darkness of the hall.

Leek jerked himself upright. In another moment or so, Rockforth would be leaving the house, and unless he took cover he would be discovered. There was no time to reach the gate, and he decided to slip through the arch in the rustic screen. The angle of the house would conceal him from the view of anyone leaving by the front door.

He was only just in time. He had barely got round the corner before he heard the front door open and shut and the sound of Rockforth's footsteps on the path. It struck him as peculiar that there were apparently no servants in so large a house. There couldn't have been, for the clergyman had let himself out. Perhaps it was their evening off —

Rockforth reached the gate, stopped for a moment with it open in his hand, and passed through. Leek waited until the sound of his footsteps had receded down the lane, and then came back to his former point of vantage. He was most anxious to get a glimpse of that other man who had been in the room. But the chair was now empty. He watched, thinking that the man had, perhaps, left the room for some reason and would come back, and waited expectantly, his eyes on the door . . .

There was no sound of footfall to warn him, but suddenly an instinct told him that he was in danger. He turned swiftly, stumbling as he did so, saw the dark outline of a figure with a raised arm, and then everything faded in a stab of agonising pain, and he fell forward among the flowers . . .

18

Mr. Budd Makes an Arrest

Mr. Budd took a long pull at his tankard of beer, and set it down with a grave face.

'I don't like it at all, Mr. Ashton,' he said seriously. 'It looks bad to me. What can have happened to 'im?'

'Perhaps he's following up an inquiry?' suggested Peter, without any great conviction in his voice.

The big man pursed his thick lips.

'Maybe,' he said, 'but I should think it was very unlikely. I've got an idea it's more serious than that.' He rubbed his chin thoughtfully. 'He wins this pool, an' he vanishes,' he murmured. 'It's very worryin' an' disturbin'.'

There was an under-current of genuine feeling in his voice.

'It can't have anything to do with his winning the pool,' said Peter. 'That's ridiculous.'

'Maybe it is,' agreed Mr. Budd, 'but it's a queer coincidence, all the same.' He drained his tankard. 'Well, we'd better get on with the business o' identifyin' Rockforth, I s'pose. P'raps we shall find some news of Leek later.'

He led the way back to the waiting car.

'Drive on up the hill until you come ter the church,' he instructed the driver. 'When you get there, stop.'

He got heavily in and Peter followed him.

'This man Rockforth 'ull be comin' out for afternoon service pretty soon,' he said, as the car moved off. 'I don't want ter go to the house if I can avoid it.' He turned to Mr. Lucas. 'You keep yer eyes open, an' tell me if you reckernise anythin' about this feller, see?'

Mr. Lucas saw, and said so at length. He had developed an ingratiating manner that was particularly repellent.

The car stopped opposite the vicarage, and almost on the exact spot where Leek had taken up his stand on the previous night.

They had a long wait, and the village

children and their parents eyed them curiously as they passed on their way to their devotions.

At last, however, the door of the house opened, and Rockforth came hurriedly out. The man radiated an atmosphere of restless activity that was curiously like some wild thing. Nothing about him was still. His hands twitched, and the muscles of his face jerked. He moved with a queerly uncertain gait, and his dark eyes turned continuously from side to side. He reminded Peter of nothing so much as a frightened and hunted hare he had once seen.

As he came out of the vicarage gate, Mr. Lucas uttered an exclamation.

'That's the man!' he whispered. 'I'm sure that's the man! He has the same hands.'

'Would you be able to reckernise his voice?' asked Mr. Budd, and Lucas nodded.

'I'd know his voice anywhere!' he declared.

'Then listen,' said the big man, and got ponderously out of the car.

'Good afternoon, sir,' he said, as Rockforth crossed the road. The clergyman stopped, gave him a hard stare, and inclined his head.

'Good afternoon,' he answered harshly. 'What are you doing here?'

'I had ter come down on business,' said Mr. Budd, 'an' I wanted another word with you — '

'You are wasting your time,' interrupted Rockforth curtly. 'I have nothing to say to you. I said all I had to say at our previous interview.'

He moved on towards the church gate, but Mr. Budd stopped him.

'It's a very small matter, sir,' he said, 'an' won't take a minute. I'd like ter know if you've ever seen this man before?'

He made a gesture towards the car, and Mr. Lucas stepped out. He was staring at Rockforth with dropped jaw, but the clergyman merely shot him a quick glance and shook his head impatiently.

'I have never seen him before,' he said. 'Good afternoon!'

He passed them, pushed open the gate leading to the church, and walked up the path.

'That's him!' whispered Mr. Lucas excitedly. 'That's him! I'd know those hands and that voice anywhere. That's him, all right.'

'All right, get back in the car,' said the stout superintendent sharply, and when Mr. Lucas had obeyed: 'There was no sign o' recognition in 'is face.'

'Not a vestige,' agreed Peter. 'I was watching closely. He gave no sign that he'd ever seen Lucas before.'

'Maybe that's just 'is cunnin',' remarked Mr. Budd. 'They're as clever as monkeys, these crazy fellers. Well, that's that, anyway. I s'pose you're quite certain, Lucas? You 'aven't made no mistake?'

Mr. Lucas was vehement in his denial.

'That's the man,' he repeated. 'I'd swear to him anywhere.'

'You'd swear to anythin' anywhere,' said Mr. Budd calmly. 'But you *an*' Walbrook can't be wrong, so I s'pose we'd better act on it.'

'What are you going to do?' asked the reporter.

'I'm goin' along ter find Collis,' answered Mr. Budd. 'Drive to the p'lice-station, will yer?'

He got back into the car, the police

driver skilfully turned it, and they sped off down the hill.

Collis was on duty when they reached the station house, and greeted them cheerily.

'Hallo,' he said. 'I didn't expect to see you to-day.'

'I didn't expect ter be 'ere,' said the big man. 'I was enjoyin' meself in me garden when I was routed out.'

The superintendent was sympathetic. He was a keen gardener himself.

'Where's your sergeant?' he asked. 'He was coming in to see me this morning, but he never turned up.'

'I'd like ter know where he is,' said Mr. Budd gravely. 'He hasn't bin seen since just around seven last night.'

Collis looked at him in blank astonishment.

'Do you mean — he's disappeared?' he asked incredulously.

'If he hasn't, it's a very good imitation,' said Mr. Budd. 'He got an all correct line in Smallwood's penny points pool last night, an' he hasn't bin seen since.'

'Good heavens!' Collis looked suddenly

serious. 'You're surely not suggesting that there is any connection, are you?'

'I'm not suggestin' anythin',' answered Mr. Budd wearily. 'I'm just tellin' you the fac's. That's not what I came ter see yer for, though. Only partly. I'm detainin' that feller Rockforth on suspicion, an' you'd better come along with me when I pull him in.'

Collis looked shocked.

'You can't do that!' he gasped.

'Can't I?' said Mr. Budd, grimly. 'You watch me! I not only can, but I'm goin' to!' He leaned forward across the desk at which he was seated. 'You listen ter me, Collis, an' when you've 'eard what I've got ter say, you'll realise that I'm justified.'

Briefly he told the startled superintendent of the events of the past few hours.

'You're justified all right,' said Collis, when he had finished, 'and I'm not going to try to stop you, but it'll create a terrible scandal.'

'It'll create a worse scandal if a few more people are murdered!' retorted Mr. Budd.

'When do you propose to arrest him?' asked Collis.

'When 'e goes back to 'is tea,' said the big man. 'An' I'm not arrestin' him. I'm detainin' him on suspicion. It amounts ter the same thing, I'll admit, but it's not so bad if there should 'appen ter be a mistake.'

Superintendent Collis looked a greatly worried man.

'I only hope to heaven there isn't,' he declared fervently. 'I'd better get on to the Chief Constable about it, though.'

'Yes, you'll 'ave ter do that,' said Mr. Budd. 'I'll 'ave a word with him, too.'

The chief constable was difficult. He disapproved of the idea completely at the beginning, but when Mr. Budd methodically paraded the evidence, he reluctantly capitulated.

'You'd better take this feller back to town,' said the big man to the constable in charge of Mr. Lucas. 'You can send another car for me.'

'All right, sir,' said the constable, and departed with his prisoner.

'Now then,' said Mr. Budd. 'This is

goin' ter be an unpleasant business, so we might as well get it over. We can use your car ter go up ter the vicarage, can't we?'

Collis agreed that they could.

'You'll 'ave ter wait here, Mr. Ashton,' went on Mr. Budd. 'You can't be in this.'

Peter made no demur. He realised that the presence of a newspaper reporter in the circumstances would be frowned on by officialdom if it became known, so he made himself comfortable in the tiny charge-room and chatted to the sergeant.

Mr. Budd went up to the vicarage with Collis, a gloomy and depressed man. He was worried about Leek, and he had no relish for the job that confronted him.

'If the old chap is guilty,' remarked the superintendent, as they breasted the hill, 'I'll swear he's not responsible for his actions.'

The fat man grunted. Never before had he been engaged on a case which made him feel so undecided. The evidence against Rockforth made it essential to adopt the line of action he was taking, but he didn't feel at all sure that he was the right man. And yet everything pointed to him. Even the motive was there. The chain of circumstances couldn't be coincidence. That was definitely impossible. And yet — somewhere at the back of his mind lurked a desperate doubt.

The elderly woman who had admitted him before opened the door and regarded them inquiringly.

'We wish to see Mr. Rockforth,' said Collis. 'Will you tell him, please?'

The woman went away, and they waited. In a few seconds she was back again.

'The master says he can't see anyone,' she announced shortly, and would have closed the door if Collis had not stopped her.

'I'm afraid he will have to see us,' he said gravely. 'Please tell him that we don't want to make any trouble.'

Her wrinkled face puckered, and she looked frightened.

'I don't think he will see you,' she said doubtfully. 'I'll — '

'What is it? Won't those men go away?' The harsh voice of Rockforth broke in from the top of the stairs.

'They say they must see you, sir,' answered the housekeeper.

He came down, a frown on his thin face.

'What do you want?' he demanded curtly. 'This persecution is really intolerable — '

'I'm very sorry, sir,' said Collis apologetically, 'but I'm afraid I shall have to ask you to accompany us to the station. Perhaps you'd like to pack one or two things.'

The Reverend Clement Rockforth stared at him, and then his already white face turned a chalky-grey, he seemed to sway back and forth on his feet for a second, and then he collapsed like the falling of a house of cards.

19

No Shadow of Doubt

The housekeeper uttered a little whimpering cry, and would have flung herself on her knees beside the sprawling form of the unconscious man if Mr. Budd had not gently stopped her.

'He's only fainted, I think,' he said. 'If you'll get some water it'll prob'ly bring him round.'

Pale and trembling, her anxiety for her master found an outlet in indignation towards Mr. Budd and the superintendent — particularly Mr. Budd.

'It's your fault, comin' 'ere an' upsettin' 'im,' she snapped angrily. 'And 'e ain't well. 'E ain't been well for a long time — '

'Get the water, please,' interrupted the big man, and knelt down with difficulty beside Rockforth. The woman looked as though she was about to refuse, apparently thought better of it, and hurried away.

Mr. Budd made a quick examination of the man on the floor and his face became grave. Uppermost in his mind when Rockforth had collapsed had been the thought that it was a sign of sudden desperate alarm — of guilt. But that thought was banished now by more urgent considerations. He looked up.

'It's worse than a faint, I'm afraid,' he said slowly. 'Who's the nearest doctor, Collis?'

'Blinder,' answered the superintendent. 'Why, what's the matter with him?'

'It looks very much ter me as if 'e's had a stroke,' replied the stout superintendent. ''E's breathin' heavily, an' his face is congested. I think if there's a phone in the house you'd better get hold of this feller Blinder.'

Collis' face was troubled.

'You don't think there's any danger of his dying, do you?' he asked anxiously.

'I don't know, but it may be serious,' answered Mr. Budd. 'We ought ter get the doctor to 'im at once.'

'I'll find out from Mrs. Sparrow where the telephone is,' said Collis, and turned away. He met the elderly housekeeper coming back with the water, and put the question.

'The telephone's upstairs in 'is study,' she replied. 'What'-cher want it for?'

Collis told her, and she looked alarmed.

'Doctor Blinder?' she said. 'What'cher want 'im for, if it's only a faint?'

'We think it would be wiser to have his opinion,' explained the superintendent soothingly.

'You mean it ain't a faint? What are yer — '

'It's possible your master may 'ave had a slight stroke, ma'am,' broke in Mr. Budd. 'We ought to get a doctor as quickly as we can.'

She broke into a wailing flood of lamentation, interspersed with angry recrimination, which the stout man eventually succeeded in stemming.

'It won't do anybody any good goin' on like this,' he said with truth. 'I'm very sorry that this should 'ave happened, but it ain't nobody's fault. The best thing you can do, ma'am, is ter calm yerself, an' try an' help.'

His words had the desired effect. With a great deal of sniffing, Mrs. Sparrow stifled her lachrymose indignation, and escorted Collis up to the Reverend Rockforth's study. After the lapse of a few minutes he came down again.

'Dr. Blinder's coming along at once,' he announced. 'I suppose we had better not move him until he's seen him?'

Mr. Budd shook his head.

'This is going to make things worse than ever,' whispered the superintendent, after a quick glance to ensure that the housekeeper was out of earshot. 'She'll spread the news round the village like lightning, and if there is any mistake we shall get it properly in the neck.'

'You're a pessimistic sort o' chap, ain't yer?' muttered the big man. 'You remind me o' my sergeant — that's the sort o' comfortin' thing 'e would have said. I know we'll get it in the neck if there's any mistake. We should 'a' got it in the neck in any case. But I should have got it in the neck a jolly sight worse if this feller is guilty an' I'd let 'im get away.'

'It certainly looks as if he might be,'

said Collis. 'An innocent man doesn't have a stroke at the sight of the police.'

'His sort do,' said Mr. Budd. 'That means nothin'. 'E's highly strung, an' nervy. It didn't want much to throw 'im off his balance.' He rubbed his chin gently. 'As soon as the doctor's been we'll 'ave a look through the house.'

'We haven't got a search warrant — ' began the punctilious Collis; but Mr. Budd cut him short.

'I know we ain't,' he said. 'But that isn't goin' ter stop me. We could get one easy enough, so it 'ull only be anticipatin' things. I wonder 'ow long that doctor feller's goin' ter take?'

Considering that he had to come from the other end of the village, Dr. Blinder arrived remarkably speedily. He was a small, stoutish man, of middle age, and all his movements were quick and bird-like. He listened to what they had to tell him with his head slightly on one side, and without wasting any time made his examination.

'He must be taken to hospital at once,' he said curtly. 'There is no doubt at all that he's had a stroke. It's not a very serious one, but he requires immediate and proper attention. I will make arrangements for him to be taken to Fallingham Cottage Hospital and order the ambulance.' He looked sharply, with a pair of shrewd, beady black eyes, first at Collis and then at Mr. Budd. 'How did this happen?' he asked. 'He must have had some kind of a shock.'

The stout superintendent explained the situation.

'H'm!' remarked Dr. Blinder. 'So that's it, is it? Well, I'm not surprised he collapsed. He's obviously in a shocking state of health — nerves all shot to pieces, and abnormally high blood pressure. It wouldn't take much to push him over the brink. Of course, he's always been queer — bit touched — eccentric. You think he's been mixed up in these murders? You've made a mistake. The old fellow wouldn't kill a beetle!'

'All the evidence — ' began Collis; but the little doctor snapped his fingers.

'I don't care a fig for the evidence,' he said. 'I'm going on my knowledge of the man. Psychology is more to be relied on than a cart-load of evidence. However, that's your affair. But you'll have to go carefully. I warn you that I shall not allow my patient to be worried in any way. It is essential that he should have complete rest, and I will not be responsible for the consequences if my orders are disobeyed.'

Collis looked at Mr. Budd. This was going to be awkward.

'How long d'you think it'll be before he recovers?' murmured the fat man.

Dr. Blinder shrugged his shoulders.

'I can't say,' he declared; 'but it will be a long time before he is in a fit state to be subjected to the slightest mental disturbance. Any such thing would, in my opinion, endanger his reason, and probably his life. Now I'll get through to the hospital.'

'That,' said Collis, 'has torn it!'

Mr. Budd nodded gloomily. It was going to make things very difficult indeed. They would be unable to question Rockforth, or make any further move until such time as Dr. Blinder raised his ban.

254

'As you say,' remarked slowly, 'that 'as torn it!'

Dr. Blinder returned and announced that he had arranged for a bed at the hospital, and that the ambulance would arrive shortly. During the intervening period, he proceeded to make his patient as comfortable as possible. With the assistance of Collis, Rockforth was lifted and carried into the big, shabby drawing-room, where he was laid gently on a couch and propped up with cushions. Dr. Blinder ordered a bowl of cold water, and with the aid of several handkerchiefs improvised a series of cold-compresses for the unconscious man's head — a treatment which he kept up until the ambulance arrived.

When it came he supervised the removal of his patient on the stretcher, gave the nurse detailed instructions concerning her charge, and promising that he would be at the hospital as soon as the ambulance, watched it drive away, took a brief farewell of Mr. Budd and Collis, and the tearful Mrs. Sparrow, and followed in his small car.

'An' that's that!' said the big man, with a weary yawn. 'Well, we'd better do what we can 'ere, an' then clear off, too.'

They had some difficulty in persuading the housekeeper to allow them to make a search of the house. It was now firmly fixed in her head that they were responsible for the sudden illness of her master — as indeed they were — and, in consequence, she was definitely hostile. By exerting all his patience, however, Mr. Budd at length succeeded in convincing her that he was only doing his duty, and she reluctantly consented not to interfere.

Before beginning the search, he questioned her concerning Rockforth's movements at the times when he would necessarily have had to be away, were he responsible for the disappearances and the subsequent deaths of Miss Mote and Mr. Gummidge. He had a list of these times, and when he checked the housekeeper's replies he discovered that Rockforth had been absent from the vicarage on these important dates. Neither was Mrs. Sparrow able to say where he had gone.

'If there's any mistake about Rockforth

bein' guilty,' said Mr. Budd, when he had finished his questions, 'then all these things we keep on findin' out is the most extraordinary coincidence I've ever come up against.'

Collis was forced to agree with him.

'It does seem pretty convincing,' he said, but his face still wore a worried frown. 'And yet, you know, I can't bring myself to believe it.'

'Well, we can't ignore all this evidence,' said Mr. Budd, who felt the same way about it himself, 'in spite of what Blinder blithered about sigh — whatever-it-is. We're dealin' with fac's, an' we're gettin' 'em, thick an' fast.'

They began their search on the ground floor, and worked carefully through the house. There was nothing of importance in the big drawing-room or in the sparsely furnished dining-room. There was a large morning-room, unused, that also yielded nothing. A smaller room and the kitchen were the exclusive domain of Mrs. Sparrow, and hardly likely to contain anything in the nature of a clue.

On the first landing were the study,

Rockforth's bedroom, another bedroom, and a bathroom. The study, a big, untidy room full of books, took them longer than any of the others, but they found nothing whatever that could be even remotely connected with the murders. The bedroom, too, was devoid of interest. The spare room had evidently not been used for some time, and all the drawers and cupboards were empty.

Mr. Budd peered into the bathroom, made a brief search of a white enamelled cabinet, which only contained medicines, and stopped for a rest.

'Looks as if we was goin' ter draw a blank,' he remarked.

'What did you expect to find?' asked Collis, wiping his face.

'Nothin' in particular,' answered the stout man. 'I was jest 'opin' that we might come across a bit o' confirmatory evidence. I'm like you. I'm not satisfied about this feller Rockforth. He fits in every way, but it seems all wrong, somehow. P'raps it's because he's a parson. I'd feel much happier if we could find one bit of real, conclusive evidence. So as yer could say — 'well, there ain't no shadder o' doubt'.'

'I'd feel happier, too,' said Collis; 'though the evidence at the moment is pretty strong. I must admit, in spite of my feeling to the contrary, that it wants a lot of explaining away, other than by the fact that Rockforth is guilty.'

'You're right,' said Mr. Budd. 'Puttin' it all together, I think any jury 'ud convict on it. But — well, I don't know.'

He twitched his massive shoulders, as though to rid himself of a burden, and sighed wearily.

'I s'pose we'd better get on with the job,' he said. 'There's only one more floor.'

There were three rooms here. Two were empty, and one was where Mrs. Sparrow slept. They found nothing to reward them for their labours but a few old trunks and rubbish, and returned downstairs tired and dusty.

'There's only the garage now,' said Mr. Budd, 'an' I don't s'pose we'll find anything there. Rockforth didn't keep a car, did he?'

Collis shook his head.

'No,' he answered. 'He either walked or rode a bicycle.'

They obtained the key of the garage, which was built on to the side of the house, from the still indignant but now resigned housekeeper, and started on the last part of their search.

The place contained an ancient bicycle, and had apparently been used as a store-room for various garden tools. There was a lawn-mower, and a collection of spades and forks and hoes, and a number of seed boxes. A bench which ran down one side was littered with all kinds of oddments, and amongst these Mr. Budd made the first discovery of any importance.

Turning over a pile of old sacks he suddenly caught a glimpse of something black and pulled it out. His ejaculation on seeing what it was brought Collis quickly to his side.

'What have you found?' asked the superintendent.

'The conclusive evidence I was askin'' for,' answered Mr. Budd, and held out the black object. 'Take a look at that.'

Collis looked and his eyes widened.

'It's a mask of black silk,' he muttered.

'Made to slip on over the 'ead,' said the big man, 'an' cover the whole face except fer these eye-holes which 'ave bin cut in it. I think that's conclusive, when yer remember Walbrook's description o' that crazy man who raved at 'im.'

Collis took hold of his lower lip between his finger and thumb and gently pulled at it.

'I think it is,' he remarked soberly.

20

Sir Mathew Franklin's Secret

Seated in the charge-room of the little police station, Mr. Budd, Peter Ashton, and Collis, discussed the discovery at the vicarage.

'The finding of that mask seems to remove any lingering doubt,' said Peter thoughtfully, 'though I'm pretty sure the poor old chap isn't responsible for what he's done.'

'I agree with you,' said Collis, 'but I doubt, if it comes to a trial, whether he'll escape hanging on that account. There's the motive to be taken into consideration, and that'll go a long way with a jury. A man who benefits to the extent of over ten thousand pounds from murdering his sister can't be as mad as he appears. At least, that's how a jury will look at it, I'm sure. And there's the cunning way in which the whole thing was planned. It was made to look as though it was the act of a madman. That was the sole reason why these other people were brought into it. If he'd only gone after Louisa Mote, or Rockforth I suppose I ought to call her, the motive would have been obvious from the start.'

'There's a mystery there,' said the reporter. 'Why was she living in the name of Mote? That's still got to be cleared up.'

'There's a lot o' things still got ter be cleared up, Mr. Ashton,' put in Mr. Budd discontentedly. 'I wish Rockforth hadn't collapsed like he had. He could have helped us a lot. Now, I've got ter work on a theory, an' it's not goin' ter be so easy.'

'What theory?' asked Peter.

'My theory concernin' the reason why Rockforth's sister called 'erself Mote,' replied Mr. Budd. 'Maybe it's a little more than a theory, really. I wish I knew what had become of Leek,' he added suddenly. 'I'm worried about that feller. He's more of a liability than an asset, I'll admit, but I wouldn't like anythin' ter happen to 'im, all the same. Where can he have got to?'

Neither Peter nor Collis could offer any suggestion.

'Just vanished into thin air,' went on the big man irritably. 'Like a candle blown out in the wind. It's very peculiar an' distressin'. Maybe we'll get on better without 'im, but I'd like to know what 'appened, just as a matter o' curiosity.'

In spite of his way of putting things, which was characteristic, Peter realised that the stout man was genuinely worried over the disappearance of his subordinate.

'What are your plans?' he inquired. 'Are you going back to town?'

'Eventually,' said Mr. Budd. 'But I'm goin' ter stop 'ere for a bit longer. Maybe if we was ter go along ter that pub, they'd rake us up somethin' to eat — '

'A very good idea!' interrupted the reporter heartily. 'I'm famished.'

'I could eat a 'ouse meself,' said the stout superintendent, rising to his feet and yawning. 'I haven't 'ad nothin' since me breakfast.'

'Come along, then,' said Peter. 'Let's go.'

'If that car comes fer me,' said Mr.

Budd, 'you might tell the driver where I am, will yer, Collis? 'E can come on down ter the pub.'

The local superintendent promised to deliver the message.

'An' keep your ears open fer any news o' Leek. That feller's always been a trouble ter me, but I'd feel happier if I knew where 'e was.'

The landlord of the local inn rose nobly to the occasion when they stated their wants.

' 'Ow would a nice bit o' cold beef an' some potatoes an' pickles suit ye, gen'lemen?' he suggested. 'Followed by stewed fruit an' custard — '

'Produce it!' cried Peter. 'In the meanwhile we will sample a couple of pints of your beer, just to whet our appetites.'

The beer was set before them, and the landlord went away to order the meal. The bar was fairly full, and the news of the Reverend Clement Rockforth's sudden illness, and the cause of it, had evidently preceded them, for there was much whispering, and many covert glances were cast in their direction.

Mr. Budd, ignoring these, drank his beer in frowning silence, his heavy face gloomy, and his manner detached. Peter concluded that he was still worrying over the whereabouts of Leek, and was partly right. There were, however, other things troubling the mind of the big man.

He had started out on the investigation with nothing to go on, and in a remarkably short space of time had succeeded in finding the people responsible. But he wasn't feeling pleased at all. He was feeling anything but pleased. He had done what it was his duty to do, considering the facts in his possession, but he wasn't satisfied. That inner voice, which at times called so loudly, kept on reiterating that it was all wrong — that instead of having brought the case to a successful conclusion, he had not yet started to uncover the truth.

He maintained his gloomy silence throughout the meal, which they ate in the small parlour, munching his food steadily, and keeping his eyes fixed on his plate. Peter left him undisturbed, until they had started on an excellent piece of gorgonzola cheese, and then he said suddenly:

'What makes you think it's not as simple as all that?'

The stout man looked up, momentarily startled. The reporter's remark had come so aptly on his thoughts.

'What makes you think that I think it isn't?' he grunted.

Peter laughed.

'Because I know you so well,' he replied. 'So you don't think it's as simple as that, eh?'

Mr. Budd swallowed the morsel of bread and cheese he had put in his mouth, before he answered.

'Well, if you must know, I don't, Mr. Ashton,' he said. 'But it's no good your askin' me why. I don't know why. It jest seems ter me all wrong, some'ow.'

'I know what you mean,' said Peter, nodding. 'I've got the same feeling. Don't you think, though, that we may both be searching for something that doesn't exist? I mean, there's no reason why it shouldn't be as simple as it appears.'

'That's the trouble,' declared Mr. Budd. 'There ain't no reason. An' yet — '

He shook his head, pushed aside his plate, and felt in his pocket for one of his black cigars. 'Fer-got ter bring any with me,' he grumbled, when his searching fingers found the pocket empty.

'Have a cigarette?' said Peter, pulling out a packet of Gold Flake and stretching across the table. The big man took one and lighted it.

'Don't know how you can smoke these things,' he said, after a preliminary puff. 'No bite in 'em. The whole thing's very unsatisfactory.'

'Well, you needn't smoke it,' began Peter, under the impression that he was still referring to the cigarette.

'I'm talkin' about this football pool business,' said Mr. Budd. 'It all fits so neatly, an' yet I can't 'elp feelin' that it ain't right.'

'Supposin' Rockforth isn't guilty,' said Peter. 'What's the alternative?'

'There isn't an alternative, Ashton,' replied the big man. 'Rockforth's got ter be guilty ter fit the fac's. Maybe I'm jest bein' silly an' imaginative; maybe it's right, after all.'

'But you don't really think so?' finished the reporter.

'No, I don't,' declared Mr. Budd. 'If I did, I wouldn't be worryin'.' He stretched himself wearily. 'Well, it ain't no use talkin' about it,' he said. 'There it is, an' we shall see what we shall see.'

The driver of the second police car arrived at that moment to report and seek instructions.

'I was waitin' fer you,' said the fat man. 'I want yer to take me up to Sir Mathew Franklin's place. I'll tell yer 'ow ter get to it — '

'What are you going there for?' demanded Peter curiously.

'I want ter have a word with 'im,' answered Mr. Budd. 'I think he can clear up a little point that I've got in me mind. You can come along, too, if yer like.'

Peter did like, and, when they had paid for their meal, accompanied the stout superintendent to the car. They were watched by curious eyes as they drove away.

'You seem to have created something of a sensation in Brimley,' remarked the

269

reporter, as he noticed this.

Mr. Budd grunted.

'Maybe I'll create a bigger one before I'm done,' he said.

There were lights in several of the windows when they pulled up before the main entrance to Brimley Court, and in answer to Mr. Budd's ring the elderly butler opened the door. He evidently recognised the big man, for his eyebrows went up a fraction of an inch.

'I'm sorry to bother yer,' said Mr. Budd, 'but I should like to speak to Sir Mathew if I could. It's very urgent, so will yer please tell him.'

The servant hesitated, and then, with a slight bow, went away. He was gone for some time, but when he returned it was with a request that they should follow him. They did so, climbing the big staircase, and were shown into the room in which Mr. Budd had had his previous interview.

Sir Mathew Franklin was seated as before behind the large writing-table, but this time his delicate face wore an expression that was almost haggard.

'Sit down — er — superintendent,' he said, indicating a chair in front of him. 'What can I do for you this time?'

'I'll stand if you don't mind, sir, thank you all the same,' said Mr. Budd. 'I don't know whether you've heard about the Reverend Rockforth — '

'I have,' interrupted the old man. 'Jordan, my butler, brought me the news. I must say that I feel most strongly that a mistake has been made.'

'I'm afraid, sir,' said Mr. Budd gently, 'that the evidence doesn't bear out that. We have discovered that one of these people who was killed was the Reverend Rockforth's sister, which means that he, as next-of-kin, would get the money she won in this football pool. It's a strong motive, an' the only motive, an' taken with the rest of the evidence, doesn't seem ter leave much room for doubt.'

Peter, watching, saw the thin hand of the man behind the desk clench until the knuckles stood out under the tautened skin, milk-white.

'His sister,' he muttered — 'his sister — '

'Yes, sir,' went on the big man softly. 'She was livin' under the name of Louisa Mote, in a little cottage near Gravesend.'

There was no doubt about the haggardness of the face now. The pale-blue eyes seemed to recede into the thin face, and the lines deepened. The white cheeks became whiter, and the thin lips bloodless.

'I believe you knew this lady at one time, sir,' said Mr. Budd, 'an' that's why I'm here. I want all the information I can get about her, an' Mr. Rockforth is not in a position to 'elp me at the moment — '

'What makes you think that I can?'

The voice that came from the man behind the desk was a hoarse croak.

'This, sir.'

With remarkable quickness, Mr. Budd stepped over to the fireplace and touched a photograph thatstood upon the mantel-piece.

'This photograph is a picture of the lady who called herself 'Louisa Mote', sir,' he said. 'It was taken a good many years ago, but I recognised it when I was

272

'ere before. It's signed 'Louisa', too — '

A queer sound broke from the old man — a cross between a sigh and a stifled groan. His thin hands went up, and for a moment he buried his face in them. When he uncovered it he appeared to have aged several years.

'You are quite right,' he whispered — 'that is a photograph of Louisa — Rockforth.'

Mr. Budd came back to the littered table.

'But she changed her name, sir,' he said; and his voice was very kind and sympathetic. 'She changed it to — Louisa Franklin, didn't she?'

Sir Mathew Franklin nodded.

'How did you know?' he asked huskily. 'How did you know?'

'I guessed, sir,' answered Mr. Budd. 'When I saw the picture, an' when I heard that you'd 'ad trouble over your marriage. She was your wife, wasn't she?'

'Until thirty years ago,' replied the old man. He passed his hand rapidly over his eyes, as though he were brushing away a fly. 'It is very painful for me to have to speak of it, but — but I think, in the

273

circumstances, I had better tell you the story.'

'I should be much obliged if you would, sir,' murmured Mr. Budd — 'much obliged.'

21

A Slice of the Past

Sir Mathew Franklin moved uneasily in his chair and fidgeted with various small objects on the writing-table within his reach. He appeared to be making up his mind how to begin, for it was a long time before he spoke.

'I shall have to go back thirty-three years,' he said at last, 'and I hope that you will treat what I am about to tell you as confidential. It is very unpleasant for me to have to refer to these private and personal matters, but it seems that the circumstances render it necessary.'

He paused, and Mr. Budd took the opportunity to lower himself gently into the chair he had previously refused.

'I can assure you, sir,' he said, 'that anythin' you tell me will be treated in confidence, unless such a confidence should interfere with the administration of justice.'

'Thank you,' replied Sir Mathew, inclining his head. 'Of course, I realise that.' He picked up a pencil, twisted it in his fingers, and laid it down again. 'I am sixty-nine now,' he began hesitantly. 'When I first met Louisa Rockforth I was thirty-six and she was twenty-five. Her brother had just been appointed vicar of this parish, and she came with him to look after his house, and act in the capacity of hostess, since he was a bachelor. She was, as you can see by that photograph, a very attractive girl, and although her brother was rather austere and remote, she was full of high spirits. It was not unnatural that I should become attracted to her. I was young, my parents were dead, and my sister was travelling abroad. I was lonely, and I think she was lonely, too. She had very little in common with her brother, and although she did her best to play the role of the vicar's sister, and take an interest in parish matters, her heart was not in it. She cannot be blamed — she was so full of life, and there was so little outlet for her in Brimley.'

The old man's blue eyes had become dreamy. He was sitting back in his chair, staring up at the ceiling with an introspective expression that told Peter Ashton his imagination had bridged the gulf of years, and he was back once more in those far-off days of which he was speaking.

'What happened was, I suppose, inevitable,' went on the soft, weary voice. 'We were thrown much in each other's company, and we fell in love. I think, considering what occurred after, that it was not really love on Louisa's side, but a desire for change and excitement. I did not, however, realise this at the time, and six months after we became engaged, we were married. We spent our honeymoon in Italy, and we were very happy. Louisa had never travelled before, and she was like a child. Everything interested her — the simplest things. It was all so new and fresh to her — '

His voice sank to an almost inaudible whisper, and ceased. Mr. Budd and Peter waited in silence for him to continue.

'We stayed away for eight months, and

then we came back to Brimley,' Sir Mathew went on eventually. 'For some time we were as happy as we had been during our honeymoon, and then gradually I began to notice a change in Louisa. She grew restless and irritable. We began to have stupid little quarrels over nothing, and these became more and more frequent and more and more serious. I, in my ignorance, put it down to the fact that she was ill, but I realise now that it was a chafing of the spirit against the routine dullness of her life. She had, in marrying me, only exchanged one dullness for another. She had never been in love with me, but in love with life. Perhaps if I had realised that at the time, things would have turned out differently. But I had been born and bred in the country, and I love its peace and its dullness, and I couldn't understand anyone feeling differently to me.' He sighed. 'When I did understand,' he continued, 'it was too late. I found, one morning, that Louisa had gone.'

For the first time a trace of emotion appeared in the thin face, and Peter saw that, in spite of the years that had passed, this man could still be stirred deeply at the recollection of the tragedy which had come into his life.

'I never saw her again,' said Sir Mathew Franklin, after a pause. 'She had gone with an artist — a man who had rented a cottage in Brimley for that summer. She wrote to me from London, asking for a divorce so that she could marry this man and begged my forgiveness. I tried to seek her out, but she would not see me, and at last I acceded to her request. The divorce was granted without very much publicity, and I tried to take up the threads of my life from the point at which they had broken. My sister, who had just returned from abroad, came to live with me, and although the village knew that something had happened to break up my marriage, very few people knew the true facts. That is the story, gentlemen. I have told it to you because I conceived it was my duty. There is no need for me to repeat how painful the recital has been.'

There was a silence in the room when he finished speaking, and for a little while it remained unbroken. No wonder, thought Peter, that Rockforth had been so bitter about his sister. He was the type who would never forgive such a course as she had taken. The old man in the chair behind the big writing-table was different. He had forgiven long ago. There had been no tinge of reproach in his voice, except against himself. Sorrow, but no anger.

Mr. Budd coughed, and broke the silence.

'I'm sure I'm very much obliged ter you, sir,' he said. 'Would you mind if I asked you one or two questions?'

Sir Mathew Franklin stroked his forehead gently with the tips of his fingers.

'If you think it necessary,' he answered. 'Having told you so much, I may as well tell you everything else I can.'

'Thank you, sir,' said the big man. 'Then, first, can yer tell me the name of this man with whom your wife went away?'

'His name was Matheson — Ronald Matheson,' replied Sir Mathew, after a slight hesitation.

'An' I s'pose after the divorce they was married?' said Mr. Budd.

'I have always presumed so,' was the answer.

'In that case she would have taken the name o' Matheson,' murmured the stout superintendent. 'That's interestin'.'

'How is it interesting?' asked Sir Mathew, a little coldly.

'It's interestin', sir,' explained Mr. Budd, 'because you'd think she would 'ave kept that name, wouldn't yer?'

'Ah, I see what you mean!' The old man nodded. 'Yes, that has puzzled me.'

'Did you know she was passin' herself off as a spinster an' calling herself Louisa Mote?' inquired Mr. Budd.

'No,' answered Sir Mathew. 'I knew nothing about her at all. I told you that the last time I saw her was the evening before she left me. That was the truth. During the divorce proceedings I did not see her, and I have not seen or heard anything of her since.'

'But you knew that she was the Miss Mote who had been murdered, sir,' said the fat detective softly, and it was more of a statement than a question. 'You knew that.'

'Yes, I knew that,' admitted the other. 'I knew it when I saw her photograph in the newspaper. It was a great shock to me.'

'An' you kept silent.' Mr. Budd shook his large head. 'You shouldn't have done that, sir. You should have notified the police.'

'What would you have done in my place?' asked the old man. 'Would you have taken the risk of raising a scandal that had been dead and buried for over thirty years? I could not see that any purpose would be served. I consulted with Rockforth, and he agreed with me — '

'He knew, too, did he?' muttered Mr. Budd. 'Well, sir, I'm afraid that you did wrong. The information that you've withheld is of very great importance — '

'In what way?' demanded Sir Mathew quickly.

'In this way,' answered Mr. Budd. 'The thing that turned our attention to Mr. Rockforth as bein' concerned in the death of his sister was partly that he had a motive. He was the next-of-kin, an' would naturally come into that ten thousand-odd that she won in Smallwood's pools. But now 'e may not be the next-of-kin at all. If this man Matheson's still alive, 'e's the next-of-kin — '

The old man uttered an exclamation and sat forward suddenly.

'Yes, yes,' he whispered excitedly. 'I see — I see. I never thought of that. Matheson — yes of course — '

'Even if he's dead,' went on Mr. Budd, 'there may 'ave bin a child. We shall have to inquire inter all that now. But you could 'ave saved a lot o' time if you'd jest said what you knew.'

'I'm sorry,' said Sir Mathew simply. 'I never realised. I was merely anxious not to stir up unpleasant memories — '

'Have you any idea, sir?' broke in the detective, 'why this lady should have adopted the name of Mote?'

'No idea at all,' answered the old man at once. 'I've already told you that — '

'I should like ter know the reason for that,' muttered Mr. Budd, frowning. 'I should very much like to know the reason. Is there anythin' else at all, sir, that you can tell me?'

Sir Mathew pulled gently at his lower lip for some time, and then he slowly shook his head.

'I'm afraid there is nothing else I can tell you,' he said.

The big man rose ponderously to his feet.

'I don't think I'll worry you any more then to-night, sir,' he said. 'I'm very glad you've told me what you have, but I wish you'd done it earlier. Good night, sir!'

'Good night!' said Sir Mathew; and then, as Mr. Budd was moving towards the door: 'If — if you find out anything you'll let me know?'

'I will sir,' promised Mr. Budd, and passed out into the corridor, followed by Peter. As they reached the hall the tiny, white-haired woman came out of a lower room and stood watching them. Mr. Budd bowed awkwardly, and she inclined her head.

'Who was that?' asked Peter, when the elderly servant had closed the front door behind them.

'Sir Mathew's sister,' grunted the big man.

'She looks like a fragile piece of china,' said the reporter. 'I don't think I've ever seen anything so dainty.'

'She may be dainty,' retorted Mr. Budd, 'but I wouldn't like to come up against 'er. I told Collis the same thin'. Well, what d'you make o' this latest development, eh?'

Peter postponed his reply until they had taken their seats in the waiting car, and were speeding down the long drive.

'It rather complicates matters, doesn't it?' he said.

'Maybe it does in a way,' agreed the stout superintendent, with a prodigious yawn, 'an' maybe in a way, it doesn't. It's confirmed my theory, anyhow. I guessed that was the situation. The thing we've got ter do now is ter trace up this feller Matheson. I think we'll find he's dead.'

'What makes you think that?' asked Peter curiously.

'The fact that this woman changed her name,' answered Mr. Budd. 'It's my opinion that Matheson died, an' that she

285

adopted the name o' Mote an' passed herself off as a spinster, so as this feller Franklin couldn't find her.'

'Why should she be afraid of his finding her?' demanded Peter. 'She had nothing to fear from him. He'd behaved very well, I think — '

'Oh, yes, he'd behaved well enough,' interrupted Mr. Budd impatiently, 'but you don't understand. This woman hid away because of her pride, not because she was afraid of him. This feller she'd run away with hadn't left her very well off — we know that. Well, she didn't want Franklin to get to hear of 'er poverty an' offer to help. An' that's what 'e would have done if he'd known — '

'I don't think that's the reason at all,' declared Peter, as a sudden idea struck him. 'In my opinion it's more likely that Matheson left her flat, and that's why she changed her name. It was pride, but for a different reason.'

'Maybe you're right,' said Mr. Budd sleepily. 'We'll find out, I dare say, when we've traced this all up. Meanwhile I'm goin' ter sleep, and I'm not goin' ter wake up until we get to London. I've had enough o' this business for one day, an' I'm goin' ter forget it!'

He huddled himself up in the corner, closed his eyes, and, to Peter's annoyance, snored unmusically throughout the journey.

22

An Unpleasant Situation

Sergeant Leek came slowly back to consciousness with an unpleasant feeling as though the entire top of his head was being crushed between the jaws of a red-hot nut-cracker. He opened his eyes, but the pain was so intolerable that he had to close them again at once. His whole body was one enormous ache, that culminated in a racking agony from his neck upwards. He uttered a groan and lay still, hoping that this would offer some relief.

Presently, after a long interval, he ventured to open his eyes again, and found that, although the pain was still severe, it was not quite so acute as before. Even as he reached this comforting conclusion, a sudden spasm made him involuntarily clench his teeth, and in doing so discover that a gag of some description had been forced between his jaws, and he was unable to move them. He tried to raise his arm to remove this obstruction, and found that he couldn't. As well as being gagged, he had been bound.

His senses were beginning to get a little clearer, and he started to wonder where he was. He remembered the lighted room and its unseen occupant, the visit of Rockforth, and after his departure, the sudden sense of danger. Had Rockforth seen him, crept back, and struck him down? Or had it been the other — the man who had been in that room?

He felt very ill. The pain in his head was still intense, and was accompanied by an overpowering desire to be sick. Once again he tried to find out where he was. His sense of touch told him that he was lying on his back on what felt like damp earth, and all around him was utter darkness. There wasn't even the faintest tinge of light anywhere. There was, however, a stale, musty smell that made him think that he was in a cellar of some kind.

He tried to move his legs, but they had apparently been bound, too, for he was quite helpless. He had another rest, staring up into the black void above him, and presently something fell with a soft splash on his face. He puzzled as to what it could be, because he was still dazed from the heavy blow he had received, and eventually decided that it must be moisture from the roof. This suggested that he was somewhere underground. But where? Was this black place the cellar of the house to which he had followed Rockforth? It was all very uncomfortable, and he began to feel annoyed. It was ridiculous, of course, but he couldn't help it. For some time he lay quivering with rage against the person who was responsible for his present plight. As he became more normal this wore off, and was replaced by an intense desire to get free.

He began to strain at the ropes that bound him, but he quickly found that whoever had tied them had done the job well, and the effort caused the pain in his head to increase so violently that he was forced to stop. The exertion almost made him lose consciousness again, and he must have actually relapsed into a semi-swoon, for the next thing he remembered was a sound that seemed to come from a long way off and which roused him to alertness. He listened, but everything was silent, and he was beginning to think that he had imagined the noise, when it came again, and he recognised it for an approaching footstep.

He rolled over on his side, and looking in the direction from whence the sound had come, saw the faint glimmer of a light in the distance. It was very dim, and was dancing and jerking up and down like a will-o'-wisp. It grew steadily larger as he watched it, until he was able to see that it came from an electric lamp held in the hand of someone who was coming towards him along a low-roofed passage-way. So he wasn't in a cellar after all, but in some kind of tunnel, and a fairly long one at that, to judge by the time the owner of the torch was taking to reach him. Nearer and nearer came the light, and now he was able to make out the shadowy figure behind it. He caught a glimpse of a long coat, and a head that was covered by a bag-like mask of black stuff, and then he closed his eyes. The footsteps came close up to him and stopped. He could hear the man breathing quickly as he bent down.

'Still senseless,' muttered a muffled voice, and the light was directed full on him. Leek remained still. The man who had been peering at him straightened up, and the sergeant opened one eye the fraction of an inch. He couldn't see much, but what he did see was sufficient. The man's hand grasping the torch was covered with large, brownish-orange freckles!

So it was Rockforth who had hit him, thought Leek. Budd would be interested to know that, if ever he were in a position to tell him.

The man went away, and Leek opened his eyes cautiously. The figure was returning along the tunnel, silhouetted against the reflected light of the torch. The visit had been very brief, and the lean sergeant wondered for what reason it had been paid. Most likely to make sure that he was quite secure.

What was this place? He had caught a glimpse of wet, curved walls in the light of the torch. What was it? It certainly wasn't a cellar, but it was equally certainly underground.

He puzzled over this for some time, but was able to come to no satisfactory conclusion. Wherever, and whatever, the place was, it was dark and unpleasant.

Leek considered the situation. There was some comfort to be found in the fact that he was still alive, and seemed in no immediate danger. That was something. His disappearance was bound to be discovered, and Budd would start making inquiries. He was already suspicious of Rockforth, and since Leek had been put on to find out all he could about the man, he would naturally associate his disappearance with him. But would he be able to find this tunnel-place in time? The sergeant concluded that there was a good chance that he would. It couldn't be so very long since he had received that blow on the head — a few hours at the most, which meant that it was now in the early hours of Sunday morning. That was awkward. Budd was hardly likely to do anything until the Monday, and in the meantime quite a lot could happen. Leek's hopes, which had risen a trifle, sank to zero. He made another attempt to free himself, but it was quite useless, and he gave it up. There was nothing for it but to wait and hope for the best. It was very cold lying on the damp ground, and from along the tunnel a draught was blowing. He was chilled to the bone, and to add to his discomfort began to feel twinges of cramp in his legs. He thought of his elation on finding that he had got a correct line in Smallwood's penny points pool. It seemed a century ago. Presently his eyes closed and he dropped into a fitful sleep — a sleep that was disturbed by vague, disjointed visions, predominant among which was the gaunt figure of a man with bony, predatory hands whose backs were covered with great brownish-orange freckles . . .

Mr. Budd reached Scotland Yard early on the Monday morning, refreshed by a good night's sleep, and his first action was to put through a telephone call to the hospital at Fallingham and inquire after Rockforth. He was informed by the matron that the vicar was still unconscious, and according to the doctor, likely to remain so for a considerable time. His condition was serious. An examination had revealed that a small clot of blood had formed on the brain, due to the rupture of a vein, and they were trying to disperse this. If they were successful, Rockforth might recover, but otherwise there was every chance that he would die without regaining consciousness.

Mr. Budd hung up the receiver, and sought an interview with the Assistant Commissioner.

Colonel Blair listened to all he had to say, and to the stout man's relief, approved.

'You couldn't have done anything else on the evidence,' he said. 'It's unfortunate that it should have affected this man as it did, but there is no blame attaching to you. It seems to me that there is little doubt about his guilt.'

'The evidence against him was pretty conclusive, sir,' said Mr. Budd, 'but it's a complicated business. I've made one or two further discoveries that don't 'elp ter make it any clearer.' He proceeded to relate his interview with Sir Mathew Franklin, and the Assistant Commissioner heard him in silence.

'An interesting story,' he commented, when the big man had finished. 'You'll have to find this man Matheson, if he's alive. If he married this woman, he's next-of-kin, and the motive for Rockforth having killed his sister falls to the ground.'

'If he's alive, sir,' murmured Mr. Budd. 'If he's dead, an' there was no child, then Rockforth's still next-of-kin.'

'It shouldn't be difficult to find out,' said Colonel Blair. 'There's another thing. If there was no marriage, and Rockforth knew it, Matheson wouldn't legally come into it at all. I think it would pay you to make very close inquiries into the past life of this woman Matheson, Rockforth, or whoever she really was. There was some reason why she called herself Mote. I think it would be interesting to find it out.'

Mr. Budd outlined the theory which he

had explained to Peter Ashton, but the Assistant Commissioner was not impressed.

'I think you'll find there's something more behind it than that,' he remarked. 'I should follow it up.'

'I intend to, sir,' said Mr. Budd, and went back to his office. He put through a trunk call to the solicitors employed by Smallwood's, and held a long conversation. When it was concluded he hung up the receiver, lit one of his thin, black cigars, and leaned back in his padded chair. The information he had obtained had given him food for thought, and with half-closed eyes, the pungent smoke wreathing round his head, he turned it over in his mind.

According to the man with whom he had just been speaking, the connection between Miss Mote and the Reverend Clement Rockforth had first been brought to the notice of the solicitors working for Messrs. Smallwood's by means of an anonymous letter. Mr. Grayle had read it over the telephone, and although it was short, it was very much to the point:

'You are looking for somebody related to the woman called Mote. Her name was Rockforth thirty-five years ago. Her brother is the vicar of Brimley.'

That was all, but it had been enough to put the lawyers on the right track. They had instituted inquiries, and discovered that the writer of the letter was stating a fact. But who had written that letter? Some scandal-loving village gossip, or — somebody else? And why had no mention been made of the marriage to Sir Mathew Franklin?

There was a puzzle here, and Mr. Budd savoured it delicately. There might be nothing more in it than a desire on the part of someone who had known Louisa Rockforth in her youth to be helpful. But if this were the case, why hadn't they given their name, and how did they associate the name of Mote with her? Had they seen a photograph in the papers and recognised her? That was possible, and was also an explanation for there being no mention of the marriage. The writer of the letter might only have known her before she had come to Brimley. All that was probable. On the other hand, without the letter it was doubtful if the relationship between the murdered woman and the Reverend Clement Rockforth would ever have been established. Was it possible that it had been written with the sole object of making this certain?

Mr. Budd pondered over this, and found that it led to a very complicated train of thought; a train of thought, in fact, which, followed to its logical conclusion, opened up such an entirely new aspect on the whole affair that he became engrossed in the possibilities it suggested.

Here was an idea that might be worth inquiring into very carefully. Smallwood's solicitors had found out all about the marriage and the subsequent divorce, but they had not been able to trace any re-marriage with Matheson, and since the first marriage had produced no issue, and they were only concerned with the question of next-of-kin, they had not bothered themselves with Sir Mathew Franklin at all. The question which interested Mr. Budd, now that this fresh information was in his possession, was — had there been a second marriage? If there hadn't, then his idea was impracticable; but if there had — Yes, if there had — what then?

He stirred uneasily in his chair. Vaguely, out of the mists which obscured everything connected with this unprecedented case, loomed the shadowy outline of a monstrous and inhuman plan — a plan so appalling that the stout superintendent's flesh crept.

He finished his cigar, lit another, and stared through heavy, drooping lids at the dingy ceiling. He missed Leek, with whom he could have discussed this new idea. The lean sergeant would have offered nothing in the way of a helpful suggestion, but he was a good listener, and Mr. Budd found that talking clarified his thoughts. It is doubtful, if Leek had been there, whether he would have learned much of what the fat man was really thinking, but Mr. Budd, who rather enjoyed playing to an audience, would at least have had the mental satisfaction of mystifying him.

What had happened to Leek? He had hoped that there would have been some word from him before this — or at least that there would have been news of him. He appeared to have vanished off the face of the earth, and behind his stolid exterior the big man was troubled. If there was any truth in this fresh idea, the melancholy sergeant might have passed from the earth in reality. There were plenty of places in the neighbourhood of Brimley where a body could lie concealed for days — even for weeks or months. But if Leek had been sacrificed to the safety of somebody, then he must have stumbled on something important after he had rung up so triumphantly on the Saturday evening. What could he have discovered?

He puzzled over this for a long time, and then, with a sigh, he gave it up and reached out a fat arm for the house-telephone.

'Give me extension 53,' he grunted to the switchboard operator, and when he was connected: 'That you, Wiles? Budd speakin'. Come along ter my office, will yer?'

Inspector Wiles, a ruddy-faced, cherubic-looking man, answered the summons a few minutes later.

'I've got a job for yer,' said Mr. Budd. 'I want to know all about a man called Matheson. I believe he married a woman about thirty years ago, who was divorced from her husband — '

He supplied the interested inspector with full particulars.

'Get on it at once, will yer,' he concluded, 'an' let me have a report as soon as yer can?'

When Wiles had gone, he resumed his musings. The inquiries he had instituted might throw a light on several points that were obscure. He could not foresee the result, but it was eventually to lead him to the astonishing truth.

23

Mr. Budd Keeps an Appointment

It was half-past twelve when Mr. Budd roused himself from his long reverie, got heavily to his feet, stretched with a prodigious yawn, and putting on his hat, made his way to the little teashop in Whitehall which he usually patronised. Sitting down at a table facing the door, he replied to the smiling waitress' greeting pleasantly, and gave his invariable order. When the two rounds of buttered toast and the pot of tea had been set before him, he proceeded to enjoy a leisurely lunch, munching stolidly and missing nothing that was going on around him, although his heavy-lidded eyes were half-closed, and he appeared to be completely oblivious to everything except his immediate occupation.

There was nothing very much he could do now except wait, with what patience he could, for the results of the inquiries he had instituted to come in. They might come quickly, and they might take a long time. There was no telling. But when they did come they ought to be worth waiting for.

He finished his toast, and squeezed the last remaining drop of tea from the pot, and, feeling considerably refreshed, returned to the Yard.

There was a conference that afternoon, which he had to attend, presided over by the Assistant Commissioner and the four Chief Constables who each control one of the four areas into which London, and that portion of the country under the direct administration of the Metropolitan Police, is divided.

There were many things to be discussed, and it was late in the afternoon before the subject of the football pool murders came up.

Mr. Budd was invited to report on the progress he was making with the investigation, and did so, stating baldly the facts which his inquiries had brought to light, and the line he was adopting concerning them. He omitted to mention any of his theories, preferring to keep these rather nebulous ideas to himself.

He was congratulated on a smart piece of work by his superiors, and murmured conventional thanks, eventually leaving the long conference-room with a sigh of relief. He hated these discussions and seldom, indeed, either profited by them, or allowed his confrères to become very much wiser by what he divulged.

However, they were part of the system, and had to be regarded as an unavoidable evil. His reticence on these occasions had, in his early days as an officer of the C.I.D., brought many a reprimand, but now all his methods had become familiar, and he was allowed more latitude. He went back to his office, and was contemplating going home, when a messenger arrived with a telegram. Mr. Budd ripped open the envelope with a large thumb, and jerked out the flimsy sheet of paper.

The message was from Peter Ashton, and was brief:

'*Have made important discovery. Meet me Hogs Corner, Brimley, ten to-night.*

*Essential keep private and confidential.
'Ashton.'*

'All right, no answer,' grunted Mr. Budd, and when the messenger had departed, read the telegram again. It had been handed in at Fallingham post office at 5.10. Mr. Budd rubbed his chin and frowned. What was the 'important discovery' that Peter Ashton had made? And where the deuce was Hogs Corner? 'Essential keep private and confidential.' That meant, he supposed, that he was to go alone. Well, there was bound to be something in it. The reporter wouldn't have wired unless he *had* found something worth wiring about, that was certain. He knew Peter Ashton too well to be afraid that he would drag him all the way to Brimley on a wild-goose chase. Perhaps he had found Leek —

The big man shook his head unconsciously. No, that wouldn't be it. If he had found Leek, he would have said so. It was something else — something that necessitated his presence at Hogs Corner — wherever and whatever that might be

— at ten o'clock that night. Since the reporter had not troubled to include any other directions, Hogs Corner was probably a well-known landmark in the district. Collis would know, if he hadn't gone back to Basingstoke. But ought he to mention anything about this appointment to Collis? 'Essential keep private and confidential.' Better not say anything to Collis, or to anyone. It would be easy to find the place. Anybody in Brimley could, no doubt, direct him.

He crumbled the telegram up and thrust it into his pocket. It was only a quarter-past six. He would have plenty of time to go home and collect his car, and also snatch a short rest. There was no knowing what the night held in store, so he might as well get a bit of rest while he could.

He caught a Streatham-bound tramcar on the Embankment, and reached his neat little villa just as the clocks were chiming seven. His dour, Scots housekeeper was out — he remembered that it was her evening off — and after eating the cold supper which she had left for him, and thoughtfully drunk two bottles of beer, he lighted one of his cigars and settled himself comfortably in an easy-chair to while away the time until he need start.

At half-past eight he took his dilapidated little car out of the garage, made sure that there was plenty of petrol in the tank for his journey, and set off for Brimley.

It was three minutes to ten when he pulled up at the pub in Brimley's narrow High Street, and getting stiffly out, entered the bar and ordered a pint of beer. He hoped that Hogs Corner wasn't very far away, or he would be late for his appointment with Peter Ashton. His question to the landlord produced a reassuring answer.

''Ogs Corner, sir?' repeated the landlord. 'No, it ain't very fur. Matter o' about 'alf a mile, I should say. You know the church? Well, yer keeps straight on past it until yer comes to a narrer turnin' — little more'n a lane it is — an' 'Ogs Corner is about two 'undred yards along it. Used ter be a farm, but it's empty now.'

Mr. Budd thanked him, swallowed his beer, and went back to his car. He had no difficulty in finding the narrow lane mentioned by the landlord, and that worthy individual had not exaggerated when he had said that it was 'little more'n a lane.' It was too narrow to take the car, and the big man had to climb reluctantly out and cover the remaining distance to Hogs Corner on foot.

The lane sloped steeply, and the surface was rough, making walking difficult. He wondered, as he stumbled along, what had induced the reporter to choose such a spot for the appointment. Most likely he had had no choice. Perhaps the discovery he had referred to was associated with this empty farm. Once again it occurred to Mr. Budd that it might be something to do with the disappearance of Leek, although he couldn't see how. Anyway, he would know what it was all about very soon, for the dim bulk of a house loomed out of the darkness in front of him.

It wasn't a house, as he discovered when he drew nearer, but the remains of a large barn that rose from behind a crumbling wall of brick. There were a pair of wooden gates, open and hanging drunkenly on their hinges, through which he could vaguely see stables flanking a wide courtyard, a cluster of outbuildings, and beyond them the house itself.

The place looked bleak and uninviting. A cold wind had sprung up and was blowing fitfully along the lane, which at this point had widened into a rutted road. It must have been an unpleasant spot even in daylight. On the opposite side of the road was a cluster of pine-trees that seemed to brood over the place like living sentinels, their branches whispering ceaselessly in the rising wind with a sound that was like the distant surge of the sea, and this seemed to enhance the otherwise profound silence.

There was no sign of Peter Ashton anywhere, and Mr. Budd began to pace slowly up and down, stopping every now and again to listen. It was getting on for twenty-past ten. The reporter was late; perhaps something had happened to him to change his plans, whatever they were?

Mr. Budd grunted, and turned up the collar of his overcoat. How long should he wait? It was most unpleasantly cold, and there was a dank atmosphere in the shadow of this old, deserted farm. Why had they called it Hogs Corner, he wondered? Maybe Hog was the name of the farmer. Well, if Ashton was coming, why the dickens didn't he hurry up? Or was he already here? Perhaps by Hogs Corner, he had meant inside the place?

The big man halted in front of the gates and peered into the courtyard. There was certainly no sign of life to be seen, but his vision didn't extend very far. The darkness over by the stables and the outbuildings was intense. He moved nearer to the gates, hesitated, and went into the courtyard. He didn't want to miss Peter if he came along the lane, but if he had meant inside there was no sense in wasting time hanging about.

He stopped to listen, but he could hear nothing except the wind in the pines — nothing at all.

And then, quite suddenly, he experienced a sharp uneasiness. A cold little

311

shiver slid up his spine, and the hairs on the back of his neck prickled. There was no reason for it. Everything was still silent. But he was quite definitely convinced that he was not alone. Somewhere in the mass of shadows which surrounded him somebody was watching . . .

'Are you there, Ashton?' he called, and waited. But only silence answered him — silence and the incessant murmuring of the pines.

Mr. Budd was not easily scared, but he was scared then. Every fibre of him screamed a warning, and he felt an almost overpowering desire to turn and run back to his car as hard as he could. He stifled the impulse. This was childish — this ridiculous fear of an old, deserted building. He took a grip on his nerves and forced himself to cross the courtyard. And with each forward step he took his fear increased. The shadows before and on either side of him seemed to be peopled with vague shapes that writhed and danced and mouthed at him. The wind suddenly died down, and the whispering of the pines behind him faded to silence. It was as if the whole place had held its breath in fearful expectancy.

'Hallo, Ashton!' called Mr. Budd loudly. 'Are you there?'

His voice echoed round the courtyard, and was blown away in a sharp gust of wind that came whirling and eddying round him, stirring the rubbish that lay scattered about, and whistling through the broken walls of the stables and outbuildings.

The fat man stopped. Before him rose the house — a rambling old place of stone and thatch, drowned in shadow — a black blot on the less blacker darkness. There seemed very little chance that the reporter was there. Having made the appointment, he would surely have kept a look-out, and he must have heard him shouting. Something had prevented him keeping the appointment, that's what it was, and he was only wasting his time hanging about the place. The best thing he could do would be to go back to the car — go home to bed.

He turned and began quickly to retrace

his steps towards the gates. Half-way across the courtyard he became suddenly *sure* that there was somebody behind him, and started to turn ... Strong hands gripped his throat from behind, and he was jerked backwards ... He tried to struggle, but the stranglehold increased ... The last thing he heard was a low, cackling laugh of triumph ...

24

Peter Ashton is Alarmed

'Another cup of tea, Jacob?' said Marjorie.

Jacob Bellamy shook his big head.

'No, thank ye, m'dear,' he answered. 'I'm not much of a tea-drinker.'

'Have a Johnny Walker?' said Peter hospitably, nodding towards the sideboard.

'No, thanks, cock,' replied the bookmaker. 'I won't 'ave anythin' more for the moment.'

'You will, won't you, Peter?' asked his wife.

'It'll be my third cup, but I think I will,' said Peter. He held out his cup. 'You still staying at the Walbrooks' flat?'

'Move back ter me own 'ouse next week, cock,' said old Jacob, 'an' mighty glad I shall be ter get there. I don't like these flats, an' I never shall. It's like livin' in a box. Yer never seem ter get enough room to breathe.'

'I detest flats,' said Marjorie, carefully pouring out tea. 'What are Mr. and Mrs. Walbrook going to do? Are they going back to their flat?'

'No,' answered Bellamy. 'They're getting rid of the rest o' the lease, an' buyin' a house in the country. They always wanted ter live in the country, an' now they can afford to. By the way,' he added, turning to Peter, 'what's 'appened ter that feller 'oo tried that dirty trick on 'em — what's-'is-name?'

'Lucas?' asked Peter. 'He's been committed for trial.'

'An' a good thing, too!' grunted the bookmaker. 'What a nasty bit o' work, eh, boy? Good thing I 'appened ter be about that night. I'm sorry fer the poor ol' vicar; 'e ain't right in 'is 'ead, but Mr. Montague Lucas, Esquire, I 'ope they put it across 'im good an' proper.'

'I don't think you need worry about that,' said Peter. 'He'll get his deserts. I shouldn't be surprised if he hangs.'

'Serve 'im right!' growled Bellamy. ''E'd 'ave killed those two as sure as a gun, if they'd bin sleepin' at the flat that night. I nearly took the law inter me own 'ands, cock, when I see what 'e'd bin up to. If yer asks me, 'e probably incited this feller Rockforth, so as 'e could rook 'im fer that five 'undred pounds.'

'You know, I can't believe that Mr. Rockforth was behind the murders of those people,' remarked Marjorie suddenly. 'It seems all wrong somehow.'

'That's what Budd thinks,' said Peter. 'I don't know what to think. The evidence against him is pretty conclusive, you know. Especially the finding of that mask in his garage.'

'Perhaps somebody put it there to make it look as though he were guilty,' said Marjorie.

Peter started.

'I wonder if that's what's at the back of Budd's mind,' he muttered.

'Nobody'll ever know what's at the back o' that feller's mind until 'e wants 'em to, cock,' said the bookmaker. 'Anyhow, there's more than the mask against Rockforth, ain't there? Walbrook identified 'is 'ands, and Lucas identified 'is hands an' 'is voice.'

'If somebody could put that mask in his

garage,' said Marjorie quietly, 'the same person could imitate his voice and those freckles on his hands. It wouldn't be difficult.'

'A frame-up, eh?' exclaimed Peter excitedly. 'That's an idea!'

'You've forgotten the motive,' put in Bellamy. 'That's the strongest evidence against 'im o' the lot.'

'But if this man Matheson is alive, it no longer holds,' said the reporter, 'Rockforth wouldn't be next-of-kin. Matheson would.'

'It's a pretty good mix up, ain't it, cock?' remarked the bookmaker. 'Looks clear as water one minute, an' the next it's like mud!'

'I think you'll find that Mr. Rockforth is innocent,' said Marjorie. 'I believe that the money was the motive, but I don't believe he had anything to do with it.'

I think we are on to something, definitely. Always supposing, of course, that Rockforth isn't guilty.'

'And he isn't, darling,' said Marjorie quickly.

'Well, accepting the fact that he isn't,' went on the reporter, 'then it must have been a frame-up. Nothing else will account for the mountain of evidence against him. And, if it is a frame-up, then Matheson seems to be the only person who would benefit.'

'Unless there was a child, boy,' said Bellamy. 'This divorce 'appened thirty years ago. If there was a child, it'd be, twenty-eight or nine now.'

'Yes, there's that,' remarked Peter thoughtfully. 'Look here, let's rake Budd in on this, shall we? I believe we've got hold of a plausible theory, and I don't think it's very far off his own. I'll ring him up and see what he says.'

His hand was stretched out to pick up the telephone when the bell rang. He lifted the receiver and put it to his ear.

'Hallo!' he called. 'Peter Ashton speaking!'

They saw his face change as he listened.

'All right,' he said rapidly. 'I'll come straight away.'

He slammed the receiver back on its rest, and glanced at the clock.

'Rockforth has recovered consciousness,' he announced. 'He is making a statement now, and Budd wants me to go along to the hospital at once.'

'Was that Mr. Budd on the telephone, darling?' asked Marjorie, and Peter shook his head.

'No; somebody ringing up for him,' he answered briefly. 'He's with Rockforth. Will you drive me to Fallingham, Jacob? You've got your car here, and it will save time.'

'You bet yer life I will, cock,' answered the bookmaker instantly. 'I want to 'ear what this statement is about as much as you do.'

'Then let's go,' said Peter. 'It's just five. We ought to get to the hospital by six-thirty, if we get a move on.'

He kissed his wife, hurried out into the hall, and struggled into his overcoat, never imagining that if he had come to his decision to ring up Mr. Budd a few seconds earlier than he had, he would have been saved a fruitless journey, and the fat detective would have been spared an experience that very nearly cost him his life.

They left the house on Putney Hill at five minutes past five, but owing to the fact that they got mixed up in the rush-hour traffic, it was nearly seven before they drew up at the cottage hospital at Fallingham.

It was a pretty little place, standing in a well-kept garden, and looked more like a row of cottages than a hospital. In the tiny vestibule Peter found a nurse on duty at a desk, and stated his business. The girl looked surprised.

'I'm sure there must be some mistake, sir,' she said. 'Mr. Rockforth is still unconscious, and nobody has been to see him except the doctor.'

'But Superintendent Budd got somebody to ring up from here asking me to come down,' said the reporter, frowning.

The nurse shook her head.

'He couldn't have done that, sir,' she declared. 'There has been nobody here to-day, except the usual staff. Our visiting days are Wednesdays and Saturdays.'

Peter turned to Jacob Bellamy, who had accompanied him inside.

'What do you make of that?' he asked.

'You've been had, boy,' said the bookmaker. 'If Budd ain't been 'ere, an'

Rockforth's still unconscious, that telephone message must 'ave been an 'oax.'

'But what could have been the object?' muttered Peter, his frown deepening. 'It's a stupid thing to do. How did anyone know that Rockforth was here, anyhow?'

'Don't ask me, cock,' said the puzzled Bellamy. 'But somebody must've done. You've bin 'ad on a piece o' toast, boy!'

'Well, if it was a joke, it's a darned senseless one!' snapped the reporter angrily.

'Some o' your pals at the office playin' a trick on yer,' suggested old Jacob, with a grin. 'Don't get cross, cock! No 'arm's bin done.'

'Except that we've wasted a lot of time, and been made fools of,' grunted Peter. He turned to the rather amused nurse.

'Can I use your telephone?' he asked.

'Yes, sir.' She showed him where the instrument was, and left him. She was talking to Bellamy when he came back.

'I've just been on to the Yard,' he said. 'Budd went home just after six.'

'An' that's where we'd better go, boy,' said the book-maker. 'Good night, miss. Sorry to 'ave bothered you.'

He took the still disgruntled Peter by the arm and led him back to the car.

'We might as well drop in and see Budd,' suggested the reporter, as the started on the journey back. 'He lives at Streatham.'

But when they reached Mr. Budd's neat little house a further disappointment awaited them. Their repeated knocking brought no response and they were forced to the conclusion that there was no one at home.

'And that's that,' said Peter, as they turned reluctantly away. 'Let's go home.'

At ten o'clock on the following morning he called at Scotland Yard, but the stout superintendent had not yet arrived.

'I don't know what's happened to him,' said the inspector whom Peter saw. 'The Assistant Commissioner's waiting to see him.'

'I'll come in again later,' said Peter, and went down to the offices of the *Morning Mail*. Mr. Sorbett was not in the best of humours that morning and he was treated to a lecture on the uselessness of reporters who could not provide a good follow up for a story, and his own complete failure to supply a continuous flow of interesting matter concerning the football pool murders.

Rendered rather irritable by this, Peter went back to the Yard at lunch-time in a bad temper, to be greeted by the news that Mr. Budd was still conspicuous by his absence.

'Nobody knows where he is,' said his friend the inspector. 'He hasn't been at home all night, and his car's missing, too. Blair's fuming like a smoky chimney.'

It was unlike the big man to absent himself without word, and Peter felt a little uneasy.

'I suppose nothing's happened to him?' he said.

'Well, that's what we're wondering,' answered the inspector cautiously. 'Don't you go trying to make a story out of this, though. We don't want the *Morning Mail* coming out with sensational headlines about it.'

''The Biggest of the Big Five Disappears,'' said Peter, with a grin. 'It *would* make a story, Patterson, and Sorbett is panting for something sensational — '

'Let him pant!' broke in Inspector Patterson. 'If you let a breath of this slip, Ashton, you'll have a black mark against your name here, and you know what that'll mean!'

'Peace, my child,' said Peter soothingly. 'You needn't worry. Seriously, though,' he added, suddenly grave, 'I don't like it, you know, Patterson. What can have happened to him?'

'He's on those pool murders, and you know what happened to Leek,' answered the inspector. 'He did a vanishing trick — ' A messenger called him and, with a word, he hurried away. Peter waited in the cheerless waiting-room for nearly half an hour before he came back, and the moment he saw the other's face he knew something had happened.

'You've had news?' he said quickly, and Patterson nodded.

'Budd's car has been found abandoned in a narrow lane on the outskirts of Brimley,' he replied. 'You've got to keep this quiet, Ashton, but it looks as though he's gone the same way as Leek.'

25

The Drain

Mr. Budd blinked painfully and opened his eyes. Finding that even with them open he could see nothing, he closed them again and tried to collect his scattered wits. His throat was sore, and he had a violent headache, and these unpleasant sensations instantly carried his mind back to that moment at Hogs Corner, when out of the darkness had come that strangling grip on his throat. He had walked into a trap. Obviously, the telegram from Peter Ashton had not come from him at all. He had been very neatly fooled!

The sender of the wire had been waiting at the deserted farm, and choked him into unconsciousness. It was lucky, he thought, that he was still alive. Remembering that those strong fingers which had closed round his throat were the same which had pressed out the lives of Alfred Gummidge and Louisa Mote, he concluded that he was very lucky indeed. And they must have been the same. In spite of the painful discomfort he was suffering, and his possible imminent danger, he felt a thrill of triumph.

His hunch that the case was not as simple as it had seemed had been justified, for Rockforth could not be responsible for his present position. Rockforth was at Fallingham Cottage Hospital, unconscious and helpless. Who, then, was the man who had attacked him at Hogs Corner? Matheson? If this was so, then all the evidence against Rockforth must have been carefully faked. Again, as he had vaguely sensed in his office at Scotland Yard, there loomed the shadowy outlines of a deep and appalling plot. Only it was no longer nebulous and insubstantial. It began to take shape with startling clarity. Louisa Franklin after her divorce had married Matheson, there had been some kind of trouble or quarrel, and she had left him — or he had left her

— and he had evolved this terrible scheme in order to get hold of the money which she had won from Smallwood's. The whole thing had been designed with the express purpose of throwing suspicion on to Rockforth and diverting it away from Matheson. But how had Matheson known that his wife had won that money? And how had he known about Gummidge and Walbrook?

Lying in the darkness, the big man tried to find an answer to this, but without success. He was beginning to feel more normal now, and cast about for a means of getting out of this unpleasant position. He had no idea where he was. The place smelt damp, and there was a draught blowing from somewhere, but the intense darkness rendered it impossible even to conjecture what the nature of his surroundings was like. He was quite helpless. A gag had been thrust into his mouth, and his arms and legs had been securely tied. 'Jest like somethin' out of one of them thriller stories,' he thought, with a curious sense of unreality. But there was nothing unreal about his danger. The man who had brought him to this place, whatever it was, must have had but one object in view.

His captor had decided that he was a source of danger, and had taken this step to safeguard himself. And the ultimate end would be death. Mr. Budd was rather surprised that he was still alive. Matheson — if it were Matheson — dare not let him go, or his carefully laid scheme against Rockforth would fall to the ground. Even by his disappearance it would be considerably weakened, for it would be obvious to anybody that Rockforth, lying helpless in the cottage hospital, could not have had a hand in that. Matheson must, therefore, have changed his original plan. What had necessitated the alteration?

The stout man thought over this while he tried to see if there was a means of freeing himself. He had been trussed fairly tightly, but when he strained his arms apart he thought he detected a slight giving of the cords. He tried again. Yes, there was no doubt. His captor had failed to take into consideration the amount of fat which covered him. It gave to the cords like compressing an air-cushion, and, by alternately straining and relaxing, he was able, at last, to wriggle one arm free. He tore the gag from his mouth, and lay panting to recover his breath. So far, so good. It would not be difficult, now that he had one hand free, to rid himself of the rest of his bonds. Presently he found himself free once more, and, sitting up, searched in his pockets for matches. Finding them, he struck a light, and, holding the feeble little flame above his head, looked around.

At first he was puzzled at what he saw. He was lying in a long, tunnel-like place, with a low, curving roof that continued down into the walls. It was built of ancient brickwork, moss-covered, and patched with damp. The floor beneath him consisted of damp mud, and the whole place was like nothing so much as a gigantic brick tube.

The match burned down to his fingers, and went out, and he struck another. The tunnel stretched away on either side into darkness, and a cold wind blew dankly.

Although the place was evidently under-ground, there was an outlet somewhere into the open. The wind proved that.

Mr. Budd got gingerly to his feet. He was just able to stand upright, with his head within a few inches of the curving roof. Between the patches of moss, and over all the crumbling brick work, was a film of greenish slime. At some time, not far distant, there had obviously been water here — water, which from the marks it had left, must have almost filled the tunnel. And then he guessed what it was. A drain! That's what it was. One of those old-fashioned culverts which are to be found in the country.

He lit a third match. This culvert was apparently in disuse, for although the brickwork was damp and glistening there was no sign of water. Most likely it only came into use in time of flood.

The cold wind was blowing from the direction that faced him as he stood, and he was just making up his mind to seek the exit when he saw a dark bundle lying in the shadow to one side. Going over to it, he struck a fourth match, and bent down. It was Leek!

The sergeant's eyes were open, and he saw astonished recognition in them as they looked up at him.

'So this is what 'appened to you, eh?' grunted Mr. Budd — and there was a note of genuine relief in his voice. He removed Leek's gag. 'How are you feelin'?'

Leek tried to speak, but the dryness of his throat and weakness from want of food prevented him.

'All right! Don't go exertin' yerself,' said the big man kindly. 'You must be feelin' pretty rotten if you've bin lyin' here all this time. Keep still and I'll untie yer.'

He had to work in the dark, and this made his progress slow; but he managed eventually to untie the knots.

'There you are!' he muttered at last. 'Can yer get up?'

'I — I don't think I can,' croaked Leek weakly. 'Me legs is numb — '

'That'll soon wear off,' said his superior. 'I'll give 'em a rub ter restore the circulation.'

He began to massage the sergeant's thin legs, and presently Leek grunted with pain as the stemmed-up blood began to flow once more.

'Now let's see if yer can get up,' said Mr. Budd. 'Lean on me.'

He groped about in the dark until he found Leek's shoulders, and supported him. The sergeant was very weak, but he managed, by clinging to the stout man, to struggle to his feet.

'That's better,' murmured Mr. Budd. 'All you want now is a 'ot bath an' a good feed, an' you'll be as right as rain. Come on — we'll try to find the way out of this infernal 'ole.'

'I believe I've caught me death o' cold,' mumbled Leek, sniffing. 'I'll never be the same man again!'

'Well, that's a comfort, anyhow,' said Mr. Budd. 'Stop grumblin' an' put yer arm round my neck. I'm not gettin' affectionate, but it's the easiest way of holdin' you up.'

It was slow work in the dark, but they stumbled on, Mr. Budd feeling his way with one hand against the curving brickwork. The tunnel took a sharp bend to the right after they had been walking for some time, and then turned again to the left. The cold wind grew stronger as they advanced, and the musty smell became replaced by a tang. Mr. Budd sniffed.

'Can you smell that?' he asked.

'I can't smell nothin',' replied Leek mournfully. 'I've got a cold in me 'ead. I keep tellin' yer — '

'A cold always attacks the weakest spot,' said the big man rudely. 'Well, if you can't smell nothin', I can. We're near water — I'll bet a month's pay!'

He was right, as they very soon found. The ground beneath their feet suddenly became soft, and they sank to their ankles in mud.

'Hold on! I'm going ter strike a match,' said Mr. Budd, and did so. Shielding the flame with his hands, he looked quickly about. Water was lapping the mud a few feet away, and beyond he could see the arched mouth of the tunnel, and a glimmer of green.

'We've got ter go careful now,' warned

Mr. Budd as the match went out. 'Test every step before yer put your whole weight down, otherwise yer may find yerself swimmin'.'

They began to move forward again cautiously. Soon they were splashing through more than a foot of water, and this began rapidly to deepen. The fat detective came to another halt, and once more struck a match. They had come to the end of the culvert. At their feet was water, and, growing thickly, screening the arched entrance to the drain, was a mass of rushes.

'You 'ang on ter the wall,' said Mr. Budd. 'I'm goin' to explore.'

He stepped forward gingerly, and was soon wading up to his waist in water. Parting the rushes, he caught a glimpse of sky and trees, saw that the culvert emerged in the rush-covered bank of a narrow stream. It didn't seem very deep, and the bank was not as steep as to be unclimbable. Here, however, was an explanation of the drain's use. It had obviously been built to carry off the flood water when the stream rose in wet weather. That was to have been their fate, he thought grimly. If they hadn't starved before, they would have been drowned when the tunnel became filled with water.

He waded back and collected the sergeant.

'You'll have to wade through the water,' he said, 'but it won't come much above yer waist.'

Leek uttered a protest.

'It won't do me cold any good — ' he began.

'It'll do it less good if yer stop 'ere!' snapped Mr. Budd. 'Come on, an' don't argue!'

He forced the reluctant Leek through the rushes and with difficulty succeeded in scaling the steep bank. Pulling Leek up after him, he leaned against a tree, panting.

'Well, that's that!' he remarked, when he had recovered his breath, 'an' I think we're very lucky to 'ave got out o' that place.'

The sergeant gave a prodigious sneeze.

'Let's get away from 'ere,' he said thickly. 'I'm froze ter the bone. Where d'yer think we are?'

Mr. Budd looked round.

'This must be the Rill,' he said, eyeing the narrow little stream that flowed gently at their feet, 'an' over there's Brimley — '

'Then let's go an' find the pub where I was stoppin',' suggested Leek, with visions of a large meal and warmth.

'Oh, no.' Mr. Budd shook his head. 'We're not goin' anywhere near that pub if I know it! We're goin' ter lie low fer a bit. This feller doesn't know we've escaped yet, an' we're not goin' ter make him a present of the information. He thinks we're nice an' snug in that drain. I'm goin' ter let 'im think so as long as possible.'

Leek looked at him in dismay.

'Well, what are we goin' ter do, then?' he demanded plaintively. 'I believe I've got double pneumonia already — '

'If you'd got double pneumonia you wouldn't be able ter speak,' said Mr. Budd. 'All you've got is a cold in the 'ead.'

'Complications may set in at any moment,' grumbled Leek. 'I ought ter be looked after — '

'You ought ter 'ave bin looked after for

years,' snarled Mr. Budd. 'You'll be all right as soon as you've 'ad a good feed. We'll go an' find a garage an' see if we can get hold of a car.'

The sky was growing light in the east and the cold chill of dawn was in the air when they eventually found what they were seeking. It was a combined filling-station and garage on the main road near Fallingham, and there was a sign outside informing all and sundry that there were 'Cars for Hire.' The place was shut, but Mr. Budd knocked up the proprietor, and after a certain amount of argument and the production of his warrant card, succeeded in hiring a decrepit Ford.

'That's better,' he said contentedly, as he drove out of the garage. 'Now to find a nice quiet place where we can get some grub, an' a rest.'

The exhausted Leek, huddled up in a rug, huskily vented his approval.

Five miles outside Fallingham they came to a small village, and Mr. Budd brought the ancient car to a stop in front of a pretty little white-stone inn, and got heavily out. Although he was dry by now, he was very cold, and his legs ached from the unaccustomed exercise which had been forced upon him. A sleepy-eyed pot-man was sweeping out the bar, and to him the big man explained their wants. The man called the landlord, who put in a dishevelled appearance, and looked a little resentful at being disturbed from his slumbers. He was, however, equal to the occasion, and in half an hour they were sitting before a comfortable fire in the old-fashioned bar-parlour, waiting impatiently for the breakfast which they could smell cooking.

After the meal, which on the stout superintendent's advice, Leek ate sparingly, they had a brisk rub down and went to bed, to sleep dreamlessly and undisturbed until far into the afternoon.

26

The Man Whom Rockforth Visited

There was no doubt that Leek had caught a cold. When Mr. Budd, refreshed from his long sleep, went in to see how the sergeant was feeling, he found him with streaming eyes and a head which he plaintively described as 'feelin' as if it was stuffed full o' cotton-wool.'

'You'd better stay where you are,' advised Mr. Budd. 'You look pretty rotten.'

'I feel awful,' rasped Leek pathetically. 'Me throat's sore, an' me head aches, and I've got a 'ot sort o' feelin' at the back o' me nose — '

'In fact, you're lousy,' said Mr. Budd. 'Well, you're all right where you are.' He sat down on the edge of the bed. 'Now, let's 'ear what 'appened to you. How did yer get in that drain?'

In between sniffing and sneezing, the lean sergeant gave an account of his adventure

'H'm!' commented Mr. Budd. 'You didn't see anythin' o' this feller that Rockforth visited?'

Leek shook his head.

'Never caught a glimpse of 'im,' he declared. ''E must 'ave crept out, an' got round behind me, unless it was Rockforth who came back an' hit me — '

'I'll bet it wasn't Rockforth,' said Mr. Budd decidedly.

'It was Rockforth who came an' looked at me in that tunnel place,' said Leek. 'I reckernised 'is hands — '

'An' I'll bet that wasn't Rockforth, either,' interrupted the stout man. 'It wasn't Rockforth who got me. 'E was in hospital then, so it couldn't 'ave bin. There's some feller who's very anxious that we should think 'e was Rockforth, an' I don't think it 'ud be very difficult to give him a name.'

'You mean someone what's impersonatin' 'im?' asked Leek.

'You've hit it,' said Mr. Budd, nodding. 'That cold 'as made yer more intelligent than usual.'

'Who d'you think it is?' demanded the sergeant.

'Matheson!' answered Mr. Budd promptly. 'I don't see that it can be anybody else.'

'Who's Matheson?' inquired Leek, to whom the name conveyed nothing.

'Oh, I forgot,' murmured the big man, 'you don't know anything about Matheson, do you? Well, I'll tell you who he is.'

He proceeded to do so, and the sergeant listened, with gaping mouth.

'An' you think 'e's at the bottom of the murders?' he remarked. 'Well, it cert'nly looks like it, don't it? P'raps it was this feller Matheson what Rockforth went to see when I follered him?'

'That's what I'm thinkin',' said the superintendent. 'It's almost certain that he lives somewhere in the district. Otherwise, he wouldn't have chosen that empty house, where 'e took Walbrook an' the others, an' he wouldn't have made the appointment with me at Hogs Corner if — '

'Maybe he did that because Rockforth lives in the district,' put in Leek, with unexpected shrewdness. 'Ter make it look bad for 'im.'

'That's possible,' agreed Mr. Budd. 'You'd better go on 'avin' colds if they 'ave this effect on yer. You're quite bright.'

'I can always put me finger on the right spot,' said the sergeant complacently. 'Shall I tell yer what they used to call me at school — '

'I'd rather not hear,' broke in Mr. Budd hastily. 'Whatever it was, I'll bet it wasn't worse than you've bin called since.'

'It wasn't anythin' bad,' protested Leek. 'It was complimentary. They used ter call me 'Bullseye Leek' — '

'I can see the likeness,' said his superior shortly. 'Never mind what they used ter call yer at school, I'm surprised you ever went to one. Tell me where this 'ouse was that you followed Rockforth to?'

As well as he could the sergeant complied.

'If you foller them directions you can't miss it,' he ended.

'I should think if I follered 'em I should find meself almost anywhere,' grunted Mr. Budd. 'Anyhow, I'll see what 'appens.'

'Are yer goin' there to-night?' asked Leek.

'I think so,' answered Mr. Budd. 'If this chap is still under the impression that I'm cooped up in that culvert place, it'll give 'im a shock, an' it's my experience that when people 'ave had a shock they give themselves away easier.'

'I wonder why 'e wanted us out o' the way?' said the sergeant. 'If 'is idea was ter get Rockforth pinched fer this business, it seems stupid ter me. Partic'larly sendin' that wire to you. If Rockforth was in 'ospital, you'd know it couldn't be 'im what was responsible — '

''E didn't think it would matter after he'd got me in that sewer,' said Mr. Budd. ''E never thought I'd get out of that. But I'm wonderin', too, why he should have wanted to get us out of the way. There was clear evidence against Rockforth, which was what he'd planned, an' there was no need ter go after you an' me. Unless,' he added thoughtfully, ''e had an idea that we wasn't satisfied — '

'I was quite satisfied,' said Leek. 'I was sure all along that it was Rockforth.'

'If I'd 'ave known that,' snapped Mr. Budd, 'I should've been even more sure that he was innocent. I was never satisfied. I always thought there was somethin' else be'ind it. Rockforth 'ad the

344

motive an' everythin' fitted, but somehow I couldn't see him murderin' people. I was never satisfied, although in the circumstances I had to detain 'im.'

'You don't even know, now, that he ain't workin' in with somebody,' said the sergeant.

'An' helpin' ter get himself hanged!' snarled Mr. Budd. 'That's a brilliant suggestion, that is! You're gettin' more normal. I thought your bright spasm wouldn't last.'

Leek looked slightly aggrieved.

'Well, you never can tell with these 'ere crazy fellers,' he said. 'By the way, I wish you'd get in touch with me digs, an' see if the wire's come!'

'What wire?'

'The wire from Smallwood's,' explained Leek, 'notifyin' me that I've won that dividend.'

'I'd forgotten all about that,' said the fat man truthfully.

'I 'adn't,' answered the sergeant. 'I was thinkin' about it all the time I was lyin' in that tunnel. I ought ter get the cheque at the end o' this week.'

'I'll bet you've made a mistake,

somehow,' said Mr. Budd; but Leek shook his head.

'I 'aven't made no mistake,' he declared. 'The third line in me coupon was an all-correct. I checked it up four times ter make sure. If you get me coat I'll show you.'

Mr. Budd brought the coat, and the sergeant hoisted himself up in bed and searched in the inside breast pocket.

''Ere you are!' he said, producing a handful of papers.

''Ere's the copy of me coupon which I took an' — '

He stopped abruptly, and his lean jaw dropped.

'What's the matter?' asked Mr. Budd.

'There's somethin' funny 'ere,' muttered Leek, gazing at the papers in his thin hand. 'There's two coupons 'ere, an' they're both filled in the same — '

'You forgot to post one, that's what you've done,' said the big man.

'No, I didn't,' answered the sergeant. 'I was very careful. I put it in the envelope, an' wrote me name an' address under the flap like what they tell yer to, an' I posted it at the post office in Brimley. I must 'ave taken two copies, though I don't see 'ow I could 'ave done that.'

'How many coupons did you have in the first place?' asked Mr. Budd quickly.

'Three,' answered the sergeant. 'One was a spare to 'and to a friend. I was goin' ter give it ter you.'

'That's the one you posted!' declared Mr. Budd, with conviction. 'You posted the spare, an' kept the others. You can forget all about that fortune. What you sent ter Smallwood's was a blank coupon, an' they won't pay yer out anythin' on that.'

Leek blinked at him miserably.

'Well, did yer ever know such a bit o' bad luck?' he muttered. 'That's what I must 'a' done. An' I got an all-correct, too.'

He was still bewailing his luck when Mr. Budd left him to find the house of the man to whom the Reverend Clement Rockforth had paid his mysterious visit.

He succeeded in discovering it without much difficulty; the white gate, the hedges of golden privet, were unmistakable. An old man was working in the garden — a gardener, evidently — and he looked up as Mr. Budd pushed open the gate. If he had required any further confirmation that he had come to the right place, the squeak of the hinge would have supplied it. The old man who was pottering about among the flower-beds, touched his hat and resumed his task. It was all very peaceful, respectable, and prosaic, thought the big man, as he walked slowly up the path to the front door. Not at all the kind of surroundings one would associate with a murderer, and yet it was here that Leek had been struck down, and it was here, also, that Rockforth had come . . .

He reached the porch, hesitated for a moment, and then pressed the polished brass bell-push.

Who occupied this neat, trim house? Was he, at last, to come face to face with the man who had killed 'Miss Mote,' Gummidge, and Stacker, and would that man turn out to be the unknown Matheson?

He heard a faint step, and then the door opened.

27

Inspector Wiles Reports

A neatly dressed maid stood on the threshold and looked at Mr. Budd inquiringly. Beyond her he caught a glimpse of a square, well-furnished hall, with solid pieces of old furniture, and a quantity of shining copper and brass. The whole atmosphere was one of prosperous respectability, and the big man felt a little disconcerted.

'Yes, sir?' said the maid interrogatively.

Mr. Budd cleared his throat.

'Is your master at home?' he asked. 'I'd like to have a word with 'im on a matter of business, if he is.'

'What name shall I say, sir?' inquired the girl.

'Mr. Smith,' replied the fat detective promptly, and unimaginately.

'Will you wait for a moment, sir?' said the trim maid. 'I'll inquire if Mr. Witherspoon will see you.'

She went away, and Mr. Budd frowned. So the tenant of this pleasant house was called Witherspoon. Was that the name which Matheson had adopted, or had he come on a wild goose chase? The house, the garden, and the maid, all spoke of affluence, and if there was money, there was no need for the owner to have plotted murder for the sake of ten thousand pounds. But the appearance of affluence might quite easily be only a surface one. Mr. Budd was too wise a man to judge entirely by outward appearances, and yet . . .

His musings were interrupted by the return of the maid with the information that Mr. Witherspoon would see him. He followed the girl across the hall, and was ushered into a small room, where an elderly, bald-headed man was seated in front of an open window, reading a newspaper. He looked up as Mr. Budd was announced, and laid down the paper.

'You wished to see me?' he asked in a thin voice.

'Yes, sir,' murmured the stout super-intendent, his vague uneasiness that he had come on a fool's errand increasing.

'Will you kindly state your business, Mr. — er — Smith?' said the bald man. 'I cannot recollect having met you before.'

'My business is in connection with the Reverend Clement Rockforth,' said Mr. Budd, and although his eyes were half-closed, he was watching the other keenly.

'Ah, yes!' The bald man frowned slightly. 'Poor fellow. I understand that he was taken suddenly ill after a visit from the police — a stroke or something of the sort. I can hardly say I am surprised. For some time he has been — well, really, I don't think I should be exaggerating if I say not quite right in the head . . . '

'Yes, sir,' interrupted the big man. 'He had an interview with you on Saturday evenin', didn't he?'

Mr. Witherspoon seemed to be a little astonished.

'He did,' he answered, after a pause. 'A rather painful interview, I'm sorry to say. I had occasion to be very firm with him, poor fellow — very firm indeed.'

'Over what, sir?' inquired Mr. Budd.

'It was in connection with church matters,' replied the bald man. 'Some of Mr. Rockforth's ideas were — well, to say the least of it, a trifle unorthodox. Neither myself nor my fellow-churchwarden approved of some recent innovations he had insisted on making, and it was decided that I should speak to him. I warned him that we should feel it our duty to complain to the bishop, unless he saw his way to conform to — er — more standardised ideas. He was extremely stubborn. As I said, the interview was very painful — very painful indeed.'

Mr. Budd rubbed his chin. Here was an explanation for Rockforth's visit that he had not expected. He had come to this house expecting to find a murderer, and he had found — a churchwarden! The thing was ludicrous.

'I see,' he murmured, wondering what the next move ought to be. 'So that's why Mr. Rockforth came to see you, sir? Did you hear anything after he 'ad gone?'

'Hear anything?' Mr. Witherspoon raised his eyebrows. 'I don't quite understand you — '

'Did you 'ear any unusual noise outside?' augmented the stout man.

'Unusual noise?' repeated the other in obvious astonishment. 'What sort of noise?'

Mr. Budd decided to be more explicit. He was pretty well convinced that this man had nothing to do with the murders, and therefore further concealment of his identity was unnecessary.

'I'm afraid, sir,' he said slowly, 'that I gave you a false name. My name is Budd, an' I'm a superintendent of the C.I.D.' He went on to explain the real reason for his visit, and Mr. Witherspoon listened with gaping mouth.

'Good heavens!' he gasped, when the big man finished. 'So that's why I found all my flowers broken down under the window the next day. I thought it was those confounded cats!'

'You heard nothing at all?' said Mr. Budd, and the bald man shook his head.

'Not a sound,' he declared. 'But then, when Rockforth left, I went out into the kitchen to put a kettle of water on the stove. It was the servant's night off, and my wife had gone out to visit a friend.'

'I see, sir,' said Mr. Budd again. 'Have you ever heard of anyone of the name of Matheson?'

'Matheson — Matheson?' Mr. Witherspoon pursed his lips, frowned, and shook his head. 'No, I've never heard the name so far as I can recollect. Tell me, is there any truth in the rumour that poor Rockforth was on the point of being arrested for these murders when he was taken ill?'

'He was bein' detained, sir,' said Mr. Budd cautiously.

'But surely,' protested Mr. Witherspoon, 'there can be no question of his being guilty? I'm sure that he wouldn't . . . '

'I'm sure, too, now,' said the fat detective. 'There was a possibility, an' it seemed pretty certain, but there's no doubt now. No, sir, you can take it from me that Mr. Rockforth 'ad nothin' ter do with the murders.'

Mr. Witherspoon sighed his relief.

'I'm very glad to hear you say that,' he declared. 'Very glad indeed. Although poor Rockforth and I did not see eye to eye over many matters, I couldn't bring myself to believe that he could be capable of anything so terrible. Is he very ill?'

'Very, I'm afraid, sir,' answered Mr. Budd, and wondered why Mr. Witherspoon had not troubled himself to inquire at the hospital into the state of his vicar's health. 'There seems ter be a likelihood that 'e may not recover.'

'Dear me, very sad — very sad,' the bald man clicked his teeth. 'And even if he does recover, he will, of course, be unfit to carry on his duties. Shocking — really shocking.'

The stout superintendent agreed that it was shocking, though Mr. Witherspoon seemed rather relieved than otherwise, and took his leave. As he walked down the path to the gate, he realised glumly that his visit had proved rather a wasted effort. If Witherspoon was other than he seemed, he was a very fine actor, and if he was really what he seemed, then Matheson had still to be found. The big man sighed as he closed the squeaking gate behind him. Perhaps there would be news for him at the Yard. Inspector Wiles was a conscientious man, and he might have discovered something of value.

★　★　★

Immediately on his arrival at Scotland Yard on the following morning, Mr. Budd had an interview with the Assistant Commissioner. Colonel Blair was a trifle disgruntled.

'It seems to me,' he said, pacing the room, 'that we are very much where we were when we started. You say Rockforth is not the man, and that Matheson is. But where is Matheson? You've got to find him.'

'I'll find him, sir,' murmured Mr. Budd, with a confidence he was far from feeling.

'Well, I hope you do,' said Colonel Blair. 'But even if you do, you've still got to prove that he's guilty. We can't afford to go making another mistake. If anyone liked to make trouble over this Rockforth affair, we could quite easily get a very severe reprimand from the Home Office. They'll say that it was the shock of a completely unnecessary arrest that made him ill, and although I realise that, in the circumstances, the action you took was justified, it's going to look bad. They'll say that we ought to have made certain before acting at all, and I'm not sure they won't be right.'

Mr. Budd went back to his office feeling that he was not very popular.

Inspector Wiles came in just before lunch, looking rather tired.

He took out a thick black notebook and consulted it.

'I've traced up the marriage,' he began. 'They were married all right — at the Bloomsbury Registry Office.'

'Well, that's somethin',' grunted Mr. Budd. 'What happened to Matheson?'

'He gave an address in Russell Square to the registrar,' said Inspector Wiles, and turned over a page of his book. 'I went round there, but it's now a block of offices. It had been a boarding-house. After a lot of trouble I was able to find the woman who had run it. She had moved to a house in Coram Street. She was an old woman, getting on for seventy-five, but luckily her memory was good. When I explained about Matheson, and mentioned his name, she remembered him. He and his wife had lived in her house for three months, and then they had gone. Matheson had told her that he had got a job in Liverpool, and that they were going to live there.'

Mr. Budd's heavy eyelids jerked open suddenly.

'Liverpool, eh?' he muttered. 'That's queer. That's where Smallwood's 'ave got their offices.'

Wiles nodded.

'I thought it was queer directly I heard it,' he said. 'But the job couldn't have had anything to do with Smallwood's. This was over thirty years ago, and they weren't in existence then. This woman couldn't tell me anything more, and so I popped up to Liverpool on the offchance that I might pick up the trail again there. It seemed to me rather like looking for a needle in a haystack, trying to find a man after thirty years without even knowing what he was like, but again I was lucky. When I got to Liverpool I went to the local police for assistance, and I found a feller who remembered the name of Matheson directly I mentioned it.

'There had been a case of forgery, and Matheson had been convicted. This feller only vaguely remembered the details — something to do with a big cheque, he thought. I looked up the records and found the whole story. Matheson had been employed in a large advertising business — designing posters and suchlike — and he had apparently forged the signature of one of the bosses to a cheque for three thousand pounds. There was no doubt about his guilt, and he was sentenced to five years' imprisonment. He was released after serving just over three and a half years, having gained full remission for good conduct. That's all I've been able to discover, sir.'

'An' that's not so bad,' remarked Mr. Budd thoughtfully. 'We can guess now why his wife left him an' changed her name to Mote. We're gettin' on, Wiles. If this feller was convicted an' sentenced they ought ter have his dabs in records — '

'They have, sir,' said Wiles, and took an envelope from his pocket. 'I've got them here.'

The stout superintendent stretched a fat arm across the desk, took the envelope, and opening it, withdrew the official finger-print records.

'These are goin' ter be very helpful,' he murmured, gazing at them. 'Very helpful indeed, Wiles. They'll make identification certain, once we can lay our hands on the man.'

'Yes, sir,' agreed Wiles, a little dubiously.

'Meanin',' said Mr. Budd, answering his tone rather than his words, 'that you don't think that it's goin' ter be so easy ter find 'im?'

'Yes, sir,' said the inspector. 'It's such a long time ago that he may very well be dead — '

Mr. Budd slowly shook his head.

'I don't think he's dead,' he said. 'In fact, I'm pretty sure he's not. I wouldn't mind bettin' that I've bin as near ter Mr. Matheson durin' the last forty-eight hours as I am ter you, Wiles. But you're right about it not bein' easy ter find 'im. I believe 'e's still alive, an' I believe he's livin' somewhere near Brimley, but I don't know what he's callin' himself now, or what 'e looks like. Once I know that' — he leaned back in his chair and clasped his hands over his capacious stomach — ' Mr. Matheson 'ull go back ter prison, only this time he won't come out again.'

28

Mr. Budd Gets Inspiration

Peter Ashton heard an account of Mr. Budd's adventure at Hogs Corner from that sleepy-eyed man's own lips when he called at the Yard later that afternoon.

'I never sent that telegram,' he began, and the big man stopped him with a weary gesture.

'I know you didn't,' he grunted. 'There's no need ter tell me that. This feller Matheson sent it — even a child could see that. He took a certain risk, though. I might 'ave got in touch with you, an' then his whole plan would've gone sky 'igh.'

'He was cleverer than you think,' said Peter. 'You wouldn't have been able to find me even if you'd tried.' He told the big man of the telephone message which had come through while he had been speaking to Jacob Bellamy and Marjorie.

'H'm, clever,' commented Mr. Budd. 'Of course, I never phoned — '

'Even a child could see that now,' interrupted Peter, and the stout man smiled.

'That's one to you,' he said. 'Well, we've got a bit farther, but not very far. We know it's Matheson we want, an' we know that 'e's somewhere in Brimley; but we don't know who he is. It's goin' ter be a little difficult to find out, in my opinion.'

'It shouldn't be,' answered the reporter. 'You've got his finger-prints — '

'We can't go around takin' everybody's prints,' said Mr. Budd irritably. 'Have a bit o' sense, Ashton.'

'I'm not suggesting that you should,' said Peter calmly. 'But you can pick out the people who might possibly be Matheson, and get hold of their prints somehow, can't you?'

'Anybody might be Matheson,' growled Mr. Budd gloomily. 'That's the trouble. It's goin' ter be a difficult job ter find 'im, I'll bet anythin' yer like.'

He was right, as the passing days

proved. Patiently, with the doubtful assistance of the sniffing Leek, whose cold was not serious enough to offer an effective excuse for not returning to work, the stout superintendent set about his task of finding the man responsible for the murders of Gummidge, 'Miss Mote,' and Stacker. Failing to find any starting point in London, he went up to Liverpool and tried to pick up the trail from there. But Inspector Wiles had done his job thoroughly, and there was no thread that he had failed to discover.

Mr. Budd interviewed the solicitors who acted for Messrs. Smallwood's, and spent an interesting afternoon going over the huge organisation which the firm of Smallwood's control. He was taken to the new building on the outskirts of Liverpool, and shown every detail of the marvellously efficient system, which receives, checks, and files over six million football coupons every week during the season.

He was shown how impossible it was for anything in the nature of a swindle to be carried out over a winning coupon. The enormous staff — over ten thousand men and women — was locked in on Saturday afternoon before the results were known, and not allowed to communicate in any way with the outside world until after the checking of the coupons had been completed. No wireless sets were permitted, and no incoming telephone calls were allowed. As a final precaution, none of the checkers knew which batch of coupons would be given out to them until the last moment, which obviated any possibility of a prepared coupon with the correct result being slipped in, since it would fail to correspond with the file number and would be immediately spotted.

The system was as near fool-and-swindle-proof as the ingenuity of man could make it. Over a cup of tea with the managing director after his tour, Mr. Budd raised the question of how the murderer of the pool winners could have become aware of their names. The managing director shook his head.

'I don't know,' he declared candidly. 'That has been puzzling us here. There is no way by which he could have found out beforehand. I can only suggest that he discovered that we distributed our cheques at the Astoria Hotel, London, and followed these people to their homes afterwards.'

'I believe you've hit it, sir,' said Mr. Budd. 'At least, you've hit it in the case of two of 'em. I never thought o' that, but, of course, it's the simplest explanation.'

The exception was 'Miss Mote.' Matheson had found out in some way that his wife had won the first dividend. He must have done that, otherwise there would have been no point in the plot at all. *How* had he done that?

The explanation came to Mr. Budd as he was dozing in the train on his way back to London, and it was as simple as the other. Matheson had known because his wife had told him.

That was it! That must be it, since there was no other means. And that meant that he had seen her on the Saturday night after the results had come through. He had seen her and she had told him, and from that he had evolved the whole horrible scheme.

The train sped on to London, and Mr. Budd, huddled up in the corner of his carriage, set his mind to work to evolve a plan that would bring Matheson within his reach. But he arrived at Euston without having discovered any workable proposition, and went home a disgruntled and irritable man.

On the following morning, accompanied by the melancholy Leek, he went to Brimley and booked rooms at the inn in the village.

'What have we come 'ere for?' asked the sergeant, watching his superior gloomily while he unpacked.

'For a breath o' country air,' snarled Mr. Budd, flinging a gaudy suit of pyjamas on to the bed. 'We're goin' ter join the 'Strength through Joy' movement.'

The sergeant sighed. He recognised the signs. The stout superintendent had reached the stage of fuming irritability which always overtook him when he found himself up against a tough proposition. Leek decided that the less he said the better, and was wise in his decision.

When they had washed, the big man took his car and drove down to the little police station to see Collis, but the superintendent was over at Basingstoke, and according to the sergeant, was not likely to be in the district that day. This put the finishing touch to Mr. Budd's bad temper, and he set off for Basingstoke in a condition of mind that can only be described as foul.

Collis was surprised to see them. He had had no intimation that they were coming down, or he would, he said, have come over to Brimley and saved them the journey. He was even more surprised when he heard what Mr. Budd had to tell him.

'Matheson, eh?' he muttered. 'You're sure of this?'

'As sure as I'm talkin' ter you,' declared the big man. 'I've got it all worked out, an' it all fits. The only thing we want now is Matheson.'

Collis rubbed his chin.

'I'll help you all I can,' he said, 'but it's a difficult job looking for a man you don't know from Adam.'

'You're tellin' me!' snapped Mr. Budd crossly. 'I know jest how difficult it is.'

'He may be anybody,' went on Collis

thoughtfully. 'You can't definitely say that he's actually living in Brimley. He may be anywhere in the neighbourhood.'

'I know all that,' interrupted the big man. 'But 'e's got ter be found.'

'How are you going to identify him when you do find him?' asked Collis. 'That's another difficulty — '

'That's the only thing that isn't goin' ter be difficult,' broke in Mr. Budd. 'I can identify 'im all right. I've got his finger-prints.'

The local superintendent shot him a quick glance.

'Oh, you have, eh?' he exclaimed. 'Well, that's different. If we can find the man, there'll be no doubt about his being the right one. That's something, anyway. The question is, how do we set about finding him?'

'We shall have to check up on everybody,' declared Mr. Budd. 'It's goin' ter be a long job, but it's the only way as I see it.'

Collis shook his head dubiously.

'There's no certainty that it will be successful,' he remarked. 'He may have been living round here for years and established a new reputation. If we knew what he looked like, it . . . '

The stout superintendent brought a huge hand down on his knee.

'Call me everythin' in the dictionary that means a fool!' he exclaimed suddenly. 'We can get some idea of what 'e looked like — '

'How?' asked Collis quickly.

'The prison photographs,' answered Mr. Budd. 'I'm losin' me grip. I should've thought o' them before. Still, it ain't too late. I can get 'em sent down at once.'

'You do that, and we stand a pretty good chance of finding him,' said Collis. 'It's fairly certain he'll have changed a lot, but we shall have something to go on, anyway.'

'Get me through to the Yard,' said Mr. Budd curtly. 'I'll 'ave them photographs here by tomorrow.'

He went back to the inn in Brimley in a more amiable mood, to Sergeant Leek's secret relief.

29

News From Collis

The photographs which Mr. Budd had asked for arrived by special messenger on the evening of the following day, and the big man opened the stout, official envelope eagerly. There were three prints, all sharp police positives, a full-face and two profiles. They showed Matheson as having been a dark-haired, good-looking man, in the twenties, with a heavy moustache. There was something vaguely familiar about the features, but Mr. Budd couldn't think of whom it reminded him.

'So that's Matheson, is it?' said Leek, peering over his shoulder.

'That's Matheson,' agreed the stout superintendent. 'Does 'e remind you of anybody?'

The lean sergeant screwed up his eyes thoughtfully.

'If it wasn't fer the moustache, an' 'is

hair was lighter, 'e wouldn't be unlike me landlady's son,' he replied at length.

Mr. Budd gave him a withering glance.

'If he was altogether different, he might be like Napoleon!' he snapped. 'I mean, does 'e remind you of anyone connected with this business?'

Leek shook his head.

'No,' he answered mournfully.

'I've seen somebody like 'im somewhere,' murmured Mr. Budd, pursing his lips, 'but I'm hanged if I can remember who, or where. P'raps Collis 'ull reckernise him.'

But Collis was not helpful.

'I don't know anyone like this,' he said, when he had examined the photographs carefully. 'But then, I don't know everybody in the district. Will you leave these with me, and I'll start some inquiries going?'

On the way back, Mr. Budd made a detour and called at the hospital at Fallingham. In answer to his inquiry, the matron informed him that there was no change in Rockforth's condition. He was still unconscious, but the doctor had hopes that it would be possible to disperse the clot of blood without resorting to an operation. The vicar's condition was still serious, however, and it was very doubtful if he would recover.

There was nothing very much the big man could do, except wait as patiently as possible for further developments. They came on the evening of the fifth day of their stay in Brimley, heralded by a message from Superintendent Collis.

They had just finished tea when it arrived, brought over from Basingstoke by a hot and dusty constable.

Mr. Budd opened the envelope, read the contents, and nodded at the waiting policeman.

'Tell the superintendent I'll do what he says,' he grunted, and the man saluted and withdrew.

'What's the news?' asked the curious Leek.

'Good, I hope,' replied his superior. 'Collis says he's got a line on Matheson. He wants us to meet 'im at Fallingham Place, that empty house where Walbrook an' the others was taken to, at ten o'clock to-night.'

'What's 'e want us ter go there for?' demanded the sergeant, raising his eyebrows.

'I dunno; he says he'll explain when we meet him,' replied the big man. 'I expect 'e's got a pretty good reason.'

Superintendent Collis had got a pretty good reason, as they discovered when they met him just before ten in the drive of the old house.

'I think I've found Matheson,' he announced excitedly, without even bothering about preliminary greetings. 'We can make sure to-night if I'm right.'

'How?' asked Mr. Budd.

'Because, according to my information, he's coming here,' answered Collis. 'I started inquiries about the district, as I said I would, and one of my men found a man who resembled those photographs who has been living for the past four years in a cottage a few miles outside Fallingham. He calls himself Randal, but I believe he's Matheson. Anyway, he comes here every night.'

'Comes here?' repeated Mr. Budd. 'What for?'

Collis shook his head in the darkness.

'I don't know,' he replied; 'but there's no doubt he does. My men have followed him, and he's come here twice. That's why I made this appointment. I thought we might wait for him to-night, and see what brings him here.'

'If he comes,' grunted Mr. Budd. 'Because he's been 'ere twice doesn't necessarily mean he'll come a third time.'

'Well, there's no harm done if he doesn't,' said Collis. 'We know where to find him. But I'm rather curious to know why he comes here.'

'I'm rather curious, too,' muttered the stout man, rubbing his chin. 'It seems rather a queer thing ter do. What time does he come?'

'On the two occasions when he was followed here,' answered Collis, 'he came about eleven, and left just before twelve.'

'H'm! Interestin' an' peculiar,' grunted Mr. Budd. 'I wonder what 'e does?'

'That's what's been puzzling me,' said Collis. 'We'll go up to the house, shall we? I think it would be better if we waited for him inside.'

Mr. Budd agreed to this proposal, and they set off up the dark avenue. It was very dark, for the night was cloudy, and, although earlier in the evening there had been a moon, there was now no sign of it. They rounded the bend and came in sight of the house — a dim, black bulk sprawling amid the neglected grounds, silent and deserted.

'I got the keys from the agents this afternoon,' whispered Collis, as they approached the porch. 'We'll have no difficulty in getting in, and we can wait in the hall.'

'How does this feller get in?' murmured Mr. Budd.

'Apparently he has a duplicate key,' answered Collis. 'He enters by the front door, anyway.'

He took a key from his pocket as he spoke and inserted it in the lock. It turned easily and he pushed the heavy door open, standing aside for Mr. Budd and Leek to go first. They entered the big hall, and Collis followed them, closing the door behind him.

30

Matheson

It was pitch black in the hall. Mr. Budd strained his eyes, but he could see nothing. Neither was there any sound except the faint breathing of the two men near him.

'We ought to have brought a torch,' he muttered.

'I've got a torch,' answered Collis, and his voice was shaking with excitement. 'Just a moment.'

There was a slight movement, and then a ray of light split the blackness, and went dancing about the bare and dusty hall.

'Move over to the staircase,' went on the superintendent. 'That's our best place, I think.'

He focused the light on the foot of the old staircase, and Mr. Budd and Leek moved towards it.

'I wonder 'ow long we shall have to

wait?' murmured the big man, and Collis uttered a little laugh.

'Not long,' he said in a strange voice. 'You won't have to wait long, Budd. Put up your hands, and don't move — either of you!'

Mr. Budd spun round.

'If this is your idea of a joke — ' he began angrily.

'It's no joke!' snapped Collis. 'I've got a gun, and if you don't do as you're told it will be the worse for you!'

'What the hell are you playin' at?' demanded the stout superintendent wrathfully.

'I'm not playing!' snarled Collis. 'You fool! Don't you understand yet? I told you that Matheson would come here to-night, didn't I? Well, he has. I'm Matheson!'

Leek's breath left his lips in a gasp of sheer astonishment.

'You — you — you're Matheson?' he stammered. 'How can yer be Matheson?'

'You've gone balmy, Collis,' said Mr. Budd. 'Drop this foolin' an' behave yerself!'

'I tell you I'm Matheson,' repeated Collis. 'Are you so thick-headed that you can't understand the plain truth when you hear it? I thought I'd settled both of you when I left you to starve or drown in that culvert near Hogs Corner, but you got away — '

'So you was responsible for that, eh?' muttered Mr. Budd.

'I've been responsible for everything!' retorted Collis quickly. 'I planned the whole thing to get that ten thousand pounds, and I'd have got away with it if you hadn't interfered. You wouldn't believe what I wanted you to believe — what I'd arranged should be believed — that Rockforth was guilty. I knew you didn't believe it, and I tried to get you out of the way. I don't mind telling you this, because in a very little while neither of you will be in a position to do me any harm — '

'Don't be too sure o' that, Matheson,' warned the fat detective.

'I am sure of it!' snapped Matheson. 'What do you think I hatched up this story about the mythical Randal for? To have an excuse for getting you both here — to this old, deserted house where nobody ever goes. You were getting dangerous. I never guessed that you had found out so much, until you told me. You told me — me, the man you were trying to find, you fool! And you gave me those photographs — the photographs that they took of me at the prison! I could have laughed in your face when you handed them over to me like a lamb. There's nothing left of them now, except a heap of ashes, and I shall find those finger-prints and destroy them, too — '

'You won't get away with it,' said Mr. Budd, with a confidence he was far from feeling. 'You won't get away with it, Matheson.'

'Won't I?' sneered Matheson. 'What's to stop me? Not you, nor that skinny-gutted sergeant of yours. You'll be dead — both of you — '

'An' so will you,' retorted the big man. 'You'll hang, Matheson.'

'I shan't,' said Matheson. 'I shall never even be suspected. When your bodies are found, there'll be nothing to implicate me. Nobody knows that I met you here. The constable who brought you that note was ignorant of the contents, and when I leave here after I've finished my job, I'm calling at the inn to destroy both it and the prints. It will be easy to get in and out without being seen, and I shall be safe — quite safe for good and all.'

'How did you manage to get into the police force?' asked Mr. Budd quietly.

Matheson laughed.

'I thought you'd be puzzled about that,' he said. 'When I came out of prison there was a war on. I joined up — they weren't asking many questions then, so long as a man was fit enough to fight — and was almost immediately drafted out to the front. I joined up in the name of Collis. I came out of the war with a good record and joined the police force. The colonel of my regiment made a personal recommendation to the Commissioner. Simple, isn't it?'

Mr. Budd was silent. He and Leek were in a very dangerous position, and he knew it. His one hope lay in playing for time, and that hope was slender.

'You seem to have won,' he remarked. 'What do you intend to do? Shoot us?'

'That is my intention,' answered the

381

other. 'I'm sorry to have to do it, but you've only yourself to blame. If you had accepted the perfectly good explanation which I was at such pains to give you, you wouldn't have become a danger to me.'

'I see,' murmured the big man. 'You know, those photographs weren't very like you.'

'They weren't, were they?' agreed Matheson. 'I've altered a lot since they were taken — my hair's gone grey for one thing, and I've shaved off my moustache. I wasn't worrying so much about those as the finger-prints, although they might have been a source of danger. Well, I'm afraid I can't waste a lot of time talking, and this time I'm taking no risks of your managing to get away.'

'A minute or two can't make much difference either way,' said Mr. Budd, 'an' I've got a very curious mind, Matheson. I'd like to satisfy that curiosity.'

'What is it you want to know?' asked Matheson impatiently.

'I want ter know how you knew who these people were who had won the dividends in Smallwood's pools,' said the stout superintendent.

'I didn't know until after I'd evolved the scheme,' replied the other. 'I only knew that my wife had won.'

'How did yer know that?' inquired Mr. Budd.

'Because she told me herself,' replied Matheson. 'I'd been searching for her for a long time. I was in the devil of a hole over some money, and I thought if I could find her I could force her to extort a few thousands out of that old fool Franklin. He's still in love with her, the old dotard! I found her, and on the Saturday night I went to see her. She wouldn't have anything to do with me, but she told me that she had won the first dividend in Smallwood's penny points pool. That started me thinking. I *had* to have money. I had borrowed heavily from money-lenders, and forged the name of a man in Basingstoke as the guarantor. The debt falls due next month, and if I don't pay up they'll call on him. Satisfied?'

'Not quite,' said Mr. Budd. 'I'd like ter know — What's that?' he ended sharply.

'What?' demanded Matheson quickly.

'I thought I heard a noise — upstairs,' said the stout man, and the other gave a harsh laugh.

'You can't catch me that way,' he said. 'That's an old trick, Budd. There's nobody in the house but ourselves.'

'I'm sure I 'eard somethin',' muttered Mr. Budd.

'I can 'ear somethin', too,' broke in Leek suddenly, 'but it ain't upstairs. It sounds like someone comin' up the drive.'

'You certainly do it very well,' began Matheson, and stopped abruptly, for there *was* a sound outside — the scrape of a foot on gravel. 'Keep quiet!' he went on in a whisper.

Mr. Budd listened with straining ears. If the person outside was who he hoped it was, there was a chance.

'There can't be anybody there,' muttered Matheson, almost to himself. 'It must have been the wind — '

His attention was distracted, and the watchful Mr. Budd saw his chance and took it. With a sudden and completely unexpected movement, he flung himself forward at full length, and as he fell, reached out his hands and gripped Matheson's ankles. His heavy impact with the hard floor winded him, but he succeeded in jerking the other off his feet. With a startled oath, Matheson fell backwards, and the pistol in his hand exploded with a report that went echoing through the empty house.

'Jump on 'im!' panted Mr. Budd hoarsely, and as Leek took a quick step forward there was a loud knocking on the front door. The torch had gone out when Matheson lost his balance, but the sergeant, groping about in the dark, found a writhing form and grasped it.

'Got yer!' he cried triumphantly. 'Jest you keep still — '

'Leggo, you fool!' snarled Mr. Budd. 'That's me — '

A shot in his ear almost deafened him, and he felt the flame sear the side of his head. The knocking was repeated, and voices called loudly. Leek, stumbling round in the dark, came up heavily against some-one, and received a staggering blow that sent him sprawling. Two further shots thundered through the house, and then Mr. Budd, scrambling with difficulty to his feet, heard the click of a lock and felt a cold wind.

'Stop him!' he wheezed breathlessly. 'Stop him!'

'Who's that?' cried the voice of Peter Ashton sharply, and was answered by a shot. 'Look out, Jacob!'

'Don't let 'im get away!' panted Mr. Budd, and cannoned into Jacob Bellamy.

'Hey, cock!' grunted the bookmaker. 'What's all the trouble — '

'Matheson!' snapped Mr. Budd. 'Did you let him get past you?' Without waiting for a reply, he went lumbering down the steps, and began running towards the dark tunnel of the drive. There was a flash of flame from the darkness, and a bullet whined past his head. Another followed, and then somebody gripped his arm and pulled him back.

'It's no good going after a man with a gun,' said Peter, as Mr. Budd struggled to free himself. 'Be sensible. If you know him, he won't be able to get very far.'

Realising that there was a great deal of truth in this, the big man stopped.

'Who was it?' asked Peter.

'Collis!' said Mr. Budd, breathing hard. The reporter whistled.

'Collis?' he repeated. 'Do you mean — that he was Matheson?'

'He was,' said Mr. Budd grimly. 'An' I never even suspected it. You turned up jest in time, Ashton.'

'I got the message you left for me, and came right along,' said Peter. 'Jacob brought me in his car — '

'Where did you leave it?' broke in Mr. Budd quickly; and before the reporter could reply, they heard the sound of an engine. It roared suddenly, died down, and then faded to silence.

'He's found it,' said the stout superintendent. 'We'd better be gettin' along to the nearest phone, an' have his description circulated. Where's my sergeant?'

They found Leek sitting on the floor of the dusty hall, groaning, with his hands pressed to his middle.

''E 'it me in the stomach,' he wailed mournfully. 'Knocked me right out, it did. Have ye got him?'

'No,' snarled Mr. Budd. 'Pull yerself together, we're goin'.'

The sergeant in charge of the little police station was surprised to see them — more than surprised when he heard Mr. Budd's conversation over the telephone with the man in charge of the Information Room at Scotland Yard. They left him sitting at his desk and gaping in stunned stupefaction.

'That ought ter get him,' muttered the big man, as they walked back to the inn. 'He won't find it as easy to hide himself, with every policeman lookin' for 'im.'

But he underestimated Matheson's cleverness.

31

The Hide-Out

Matheson drove through the night without thought of direction. His carefully laid plans had been wrecked at the last moment, and fallen in ruins about his head. All his trouble and risk had come to nought, and he was now a hunted thing, fleeing from the law he had for so long represented. He cursed under his breath as he swung from the main road into a secondary road, and sped on. In a very few minutes the hunt would be after him in full cry, and he knew enough about police organisation to be certain that he could not elude the men who would be looking for him for long. It would be fatal to go very far in the car. A description of it would be circulated throughout the country, and it would be more of a liability than an asset. Equally certain was it that he could not hope to get away on foot. He was known in the district, and would shortly be known everywhere that was within reach of telegraph and telephone.

Was there time to reach his house in Basingstoke? That would be the first place to come under observation, but if he hoped to get away he would have to have money, and there was nearly a hundred pounds in his desk.

He glanced about him and discovered that he was not very far away. Should he risk it? Without money it was hopeless. With money there might be a faint chance, if he could manage to elude the watchful men who would be searching for him.

He made up his mind to chance it. It was scarcely likely that they would have had time yet to take any action, and he would only need a few seconds. He increased his speed, avoided the main streets of the town, and reached his small house on the outskirts. Stopping the car, he got out with a wary glance round, and hurried up the little path to the front door, opening it quickly with his key. The hall beyond was in darkness, and there was no sound. His elderly housekeeper would long since have gone to bed, and there was no need to disturb her. He felt his way to the small room which he used as a study, and switched on the light. Crossing to the roll-top desk which stood in one corner, he unlocked it, threw up the top, and pulled open a drawer. There was a packet of notes inside and these he transferred to his pocket. Now, if he could get away, as he had come, unseen, he might be able to think of some place where he could hide until the hue and cry had died down. He was at the door when the idea occurred to him. It came suddenly in a flash of brilliant inspiration — the one place where no one would ever dream of looking for him.

He hurried along the passage into the tiny kitchen, opened the door of the larder, and inspected the contents. There was a certain amount of tinned food, some bread, and a nearly new pound of butter. Working rapidly he transferred the edible contents of the larder to the kitchen table, found a sheet of brown paper and some string, and made the whole lot up into a parcel. There was enough there to keep him from starving for a day or two, and when that was exhausted — well, perhaps he would be able to think of some way of replenishing his supply.

With the parcel under his arm, he let himself out of the house, closed the door gently behind him, and went back to the car. The street was still deserted, and he breathed more freely as he slipped behind the wheel and pressed on the starter.

The engine started quickly and smoothly, and turning the car round he shot away in the direction from whence he had come.

So far, so good. The next step was to abandon the car, and find some other means to take him to his destination. The better way would be to walk. He could take to the woods then, and the parcel wasn't heavy.

He drove on until he came to a cross-road, ran the car into a hedge at the side of the road, and switching off the engine, got out. With his package of food tucked under his arm, he set out on his long walk to the sanctuary he had chosen. He knew the district like a book, and chose his route without hesitation, taking short cuts across fields, and keeping as much as possible to the friendly cover of the woods. He came at last to the fringe of the thick belt of trees that bounded the grounds of Fallingham Place, climbed the barbed wire fence that separated the wood from the estate, and made his way towards the old house.

It loomed up out of the darkness before him, lightless and deserted, and he chuckled softly. It had been nothing short of a stroke of genius that had prompted him to come here to hide, he thought. The police would never think of looking for him here, and even if they visited the place, they would be clever if they trapped him. There were countless places of concealment, and he could remain hidden for days, for weeks if need be, so long as he could find some means of supplying himself with food.

He forced his way through a thick shrubbery, crossed a patch of ground waist-high with weeds and rank grass, and eventually found himself at the back of the house. He searched about until he found a small window, and forcing this, climbed inside. It was a relief to feel the darkness of the old house round him. It seemed to envelop him like a friendly cloak, offering safety and succour. Here he was hidden from the vigilant watchers who would be on the lookout for him, with time to rest and think and plan for the future.

His spirits rose as he felt his way towards the kitchen. He would beat them yet, in spite of the bad luck which had nearly brought about his downfall. The kitchen, he remembered, had wooden shutters to the windows. It would be possible to light one of the candles which he had brought with him without fear that it would be seen by anyone who might chance to be about. Not that there was likely to be anybody. It would only be visible from the back, and it wasn't likely there would be anyone in the woods at that hour.

He reached the room he sought, and unpacking his parcel, lit a candle and stuck it on the built-in dresser. He was tired and hungry. Opening a tin of salmon, he made a hearty meal, and lighting a cigarette, settled himself in a corner with his back against the wall, and began to plan the future.

He had, he calculated, enough food to last him nearly three days, if he were careful. After that he would have to find means of getting more. It occurred to him that it would be comparatively easy to break into one of the near-by houses for this, but he rejected the idea almost as soon as it entered his head. That would be fatal. It was bound to reach the ears of the police, and they would guess instantly that he was still somewhere in the neighbourhood. He would have to adopt other methods. He had plenty of money, that was an advantage. Perhaps it would be possible to venture out in the dusk of the evening and buy what he wanted at one of the village shops in Fallingham. It all depended on the attitude the police took towards his escape. If they thought, as he hoped they would think, that he had succeeded in leaving the district, then the risk would be practically nil. He was not well-known in Fallingham, and if he could adopt some simple form of disguise in case he ran into anyone who might recognise him, it would be easy.

But he had nothing that would serve as a disguise, and there was certainly nothing in the house except a few old sacks. A few old sacks! Here was an idea, an idea as good as the idea of making Fallingham Place his hideout. An old sack and the soot from the chimney would turn him into a passable imitation of a sweep in a few seconds. Who would look twice at a sweep, buying food on his way home after a day's work? It was a good idea — a very good idea — and he decided to adopt it. That disposed of the food question. The next thing to decide was, how long was he going to remain in hiding.

That would depend on the circumstances. The longer he stayed, the better chance he would have of getting away. He sat thinking and planning until he dropped asleep from sheer weariness . . .

★ ★ ★

As the days passed and there was no news of Matheson, Mr. Budd began to get irritable and uneasy. Every port and place of embarkation, every railway station, was watched, and it was next to impossible that the man could have succeeded in getting out of the country.

'Where can he have got to?' grunted the stout superintendent to Leek for the hundredth time.

''E's lyin' low somewhere, that's my opinion,' answered the lean sergeant.

'Of course he's lyin' low somewhere!' snapped Mr. Budd. 'Any fool knows that! But where?'

'There's lots o' places in the country where a man could 'ide,' said Leek. 'You can bet yer life that's what 'e's doin'. Campin' out in some wood or other where no one ever goes. Off the beaten track, as you might say. That's why 'e took all that food from 'is house.'

'The woods and commons an' likely places are bein' searched,' remarked Mr. Budd, taking the butt of his cigar from between his teeth and inspecting it with a frown. 'There may be somethin' in what you say, though, for once.'

'It's always been my theory,' said the sergeant complacently. 'There ain't no other reason why he should 'ave wanted the food.'

The big man pinched his fat chin.

Leek's idea was, surprisingly, a sensible one. If Matheson had intended to seek refuge in a lodging-house or similar place, he would scarcely have burdened himself with a parcel of food. When that had been reported to him, the fat man had come to the same conclusion as the sergeant, but what troubled him was that Matheson had not been found before this. He couldn't have got very far on foot, and with every policeman in the county looking for him, and every likely hiding-place subjected to a rigorous search, it was surprising that there had been no news of him. Since abandoning the car, he had completely disappeared.

There was one consolation, however. If this idea of Leek's, and also his own, was right, it could only be a question of time before the man was caught. The food he had taken would not last for ever, and he would be forced out into the open to get more, and that was when they would have him. It was merely a question of waiting patiently — if this was really what Matheson had done. That was the question that was bothering Mr. Budd. Had that food been taken genuinely for use, as they believed, or had it been taken as a blind to make them think just what they were thinking? In that case, Matheson might have planned a means of escape that would prove successful, and Mr. Budd went cold at the thought. There would be a severe reprimand for him if the man succeeded in getting away, and although the big man could not see how he could be clever enough to evade the wide-spread net, it had to be taken into consideration that he possessed an unusual knowledge of police procedure.

He dropped the cold butt of his cigar into the wastepaper basket and fished a fresh one out of his waistcoat pocket. When it was alight, he leaned back in his chair and, surrounded by clouds of acrid smoke, tried to grapple with the problem by putting himself in Matheson's place . . .

★ ★ ★

All that day Matheson had eaten nothing. The last of his supply of food had given out on the previous night, and so had his supply of candles. He would be forced at last to put the plan he had evolved into execution.

The light was fading from the sky when he began his preparations. He found an old sack and blackened it with soot from the chimneys. There was plenty of soot. None of them had been swept for years, by the look of it, and when he had finished with the sack, he rubbed soot well into his face and hands and over his clothes. There was a cracked mirror in the bathroom upstairs, a relic of the last occupant, and when he had finished he surveyed his appearance with satisfaction. Certainly there was no resemblance to the rather dapper Superintendent Collis. His grey hair was concealed under the film of soot, and it also had the effect of smoothing away all the character from his face. Nobody would recognise him.

He came back to his headquarters in

the kitchen, hesitated for a second, and then went through the scullery to the back door. He felt an almost overpowering desire to give up his enterprise and remain in the shelter of the house. The surrounding walls gave him a feeling of security that was very comforting. But he had to have food, and he forced himself to unlock the door.

It was very still and peaceful outside in the half-light. Away beyond the neglected grounds, the wood showed up dimly against the darkening sky. He had decided to go through the wood and work his way round to the Fallingham road. It was safer than leaving by the main entrance. He stepped across the threshold and closed the door behind him — and the peace of the evening was instantly shattered.

From the bushes sprang men — big men whom there was no mistaking, in spite of the plain clothes they wore. They bore down upon the startled Matheson, and his lips curled back until his teeth showed up against his black face with almost uncanny whiteness.

He crouched back against the closed

door of the house which had given him sanctuary, snarling like a trapped animal, and his hand went to his pocket. But before he could reach the revolver his wrist was gripped and twisted up behind his back.

'You look like a black and white minstrel, Matheson,' murmured Mr. Budd, surveying him sleepily. 'Maybe you'll be able to entertain the magistrate with a song an' dance!'

Matheson said nothing, but his heart was cold, for he knew that the end had come.

32

The House-Warming

'It's a beautiful place,' said Marjory Ashton enthusiastically. 'I think you are very, very lucky.'

'It is nice, isn't it?' said Molly Walbrook, looking about her with the proud eye of ownership. 'We searched and searched until we found exactly what we wanted. I've always dreamed of a house like this.'

'An' you're luckier'n some people,' grunted Jacob Bellamy, just managing to prevent himself adding 'cock.' 'Your dream's come true.'

'If them roses are well pruned back,' murmured Mr. Budd, 'you ought ter get some fine blooms. They've bin a bit neglected an' grown straggly, but if yer cut 'em back they'll soon get strong an' 'ealthy. Don't be afraid ter use the knife. The more drastic you are, the better they'll be.'

'Mr. Middleton has spoken!' grinned Peter. 'For Heaven's sake, keep off the subject of roses, Budd, or we shall never get a word in edgeways.'

They were standing on the smooth lawn of the house which Harold Walbrook had bought with part of the money he had won from Smallwood's. It was a lovely old place, half-timbered, and standing in an acre and a half of wooded, matured gardens. From the lawn on which they stood they could see for miles across open country, a wonderful view of downs and meadows and wooded hills.

The Walbrooks had invited them down for a house-warming party. — Peter Ashton and his wife, Mr. Budd and Leek, old Jacob Bellamy, and one or two friends of their own.

'Yes, it's a lovely place,' said Marjory again. 'You ought to be very happy here.'

'I think we shall,' said Walbrook. 'I've always wanted a house in the country — the real country — and so has Molly. And now we've got it.'

'We followed the trial in the papers,' said his wife suddenly. 'They tried hard to make out that that man was insane, didn't they?'

'They did,' said Mr. Budd grimly, 'but they didn't get away with it. The whole thing had been too carefully planned for a madman.'

'Both Matheson and Lucas are being executed next Tuesday,' said Peter.

'Serve 'em right, too!' grunted Bellamy. 'It was a cold-blooded business.'

'What happened to Rockforth?' asked Walbrook.

'He died, without recoverin' consciousness,' answered the big man slowly. 'The doctors was goin' ter operate, but they decided that he was too weak ter stand it. I think it was the best thin' that could 'ave happened to 'im. They told me that even if he had recovered, he would have been stark ravin' crazy.'

'Poor old man,' said Molly softly.

There was a moment's silence, and then Walbrook said:

'What was the idea of that shooting? You know when I mean. That day at the empty house — '

'The idea was Matheson's,' replied Mr. Budd. 'He wanted to make certain that no suspicion could possibly attach to him,

405

an' so he instructed Stacker, who had been a sniper in the army, ter get up that tree an' give us a scare.'

'Did Stacker know him?' asked Bellamy. The fat man shook his head.

'Matheson didn't think he did,' he answered. 'He issued his instructions as the great unknown. But Stacker did know 'im, I think. That's why he wrote the letter to Ashton.'

'He must have written that the night before the shooting episode,' said Peter.

'He did,' agreed Mr. Budd. 'An' we showed it ter Matheson — was as good as signin' Stacker's death warrant.'

'But surely,' put in Marjory, 'it was dangerous for Matheson to arrange for the man to shoot at you all. He was there himself, and he might have been hit — '

'Nobody was ter be hit,' interrupted Mr. Budd. 'Those was Stacker's instructions, so Matheson told me. It was jest done to give him an additional alibi, if necessary.'

'What'll happen to that ten thousand pounds now?' said Walbrook. 'There's no next of kin — '

'It'll go to the State, so Smallwood's

tell me,' replied Peter. 'I asked them.'

'So all that killin' was fer nothin', cock,' muttered old Bellamy. 'All fer nothin'.'

'Yes, a lot o' innocent people were sacrificed to Matheson's scheme,' said Mr. Budd. 'That's why I'm glad he didn't get away with the 'Guilty but Insane' verdict that the defence was tryin' for. If ever a feller deserved hangin' it's 'im.'

'Let's talk about something more cheerful,' said Marjory.

'We'll go and join the others,' said Harold Walbrook. 'They'll be wondering where we've got to.'

They returned towards the house, and the lank form of Leek fell into step beside Mr. Budd.

'Beautiful 'ere, ain't it?' sighed the sergeant. 'It makes me mad when I think what I've lost.'

'What d'yer mean, what you've lost?' grunted Mr. Budd.

'I might 'ave had a place like this, if I'd sent that coupon o' mine prop'ly,' explained Leek. 'Think of it! A nice 'ouse like this 'ere, an' the rest o' me life spent in leisure.'

'The only difference is, that you won't have the house,' said Mr. Budd rudely, and it was not until they were halfway through dinner that the lean sergeant realized what he had meant.

THE END

THE FACELESS ONES
GRIM DEATH
MURDER IN MANUSCRIPT
THE GLASS ARROW
THE THIRD KEY
THE ROYAL FLUSH MURDERS
THE SQUEALER
MR. WHIPPLE EXPLAINS
THE SEVEN CLUES
THE CHAINED MAN
THE HOUSE OF THE GOAT

Other titles in the
Linford Mystery Library:

BLOOD MONEY

Catriona McCuaig

1948. Midwife Maudie Rouse looks forward to working with Llandyfan's handsome new doctor, Leonard Lennox, but is he all that he seems? When a young woman named Paula Mason turns up claiming to be his fiancée, this sets into motion a train of events that leads to her murder. The doctor is arrested, but the facts don't add up, and Maudie is determined to investigate. But could she be in danger of being murdered herself?

THE HOUSE OF THE GOAT

Gerald Verner

Investigating the murder of a shabby man who had asked directions to the home of Lord Lancroft before being found brutally stabbed, Superintendent Budd has only one clue. Inside the man's jacket is a piece of paper, on which is written the Lord's name and address, and the words 'The House of the Goat' . . . And when an ancient mummy is stolen in the search for a mysterious ring, nothing is as it seems . . .

CODE OF SILENCE

Arlette Lees

When Sterling Seabright is found strangled in the woods outside the small farming community of Abundance, Wisconsin, even her closest friends are shocked to learn of her secret life. When a second body is found murdered in a cabin by the lake, it's up to Deputies Robely Danner and Frack Tilsley to discover the link. Sterling's classmates hold various pieces of the puzzle, and although they may be talking among themselves, Robley and Frack are unable to break their code of silence..